"Innocent!" She threw up her hands

"How can you use that word to describe *me*?" she insisted.

"Candy, just because you knew a man and had his child doesn't mean you're not innocent. You're as green as a seedling. I know people who would give anything to go back to where you are now. I don't know how long it took me to crystallize my feelings about you," he said softly. "I've always known in theory that it's what you leave behind in this life that matters. It's the same reason that *you* fight to keep the world clean, Candy. You know how important that is to you."

He took her into his arms and whispered into her hair. "The truth of it is, I don't want to get old and see nothing emerge from my life but material things. And I don't want to know that you're somewhere, fighting just to stay alive."

Dear Reader:

Romance offers us all so much. It makes us "walk on sunshine." It gives us hope. It takes us out of our own lives, encouraging us to reach out to others. Janet Dailey is fond of saying that romance is a state of mind, that it could happen anywhere. Yet nowhere does romance seem to be as good as when it happens *here*.

Starting in February 1986, Silhouette Special Edition will feature the AMERICAN TRIBUTE—a tribute to America, where romance has never been so wonderful. For six consecutive months, one out of every six Special Editions will be an episode in the AMERICAN TRIBUTE, a portrait of the lives of six women, all from Oklahoma. Look for the first book, *Love's Haunting Refrain* by Ada Steward, as well as stories by other favorites—Jeanne Stephens, Gena Dalton, Elaine Camp and Renee Roszel. You'll know the AMERICAN TRIBUTE by its patriotic stripe under the Silhouette Special Edition border.

AMERICAN TRIBUTE—six women, six stories, starting in February.

AMERICAN TRIBUTE—one of the reasons Silhouette Special Edition is just that—Special.

The Editors at Silhouette Books

LINDA SHAW
Kisses Don't Count

Silhouette Special Edition

Published by Silhouette Books New York

America's Publisher of Contemporary Romance

SILHOUETTE BOOKS
300 E. 42nd St., New York, N.Y. 10017

Copyright © 1985 by Linda Shaw, Ltd.

Distributed by Pocket Books

ISBN: 0-373-09276-8

First Silhouette Books printing November 1985

10 9 8 7 6 5 4 3 2 1

America's Publisher of Contemporary Romance

Printed in the U.S.A.

LINDA SHAW

is the mother of three children. She enjoys her life in Keene, Texas, where she lives with her husband. When Linda isn't writing romance novels, she's practicing or teaching the piano, violin or viola.

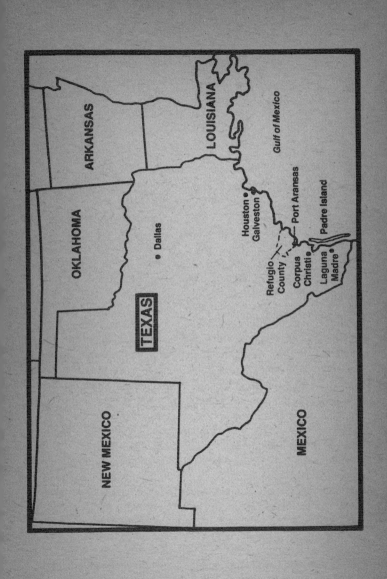

Chapter One

If there was another way to do it, Candice Burrows thought as she took an inhalation of compressed air and watched her exhaust bubbles swell until they looked like eager, flattened mushroom caps racing to self-destruct on the surface of Corpus Christi Bay, she didn't know what it could be. She'd hardly thought of anything else for weeks.

At least no one knew she was leaving. None of the oil-spill research team knew. No one at the Worthington Foundation. Agatha didn't know. And certainly not Victor.

Scooping some sediment of the bay into a sample bottle, she watched the sand rouse in a miniature explosion, drift ambitiously for a second, then settle indolently back down to the ocean floor again. She wanted to memorize everything—the way the surface fragmented above her, the July sun bursting wrathfully above it, the sloping shallows.

Strange how she never felt she was trespassing in this watery world, not as she often did in the human world. Did astronauts feel like that? If she were an astronaut instead of a marine biologist, perhaps she would be running away to the moon instead of to St. Paul, Minnesota.

Enough daydreaming. Candy clipped the bottle to her belt and glanced at her underwater wristwatch; only four hours left to wrap everything up into a neat little package. She tumbled in a somersault and gave her fins a languid kick that propelled her forward and scattered the browsing fingerlings. Keeping on a parallel with Mustang Island, she gained speed and watched the beach reel past, with only the bubbles roaring out of the regulator to keep her company.

For weeks now Candy had reminded herself of a petty thief working out a caper to steal the crown jewels. Her checking account had mercifully been put out of its misery. Her plane ticket to St. Paul was squirreled safely away in her bureau drawer. Her off-season wardrobe, less than a dozen articles but selected with agonizing care and expense, had been smuggled out of the house and into a locker at the airport. Of Amber's baby things, she planned to take a minimum of paraphernalia; luggage and babies didn't mix.

The crucial thing, she thought, was to give the impression of life going on as usual. She'd had Tom take the boat out early. Today she and the team were gathering bottom sediment from Laguna Madre to the Shamrock Island oil field.

And tonight? Tonight was the reason she hadn't left at least a week earlier, before Victor would get into town. Tonight was the birthday party.

No amount of wheedling could talk Agatha out of the party. Amber was two and Candy was twenty-six. Goodness gracious, the older woman had argued, how many times did you run into that in your life? Despite her sixty-six years, Agatha had made the cake herself.

Candy practically owed her life to Agatha. There wasn't much she could do but shake her head at the dear friend who had provided room, board and TLC for the past two years and say, "It'll be a wonderful party, Agatha."

So, here she was—having no choice but to leave in the middle of the night when Agatha's big house off Holiday Beach was listless with fatigue and the crickets were delirious and the frogs were raising a ruckus. She would take her manuscript on ecosystems, her notes and her beautiful sleeping daughter and sneak away into the night like some vandal hustling stolen hubcaps.

Unforgivable! But Victor was a man of enormous charms. He would come to the beach house and stand there in all his Jeb Stuart, Confederate cavalry appeal and smile that lazy Georgian smile of his and ask Agatha where his daughter was, please, ma'am, and Agatha, if she knew, would tell him everything. Candy was a connoisseur of Victor's smiles. She's been seduced by that smile.

"Get an abortion, darlin'," Victor had said after their flaming year-long love affair. "I can't get married now."

Candy had been as stunned as if he'd run her through with his cavalry sword. For a moment all she could do was stand and gape at her life's blood spilling out into her hands. "You mean..."

"I mean that I can't saddle myself with a baby. Come on, Candy girl, be realistic. You better than anyone know what's at stake here."

"W-well, then," she had stammered, fighting her way out of the paralyzing shock, "we won't get married. It's kind of the thing, you know. People raise their children...I can live with that."

"It's the future, Candy. My future. They're buying the movie rights now. Those POWs would never have been released if it hadn't been for my book, and you know it. I'm on my way to being somebody, girl. Can't you see that I can't be tied down? In a year, five years, it might be too late."

All Candy could see was a man whom she had loved shattering her life without a second thought. Unspeakable things broke up inside her. She felt like a prostitute. She felt cheap. She felt raped.

"Please don't do this to me, Victor," she pleaded with him. "It's wrong. It's not fair."

Here Victor had smiled his splendid smile. "There's nothin' to an abortion, sweetheart. If I were in your shoes, I wouldn't hesitate. The truth is, Candy, I'd be a lousy father. I'm not cut out for it. That's just the way I am, you know?"

She had known more than he counted on. For the first time since she'd fallen under the spell of that smile—or had it been a curse?—she had refused Victor something. Now, over two years later, with his silver-lined dreams of becoming another David Halberstam or Gay Talese slowly tarnishing, Victor had strolled back into her tediously restructured life.

POWs were passé now, he said with a bewitching grin. Now he was working on a book about the Shah of Iran. It wouldn't be a Pulitzer prizewinner, of course, but it would make him a lot of money. He couldn't go back to being a mere reporter, could he? After having been on The New York Times Best Seller List for nine months?

He'd pulled out that ridiculous pavé-studded ring, and she had stared down increduously at his sixteen-thousand-dollar penance. They'd been standing outside one of the labs at the Worthington complex, and Victor had pushed her up against the bricks and trapped her body with his.

He propositioned her with a disrobing stare. "I've missed you."

Everything was cold and embalmed inside Candy now. "I'm not listening, Victor."

"Don't be like that, sugar. D'you know how long it's taken me to get up the courage to say this? Admit it, now— you've never really closed the door on what we had.

Haven't you always thought, way back in your mind, that we'd have another go?''

He drew her eyes back to his with a fearful magnetism and charm. ''Things haven't gone right since we split up, Candy. I've tried, but I never could find what we had. That shouldn't surprise you. Look, take the ring. We'll get married. We'll have all the babies you want. I need that now. I need roots, a sense of destiny. You're the only one I want that with, darlin'.''

It hadn't ended nicely. Victor never yelled or lost his temper. His cruelties were always inflicted with infinite finesse.

He smiled. ''I don't want t'get tough, Candy. It isn't me. I don't enjoy it. My lawyer said...''

Which was Victor's way, of course: the polished hesitation, the perfect pause, the cruel and murderous silence. In that one instant Candy thought she could have killed him.

''I see,'' she said as her fists quietly closed upon her bitterness. ''Well, go ahead and get your lawyer, Victor. Take me to court. My life-style is impeccable.''

''But can you provide for our daughter, sweetie? Look at you. You live off an old woman's charity.''

''It's not charity. I earn my room and board. I received an advance on the book. Once it's finished I—''

He ruffled her hair as if she were a puppy. ''And I really respect that, Candy. You were picked up by a fine publishing house, but you and I both know you won't get rich on a textbook.''

''I don't care about rich. I care about surviving. And Amber.'' Candy's determination was a fire licking the curves of her cheeks. ''And I might just surprise you and make some money on this book. You're not the only one who can write.''

''If you want to make money, forget the text. I'll pay you to type and edit my book as you did the other one.''

"I'm not in the typing business anymore, Victor," she said and started to leave.

He forced the ring onto her finger, and when Candy jerked back her hand, he clasped her head in his hands. Gone was the old southern gentility and in its place a hard, contemporary ruthlessness. "Sweetheart, don't push me to this. Don't force me to remind you of your medical history."

So! He'd finally said it! Memory was a fiend that laughed at Candy from a distance. "That was before I even knew you, Victor. I don't take so much as an aspirin now."

"There's an old saying, sweetie pie." Amusement rumbled in Victor's chest. Candy's addiction—the fact that it was a medical one was of no big concern to him—still intimidated her. "Haven't you heard that necessity is the mother of invention?"

What was it her grandmother had told her so many years ago, Candy reflected, back when she was just a skinny adolescent and her father had dropped out of her life only six months after her mother? "Wife first, Candy," she had counseled with a wag of her finger that had seemed stodgy and old-fashioned at the time. "Wife first, mother second."

Candy twisted off Victor's diamond-studded bribe and dropped it into the pocket of his Frost Bros. jacket. "This is the first time in my life I've looked at myself and seen something good. If you take one step toward Amber, I'll—"

Victor stopped her declaration with two fingers upon her lips. "You won't do anything, pretty girl. Not if you don't want to wake up one morning and find her gone."

Leaving her speechless, he had serenely kissed the end of her nose and sauntered off toward his BMW.

The fingers of Victor's threat were serious and long-reaching. Even here, out in the bay, Candy could feel them snaking out like tentacles and coiling about her throat. Victor was coming. To Texas, he had said, for Amber's second birthday, and he would arrive today or the day after.

If she was anything, Candy thought, she was a woman who learned her lessons. More than she hated leaving her beloved Agatha and the team, more than she dreaded the thoughts of starting a new life somewhere else, she feared Victor.

Swimming with strong and untiring skill, Candy allowed herself ten minutes to pick up her canister near Benjamin North's new drilling rig in the shallows around Shamrock Island.

Several months ago she had placed the canister near the TempCo Oil site and had laboriously established a colony of flagellates. She wanted to see how the drilling process would affect the phytoplankton food chain: the little undramatic spills of oil men, careless disposal, sloppy fueling. Now she swam close and squinted through the cloudy water where the concrete piers thrust up from the floor like the ruins of some once-majestic Atlantis courtyard.

The water throbbed against her eardrums. Pausing, Candy resettled the flanges of her mask and studied the scene again. Where was her canister? Surely she hadn't become disoriented and passed it.

Backtracking, she uneasily approached the rig again and strained her eyes for sight of it. One could expect a certain amount of drifting, but to disappear altogether? There was no mistake. It was gone.

Damn! Of all days for something like this to happen. It could cost her the whole afternoon.

Filling a sample bottle of sediment and one of water, prying a mussel from the bottom of a pier, she secured all of them to her belt and started swimming impatiently in the direction she'd come from. When she reached the boat, one dexterous kick sent her spiraling up to the surface.

She pierced through the water, looked around and grasped the bar on the portable ladder, and, pulling off her mask, heaved herself over the side.

"Well," Tom said as he helped her off with the air tank. "I was beginning to wonder if you'd turned into a mermaid down there."

Tom Paughteck was twenty-two, the oldest of her trio, a shy, freckled chemistry graduate who watched her from a distance with longing, virginal eyes. Only once had she and Tom ever acknowledged his feelings, one night after they'd worked too long and too hard to resist laughing and falling into each other's arms. It was the first time a man had touched her since Victor. Candy had fought him with a wildness that embarrassed her, even now.

Brusquely she said, "Care to commit mutual suicide?"

Miller, the second male member of the team, was a third-year biologist at Texas A & M. He was logging his samples, and he exchanged a grimace with Tom. "What's the matter?"

"Where's Wendy?" Candy squinted and gazed out over the bay.

Tom shrugged. "She went down for another sample. What's the matter?"

Sighing, Candy said, "Well, you might as well know, it's gone."

Tom exchanged another wondering glance with Miller, then shrugged at Candy. "What's gone?"

"The canister." Candy met his incredulous eyes.

"Impossible," Miller declared. "It must have drifted."

Shaking her head, Candy shielded her face against the ferocious sun. Before she could explain, Wendy's head bobbed up through the surface. The water was only six feet deep where she was, and she was goggle diving. Waving with one hand, she pushed back her goggles with the other, and Miller began cranking up the anchor.

Miller, with his wild punk hair, was the Rod Stewart of modern science, Candy had often said. He laughed at her. "Maybe a shark ate your canister, chief."

Grimacing, Candy watched Wendy make her way to the boat. Miller heaved her on board as if she were a piece of driftwood.

"You'd better take a look at this," Wendy puffed and fished some hydrophobic seaweed from a wire net.

Candy spread the dying ribbon in her palm. "Great, just great."

"None of it looked like this last week." Wendy braced her hands on her knees and caught her breath. "I swear."

"I'll put it on the GC," Tom said. "I can tell where that oil came from."

"We don't have any of TempCo's oil to compare it with, Tom," Candy said.

Candy stared hard at North's drilling platform. Oil had individual characteristics like humans and, like humans, it could be "fingerprinted" with the help of a gas chromatograph. Tom was the GC operator, and all he needed was a drop. If Benjamin North's rig was spilling oil into the bay, the least he would get would be a five-digit fine.

On deck, the TempCo crew moved about like ants. From the mainland, a helicopter lumbered slowly toward it, and the noise deafened the team as it passed over their heads. They all watched until it landed on the island and settled down to wait like a black beetle drooling for its lunch. Its passenger was met by an outboard and taken to the rig.

"I think I know why my canister disappeared," Candy said grimly. "They've leaked something or spilled something over there, and it killed the algae. To keep us from finding out, they took the canister."

Tom's expression agreed. "They obviously fixed the leak."

"Couldn't have been much of a repair job," Miller offered another opinion. "It hasn't shut down that I know of. How much does it cost an operation the size of North's to shut down?''

As Candy pondered, the sides of her mouth curved attractively downward. ''It depends on how much interest he's paying, of course, but I'd say twenty, twenty-five thousand dollars a day.''

Miller popped the cap off a can of Pepsi, guzzled it down and wiped his mouth with a dramatic sigh. ''That's why I say he hasn't shut down. North is hurting really bad for money.''

Some said that Benjamin North had amassed his empire by default: tricky oil wells, political boardrooms and the lucky end of several lawsuits—not dishonest but far from lily white. Now rumor had it that the empire was on the decline; North, the old, ailing crocodile who'd been known to swallow people whole, needed money badly. The *Quarterly Review* had featured an article: ''The Decline and Fall of Benjamin North.''

Pressing her fingers to the bridge of her nose, Candy said, ''I think I'd better talk to them up on the rig.''

The words were hardly out of her mouth before Tom's head was shaking back and forth. ''It's a mistake, Candy. Let the foundation handle it. That's what Cavanaugh gets paid for.''

''I don't have time to wait for Cavanaugh.''

The three scientists exchanged a puzzled look, and Candy turned up a palm. ''I just want to know what happened to the canister, that's all. And I'll get you an oil sample.''

Motioning to the platform, Candy emphatically unbuckled her belt and dragged a faded man's shirt over her swimsuit. ''And don't be shy when we approach. I want everyone on the platform to see us coming.''

''No one could miss you, babe,'' Tom mumbled as he dragged his hungry eyes from her derriere and reached for the crank of the motor.

Tom Paughteck never argued with Candy, not because she was the unspoken leader of the team but because he was in love with her. She wasn't what he'd call beautiful. She was much too aloof for that. *Intriguing* was the word for Candy, mysterious. She was a good five feet eight without her shoes, which was usually the way he saw her during work hours—barefoot and wearing a slender swimsuit, or a bikini bottom and a cotton knit shirt that could drive him to near-insanity when it molded to her like a second skin.

From the back, with her long tanned legs and firm hips, plus a sensually aggressive walk and a mop of short, frilly black hair that perpetually looked as if it had clashed with an eggbeater, Candy promised to be a sexual lioness. But when she turned around she was all challenging blue eyes that didn't miss a thing. She had a straight, slender nose that was delectable enough to nibble but which never let anyone get that close, and a mouth that would have been devastatingly naughty on anyone else but that was almost always talking about cytoplasmic modification or unicellular protists or some such. Candy was enough to discourage all but the most stouthearted and dedicated male.

Knowing that it wouldn't do him one whit of good to protest, Tom yanked on the cord. The engine sputtered once, then exploded to life. He brought them around in an arc and leveled out until they were slicing across the bay like a knife easing through frothy cream. The prow lifted out of the water, slapped the waves and jarred their skulls.

"How much do you want t'bet that North doesn't know about the canister?" he yelled to Candy.

Used to Tom's sudden detours of mood, Candy laughed. "Lay your money down, Tom."

Tom's grin was boyish and hopeful. "Dinner tonight?" He winked. "For all four of us. If North knows, you buy. If he doesn't, I buy."

The edge of Candy's composure cracked as she thought about what she would be doing tonight. She plucked at a rebellious wisp of hair. ''Sorry. I can't.''

''Why not?''

What excuse was better than the truth? ''It's my birthday,'' she yelled back. ''There're plans.''

Squealing, Wendy pounced like a kitten on a bright ball of yarn. ''Your birthday! You said it was Amber's birthday.''

''It is.''

''You mean, you've got the same birthday? Hey, that's serious genealogy. Hear that, Miller? Candy and Amber have the same birthday.''

Miller looked at his female teammate as if she were losing her mind. He shouted, ''I'm not deaf, you know.''

She glared at him. ''You know, Miller, if you'd quit guzzling caffeine all day long, you might find the world is a nicer place.''

''What d'you want me to do, hard drugs?''

Tom cackled. ''Might be an improvement.''

Candy had never been part of their camaraderie. Accepting her exclusion, she stared out over the horizon where water and sky met in a shimmering blue seam.

Wendy inched closer. ''How did you manage the birthdays, Candy? Maybe I'll do that when I have children. What d'you think?''

Candy smiled. ''Ours was an accident.''

An accident of about one month. . .early labor. . .the ambulance. . .all that blood, all that emergency surgery. Now Ms Candice Burrows was truly liberated; she didn't have to worry about ever getting pregnant again.

''Well—'' Wendy tapped her jaw ''—tomorrow night we'll give you a belated birthday party, Candy. A real bash where the appetizers cost as much as the entree and they bring you three kinds of wine. And none of this betting stuff. This is on us. Okay, guys? And if you want to, you can invite someone. If Amber's father—''

Tom flashed Wendy a blistering warning, but it came much too late. A pained smile flitted across Candy's face, and she looked quickly away, pretended to be absorbed with the rig as they closed the distance.

Grinding his jaw, Tom eased back on the throttle and swung alongside the piers with a sputtering growl and a wave that threatened to dash them against the concrete.

The men on deck had seen them approaching. Someone had fetched the bullhorn, and he leaned down to bark, ''Who are you? What do you want?''

With a motion for Tom to cut the engine, Candy placed her hands beside her mouth. The men up there knew exactly who she was; they and the team had waved to one another as they'd gone about their work week by week.

Candy refused to acknowledge the disapproval creasing Tom's face. She raised her voice. ''I'm coming up.''

Reuben North was a born diplomat. Being the son of a man like Benjamin North, he'd almost had to be. In less than a decade he had established one of the most respected public-relations firms in New York City, and, according to *Business World*, he employed some of the most exciting talent in the country. Reuben was also exceedingly clever. He looked for genius where it is almost always found, tucked away in unappreciated, unpopular places after mediocrity has diagnosed it as below standard.

Once his cleverness had created a self-perpetuating business that hardly needed him around, however, Reuben learned the secret every little girl learns at the age of five— that building the playhouse is all the fun. What d'you do with the damned thing once it's done?

The obvious answer: play another game. Except that Reuben was thirty-five years old, and he had wearied of games.

So today, the man whom financiers and powerful men behind the scenes had come to know for his graceful wit and formidable success had climbed out of a Bell-Jet helicopter with an uncharacteristic groove etched between his brows. The flesh over his patrician cheekbones was more stretched than usual. A muscle flexed repeatedly in his jaw, and deep lines marked the distance from each nostril to the sides of his mouth.

Reuben planted his feet firmly upon the deck of an oil rig that he'd pleaded with Benjamin not to sink. His pleated slacks whipped about his legs, and he pushed up the sleeves of an unconstructed Belgian linen jacket. Long ago he had ceased to care about the impression he gave strangers; some told him later that they had first mistaken him for a European symphony conductor, or a Riveria beach bum. One woman cooed and said she'd thought he was a cat burglar—everything but a Texan, so Benjamin complained, as if it were an unforgivable sin against Sam Houston and Stephen F. Austin!

Lord, he'd forgotten just how hot Texas could be!

Shrugging out of his jacket, Reuben slung it over his shoulder and pushed sun-bleached brown hair out of his face. From behind wire-frame sunglasses, he searched for Pete Dysan, who had located him in Rome two days ago and had begged him to please come quickly and not say a word to Benjamin or his mother.

Pete Dysan was Benjamin's accountant. He looked like a little boy constantly screamed at by his mother and who has compensated with a neat haircut and an alarming handlebar mustache. He was approaching at a dead run.

As they shook hands the crane operator lifted his hoist and swung it out over the deck. A woman was standing on the platform as it came into view. Her arms, slender, darkly tanned, were outstretched, and her hands clasped the chains with the vigor of a healthy young man. She wore a blue bikini over which flapped an unbuttoned man's shirt, and her assertive hair, as thickly black as the oil his father pumped from beneath the sea, was whipped by the wind so that she had to tip up her face, charmingly, Reuben thought, to keep it out of her eyes.

The operator put her down as gently as thistledown, and curious roughnecks began gathering around like honeybees. Squinting, Reuben watched and waited with the rest.

"She's out of a Port Aransas laboratory," Pete explained. "She and some scientists patrol the gulf like Nader's Raiders."

"Well, what d'you know?" someone hooted. "The Mr. Clean lady herself."

"No 'mister' in that wet suit. Get a load of those legs."

"Get 'er off the rig!"

"Buzz off, man."

"A woman's bad luck on a rig."

"Sez who?"

The woman appeared to hear none of the resounding wolf whistles; she waited—tall, aloof, much above the stamp of public opinion one way or another as her eyes met those of Stretch McPherson, the rig's driller.

After one compelling look from Stretch, the roughnecks grudgingly fell silent.

Pete twirled the ends of his mustache and said to Reuben, "I've always wondered what it's like with a woman like her. D'you think she knows the effect she has on people?"

Her poise did seem to be uncanny, and it was literally placing the men under a spell. Stretch caught Reuben's eye and, as a shrugging courtesy to Benjamin, passed the decision on to him.

Personally, Reuben didn't want a woman on the rig; most of these men worked two weeks at a time without going inland, and this woman—what was she? Mid-twenties? A good eight or nine years younger than himself? This woman was like some mysterious collector's item from the ocean that everyone wanted a closer look at.

Still, Stretch knew these waters and these people better than he did. Reuben signaled the driller to carry on.

"So, Pete," he said and reluctantly turned away from the goings-on. "You've gotten me out here. Lay it out now, nice and easy, and don't tell me that Dad's in trouble. He'll be that until the day he dies."

"Which may be a good deal sooner that we thought."

For Pete to exaggerate about Benjamin North was like a banker joshing about the prime interest rate. Reuben automatically started to smile, then felt sticky-palmed and unnerved. "What are you saying?"

"That your father's sick, Reuben. Real sick."

"No one said anything to me."

"No one knows it. Well, your mother knows. I talked to his doctor. No pressures, he said, or it could kill him. We've got a problem here, Reuben. I can't take the responsibility for all this drilling and stuff. I'm an accountant, for God's sake."

Benjamin? At death's door? Reuben couldn't begin to fathom the complications his father's death would create for four corporations and a wife and three married daughters who went through money like water through a sieve. He shifted his weight to the opposite hip, took a few uncertain steps away, then turned back.

"Stretch can handle this gastric menace," he pointed out. "If you'll remember, Pete, I didn't want Dad to stick it out here to begin with."

"Look, Reuben, Stretch can drill a well, but he can't save this rig." As he explained Pete fervently stroked his mustache. When he caught Reuben staring, he slipped his hands in his pocket.

"Why am I getting the idea," Reuben asked, scowling, "that you're dancing with me? Why don't you just come out with it, Pete?"

When Reuben swiveled a quarter turn, not really intending to do more than get an idea of where the woman had gone, she was in the process of surveying the deck. The aching sun had fractured light into her face, and she was momentarily blinded.

As she shielded her eyes and stepped into the lanced shadow of the trapezoid that reached skyward, Reuben's mouth suddenly went dry. It wasn't because women didn't interest him anymore; they did. But the women he knew well were those who looked out for themselves, spoiled and glamorous big-city women who took more than they gave and who had long ago lost their innocence. This woman was as different from them as jewels from beads.

"Spit it out, Pete," he said and tried to concentrate on what the accountant was saying.

"TempCo's out of money," Pete told him flatly.

But Reuben, despite his good intentions, was a million miles away. He was imagining the woman in some other place from the rig or the crowded bars and bohemian streets he was used to. In his fantasy she walked along the beach at night, alone and barefoot with the water swirling around her feet. Her loose pants were rolled to her knees and wet. Her blouse was silky and free, whipped by the wind so that her breasts were a mystery. Again he saw her—wet, wrapped in a towel, beaded droplets glistening like spilled pearls upon the tops of her shoulders as she smilingly bent over a child's uplifted face.

Pete's words finally crashed into the back of his head. Turning, he asked, "What did you say?"

"Out of money. Like in bankrupt."

Reuben lifted a hand to his mouth, swallowed, then laughed from sheer incredulity. "That's impossible. There're two producing wells here."

"Well, if this third one comes in, TempCo might just break even. If it's a good one. Your father has everything riding on this one, Reuben. Just...everything."

Still slack-jawed with amazement, Reuben scowled at the accountant's features. "Pete, never in all of Benjamin's sordid and gory past has he staked everything on one throw of the dice."

"I wish I didn't have to be the one to tell you this."

Swirling his jacket around, Reuben draped it over an arm and curved his back as if to protect his vitals. In the edge of his vision he could still see Stretch and the woman walking toward the sheet-iron shed that served as the rig's office.

"Maybe you'd better start over," he said numbly.

They walked as Pete told the unhappy tale. "You have to understand your father's frame of mind the past few years, Reuben. He's watched himself getting old with not much security to show for it. Lucas Stanford's the only partner who showed much profit in those early years, so when the geology reports came in on this one and looked pretty good, Benjamin gambled big. He collected every penny he could get his hands on, mortgaged the rest, and bet it all."

Reuben had a sickening thought. "Did Lucas Stanford cheat my father?"

Pete shook his head. "Controlling interest. Fair and square."

Fury surged up into Reuben's throat that Benjamin could have done this to his family. One of the roughnecks walked over with soft drinks and gave one each to Reuben and Pete.

"The thing about these wells is," Pete's voice droned on between sips, "at least they're all Benjamin's. And they haven't cost an arm and a leg. But Benjamin's cut a lot of corners too. You know what fancy safety devices and such can cost. Up till recently, the Coastal Zone Management hasn't pressed too hard, but the locals have gotten themselves some help. These scientists know their stuff, Reuben. They can pack some pretty heavy lawsuits sometimes.

The OCS will cancel leases on their evidence alone. *She*, for instance, could mean big, big trouble for your daddy."

Reuben thought, as he wiped the mouth of the bottle and placed it to his lips, turning at the same time to search for the woman, that the trouble she could cause wasn't remotely the kind Pete had in mind.

The sun wasn't in her eyes when he found her this time. She didn't even seem surprised that he was looking. With a cool unconcern she moved her gaze up and down his length, and Reuben winced; women didn't generally look at him without doing something: smiling was common, an invitation. But he got the distinct impression that this woman could live perfectly well without him and fully intended to do so. He had the wildest, most insane compulsion to walk up to her and take her by the shoulders and demand where she'd been.

But before he could do anything, she was moving away, as if she had second-guessed him and refused. How long had it lasted? Two seconds? Five seconds? But something had happened. He wasn't sure what; a line crossed, perhaps, a challenge accepted by a polar opposite.

Clearing his head, he heard his own voice asking Pete, "How much will the repairs cost?"

Pete made some mental calculations. "About ten thousand. But to replace the defective equipment—"

The woman was forgotten. Reuben even forgot how much he resented being here. As he came around, tight-jawed and wound like a spring, he gritted out words he couldn't believe he was asking. *"What defective equipment?"*

"Well, not actually defective." The anxious shadows beside Pete's nose darkened, and he succumbed to the temptation to fondle his mustache. "Just not the best. Your father always meant to replace this or that, but things kept happening. This past week we had a really bad pressure foul-up. When I told the doctor that I had to talk to your dad, he said a few nasty words to me. That's when I called you.''

Reuben swore bitterly under his breath. ''Good ole Reuben.''

''What?''

Waving him away, Reuben bent his head to ponder how to best go about dealing with this. He glanced over his shoulder, but the woman had disappeared somewhere with Stretch. ''Well—'' he looked Pete straight in the eye ''—I guess I'll have to fix things, then, won't I?''

Pete grinned, his eyes a child's trusting eyes. ''Man-oh-man, I was hoping you'd say that.''

Starting across the deck, Reuben belatedly watched the toes of his shoes as he talked. ''The first consideration is to make some sound repairs to hold what we've got. I'll worry about bringing in this new well when I make sure it won't be spread all over south Texas.''

Pete fished a handkerchief from his trouser pocket and mopped his sweating face, then twirled the ends of his mustache neatly back into place.

The animosity of oilmen for environmentalists has always been a natural phenomenon, not unlike the traditional suspicion of the bootlegger for the revenuer. As Candy stepped off the hoisted platform onto the deck of TempCo Oil, she regretfully guessed that she wasn't going to change that attitude very much.

Yet she offered her most pleasant professional smile to the sunburned, gaunt-shanked replica of Gary Cooper who ambled toward her and removed his hard hat with old-fashioned Texas gallantry. ''Howdy, ma'am.''

''I'm Candice Burrows,'' she said with an equally gallant bow. ''Thank you for bringing me up.''

They had to shout to be heard over the clanging uproar at the rotary table as over a dozen masculine eyes exchanged knowing looks. Candy felt as if she were being stripped naked.

During the past months Stretch McPherson and the men had cracked a lot of salty jokes about the two female scientists who frequented their waters. There was considerable guffawing and wisecracking about mermaids and deserted islands, and he had done his share.

"They call me Stretch, ma'am," he said and grinned to reveal a mouthful of crooked white teeth. "I'm the driller. What's on your mind? Somethin' wrong?

Candy didn't want to come off sounding like a snooping scientist, so she pretended to be awed by the drilling. "How many wells go down underneath us?"

That was like pushing a "start" button with Stretch. "Could I offer you the guided tour, ma'am?" he said, settling his hat with energy and gesturing outward with an arm.

Her smile was just right. "I'd be honored, Mr. Stretch."

"Stretch," he corrected and chuckled. "Just plain Stretch."

Candy politely nodded to a few of the men as Stretch explained some general things she already knew. Meanwhile, she scoured the deck for some sign of her canister. Nothing. Beyond her, fifty feet away, two men in street clothes walked into her field of vision.

Caught against the merciless dazzle of the sun, the taller man could have been hurled from the sky, and Candy shielded her eyes. She saw a breathtaking, godlike creature, a pagan son of Merlin swathed in flames. The angle of his head made him seem to be surveying everything with ruthless detachment, as if he were about to bring it to its knees with a snap of his fingers.

Candy's heart gave a foolish, unexpected kick, and she darted her gaze back to Stretch. She tried to be interested in what he was saying, but half her mind kept straying back to the sun god. Silly female! she called herself. Yet, as helplessly as a silly female, she turned to look again.

There wasn't the slightest godlike thing about him now. He was merely a not-too-handsome man whose six feet of beautifully articulated bone and muscle was lounging back on itself, hinting that he hadn't gotten much sleep lately. One of the roughnecks was placing a bottled Coke into his hand.

Mesmerized, Candy watched his arm come up and his head tip back as he sent the stinging liquid sluicing down his thoat. The wind was molding soft, expensive clothes to his body. His teeth bared as he sucked in his breath, and as he spotted her, he lowered the bottle and rearranged his mouth, drawing his dark glasses down the bridge of a startlingly wonderful nose. In that second his quick brown eyes slammed into her own blue ones with the force of a meteor.

Since Victor's jilting, Candy had made a practice of never looking men straight in the eye; it only gave impressions that she was unprepared to back up and reminded her of irreparable failures. But the presence of this man was staggering. She couldn't move, and she couldn't think. She couldn't do anything.

As he slowly lowered the bottle to his waist, she flashed him the message: *I refuse to do it. Every woman must fall at your feet. I refuse to do it.*

"This way, ma'am," Stretch was saying.

"What?" Dazed, Candy wrenched her head around. "I'm sorry. What did you say?"

"This way if you want to see the control room."

"Oh, yes. Certainly."

Out of sync with herself, Candy stumbled alongside him to the elevated iron shed with a stairway plunging down beside it, and as they started down a man came charging up. She stepped back to keep from being caught in a head-on collision.

"Hey!" The man took one look at Candy and stared at Stretch in bewilderment. "Who is this? What's she doing here?"

Stretch placed his hand on her arm. "Just a minute, ma'am."

Candy overheard the roughneck saying something about a build-up of pressure as he shoved a clipboard into Stretch's hands. "Estes thinks it's probably a stuck valve."

The driller glanced over a column of figures and looked at his wristwatch. When he saw Candy watching, something passed over his face, and Candy guessed that he was wishing she were a thousand miles away.

"Are you outfitted with adequate storm chokes, Stretch?" she asked.

Storm chokes were a safety regulation of the Department of the Interior so that in the event of an explosion or pressure change the flow of oil would be shut off automatically. But cut-off valves, like everything else, came in varying degrees of sophistication.

"I'd better look at the gauges," he said to the man.

"Should I have Mr. North get Cantrell out here?

Mr. North? *What Mr. North?* Candy made the connection instantly. Of course, the man she'd been watching. He was a North. A brother? She doubted it. A nephew? More likely a son. Yes, there was a son, wasn't there?

"We can't afford to shut down this rig," Stretch was telling his man with an apologetic nod to Candy. "Ma'am, I hate to do this, but I'm afraid I have to ask you to leave the platform."

She hadn't even told him what she'd come for. She pulled one side of her mouth down and shook her head. "I want to talk to you about a canister, Stretch. One that oddly disappeared. Now, I—"

Out at the rotary table two coveralled men were preparing to add a section of pipe, to send the bit deeper and deeper into the reluctant ocean floor. Before Candy could get the words out of her mouth, Stretch was waving his gloves in the air.

"Hold up on that, Buddy!"

Hardly had he done so when Candy sensed things beginning to happen. She didn't actually see the man, North, moving toward her, but somehow she knew that he was. As she whirled around he was coming at a dead run, his legs a sprinter's legs, long and driving beneath his straining slacks.

From somewhere beneath her feet thunder rumbled ever so slightly. From the side of her vision Candy glimpsed the men wheeling away from the rotary table. Then she saw oil bursting from the wellhead.

"Hit that alarm!" Reuben North yelled as he ran toward her through a slippery, slimy geyser of crude oil. *"What happened to the damn storm chokes?"*

The noise was loud, very loud. Candy felt something make connection with the back of her head, but even as the force snapped it forward like a blossom on a stem, it didn't hurt. It occurred to her as it was happening that it did make the image of the running man blur around the edges.

Then everything blurred.

Then there was nothing at all.

Chapter Two

In his high-school yearbook Reuben North was voted the most popular boy of the senior class. There was hardly a girl who didn't dream of at least one night locked in his arms or a boy who didn't secretly wish that Reuben would drop off the face of the earth. In Reuben's last year at Texas University he was proclaimed the official "Man Around Campus," though by then female spirits had waned slightly because of his much-publicized engagement to Miss Emma Stanford, daughter of Lucas Stanford III, for which the entire male segment of university society breathed a fervent prayer of thanksgiving.

Lucas Stanford I had been a cattle baron and oil tycoon, the ultimate embodiment of leadership. He and those like him set the tone of Texas "mystique" for decades to come. They decided who would be allowed to join their group, who was good and who was bad and who stayed and who left. Emma's money was Stanford family money. Old, old money.

Reuben was from slightly less impressive stock. His grandfather had been a penniless ranch hand from West Texas who had stretched barbed wire across the poorest, most maligned part of the state. Benjamin, the second generation of Norths, had had the questionable taste to become a millionaire before he was thirty. Since his family had not been part of the elite, he determined that his children would be.

Though Benjamin never came right out and said that he was disappointed in his only son—Reuben was too smart for his own good, Benjamin often said—Reuben always knew that he didn't have enough of the ''killer instinct'' to suit his father. Benjamin was also very big on killer instinct. The only time Benjamin had ever complimented him was after Reuben had bailed him out of trouble for giving some bad advice to the governor of Texas regarding campaign donations the month before the Watergate hearings were televised.

''Good ole Reuben,'' Benjamin said fondly. ''He can come through in a pinch.''

Benjamin aside, Reuben possessed an uncanny knack for pleasing people. He knew how to create television advertising for a disenchanted public. He was also a trendsetter in delicate marketing concepts for products imported from the Republic of China. His fresh ideas found favor with troubled companies like the Chrysler Corporation, Johnson & Johnson and Braniff Airlines. Whatever needed fixing, Reuben could. And he usually did.

When Reuben moved to New York City, Emma Stanford took up residence in a fashionable Park Avenue apartment. She blended easily into the silky social strata of the very, very rich, and the engagement survived. Emma and Reuben were seen at everything worth being seen at, but people who knew them well smiled and murmured that Reuben went his way when the evening was over and that twenty-year-old men were seen escorting Emma back to her apartment late at night—a generous estimate; they were closer to eighteen.

The North family wasn't at all worried. At some point in the future, they said, they were sure that the North fortune, presently in decline, would merge with the multimillion-dollar Stanford fortune and recover.

When Reuben became dissatisfied with the boring easiness of his life, he took the logical step and talked seriously to Emma about getting married and having children. Emma stopped him with a look down her costly nose. She would love to get married, but from the beginning they had decided not to have children. Why was he so suddenly hung up on this fulfillment thing, anyway?

Perplexed, Reuben considered breaking the engagement. But to do what? To go where? No other women appealed to him for more than one night, and sometimes not that long.

Though it didn't seem possible, Reuben found himself disgusted with everything. He found himself talking more but smiling less. Finally he stopped talking. There was nothing he wanted to say.

Until he sat in the helicopter and gazed down at the unconscious woman surrounded by the scattered contents of a first-aid kit and to whose head he pressed a handful of gauze. As he pondered Candice Burrows—her whole body saturated with crude oil, nothing about her being its best, her regal bearing having been violently erased and the years of unhappiness more honestly traced in the bones of her face—he thought of a dozen things he would like to say. Life suddenly became quite serious and not at all easy.

Reuben had never been much of one to call sex love; love was a growing process between two people that took a long time. But chemistry? Yes, and whatever the particular formula was that he was feeling now, it was potent. It made him wonder a little crazily what it would be like for Candice Burrows's hands to touch his quivering skin, for her parted lips to graze the muscles spanning his back.

Yet if she did none of those things, and he guessed parenthetically that she would not, he would want to know her anyway. So why the chemistry? And why was he sitting here like some irreverant Attila the Hun, staring at her near-nakedness, when she had come within millimeters of having her neck broken?

Very carefully he plucked oil-saturated tendrils from her cheeks and then, realizing that he was completely helpless for the first time in his life, he thoughtfully spread her long, slender fingers upon the bend of his knee.

"Don't you do it," he muttered in wonder as he bent over her and willed the helicopter to hurry faster across the sky. "Don't you dare slip away, Candice Burrows. Not when I've just found you."

In Candy's delirium sound was drifting through her mind like lyrics to some long-forgotten song. It was the darkest hour of night; shades of black enveloped her—velvet, seductive, lethal. The sound became more intense, and she groped for a telephone, then realized the sound wasn't a telephone at all but a thunderous roar, the fury of a river gushing not around her but through her.

Suspended between heaven and earth, Candy roused and felt her head.

"Be still, Miss Burrows." A voice carried through the hollow black chambers, its rich depth one of authority she dared not disobey. "Please don't move. You're doing fine, but you must be still."

Candy gripped the hand that rested upon her arm and found the symmetry of five powerful fingers, the commanding bones of a wrist, a firm and reassuring palm.

"Who...where..."

The sound of her own voice helped bring her partway back from her illusion, and she felt as if she had vanished completely. The blackness wasn't the normal emptiness before waking but some hellish, Styxian void that threatened to suck her down into its depths.

Feeling beyond the hand, she found the man's arm; it oddly had much to do with her, and when she whimpered and pulled herself up, it closed about her back like a promise. His shirt was unbuttoned and reeked of the same stench as she did, but it didn't matter.

"I'm here," he said.

"A dream," she murmured as her fists filled with his shirt and her cheek pressed against the wet down on his chest.

"It's all right," he whispered. "Shh."

"Someone keeps calling. The telephone..."

"We'll be there soon."

Yes, Candy thought, it was a dream. If she concentrated hard she could force herself up through the darkness where the sunshine could splash her face. But she was loathe to leave the comforting safety of his embrace.

"Are you God?" she asked. Idiot, she knew he wasn't God, but she needed a different vocabulary for this darkness. "Tom?"

"Tom is fine."

"Tom is on the boat."

The phone...no, not a telephone...the *sound*, the sound was battering the bones of her head now. It went all over her body and shook it like a dog mauling a rag—*Blue Thunder* in Dolby stereo with the volume turned all the way up.

Candy pressed farther and farther into the man to escape the vibration and felt strands of her hair being plucked from her face where they stuck. Warm lips pressed against her ear. Then, somehow, she knew the truth.

"I can't see," she whispered in horror. "Help me, I can't see."

The words he spoke were drowned somewhere in the pools of her fear.

Later—or was it only seconds?—Candy roused again. The man was still there, and he didn't flinch or move away when she stirred and timorously placed a hand upon his jaw.

"You *are* real, aren't you?" she whispered through her daze. "I thought I was dreaming. Where. . .what is the sound?"

"You're in a helicopter."

She didn't release his face but reached up, pressed her own cheek to his. A stubble of new beard was rough beneath her curious fingertips. With a boldness that was strikingly out of character, she found his mouth, well-defined and slightly parted, and a row of smooth, straight teeth. His nose was long, cleanly planed with a fine, definitive hook at the top. Eyes, brows, craggily hollowed cheekbones, a forehead that was high and intelligent but strong, one that could and would make its own rules. How strange it was to see a man's character by feel.

"You've hurt your head," he said. "No, don't touch it. We're taking you to the hospital. You're going to be all right."

"Are you sure?"

"Yes."

How could he be sure? Yet he had said so. Such a mouth wouldn't lie. She touched her fingertips to his lips and whispered urgently, "I'm not going to die, am I?"

"No."

From beneath the stench of crude oil came the distant fragrance of spice. How sweet. Her father had worn Old Spice, but she had been very young then. "I'm going away, Candy," he had said. "Grandma will take care of you now."

"But she died," she told Reuben and trailed her fingers along the strong corded column of his neck. "Grandma died."

Abruptly, like some foolish, witless girl, she began to whimper. She couldn't stop, and she hated the pitiful, weak sound of it.

"I know," he said. When she buried her face in his shirt, she felt his lips find her ear and kiss it ever so softly: once, twice. "I know."

Ordinarily she would have repulsed any man who dared touch her, but now she grasped his shoulders, pulled herself up, and strained to see him so badly that her head threatened to crack. She shook him.

"Can they fix me?" she cried. "Can they make me see again?"

"At the hospital they'll take care of you."

Even in her anguished delirium, Candy remembered her plans. She couldn't go to some hospital. Victor's plane could arrive at any time. If he found out she was in the hospital, much less hurt and unable to see, he would take Amber, she knew it. Her daughter would be one of those ghastly statistics on the television news and thumbtacked to hospital bulleting boards: HAVE YOU SEEN THIS CHILD?

The face above her came into focus. With inner eyes, eyes-behind-eyes, she could see its cruelty now as clearly as she could not see it when she had first loved him—Victor's lying eyes and his beautiful, expert mouth that had whispered all those promises and touched all the magical places.

"No!" She thrust hard away from him. "No, Victor."

He held her as a man would hold the victim of his crime. "Be still."

Victor had said that, too. Candy's head snapped back. Lightning pain flashed through the back of her skull, and she didn't have the strength to win against him.

"I won't let you take her." Her words didn't even sound like her own as they echoed against the burnished walls of her terror. "I'm going away, Victor. You'll never find me. You'll never take her away from me."

The cruel trick of waking up in blackness made Candy remember almost everything. With a perfectly coherent embarrassment she even knew who the man had been—that sprinting man of those last seconds: Mr. North, the man who had held her in his arms. She could remember his clothes now, his wild, windblown hair and the explosion of his fear.

Dear God, she thought. Time had stopped. She was invisible. Someone had taken off her shirt and swimsuit and cleaned off the worst of the oil. She lay barelegged upon a hard examination table and was wearing a dreadful hospital gown. A band of gauze circled her brow like an Indian's headband, and she gingerly inspected it, collided with an arm.

Her voice cracked. "Who-who are you?"

"I'm Dr. Webster, Miss Burrows. You're in the emergency room of Alexander General. How are you feeling?"

How did he expect her to feel? She was terrified. "I can't see."

"Yes, I know. Take it easy."

Men always said that. "Take it easy," they said to their women. "Take it easy," to their horse. She hoped he wouldn't tell her now that everything was going to be all right.

"Everything's going to be all right," he said.

He was holding her face and spreading her left eye excruciatingly wide. He bent over her as if he were viewing obscene pictures inside her head.

"What d'you see?" she asked.

Dr. Webster operated upon the premise that people are much better off in ignorance than knowledge about themselves that might be misused. "Nothing much to worry about."

"What's wrong?"

"Please don't upset yourself, Miss Burrows."

Ludicrous. She was trapped here in some sightless horror chamber, unable to even pick up the telephone and warn Agatha about Victor, and he was telling her not to be upset.

She pushed his hand aside. "I'm sorry, Dr. Webster. I, uh—we're going to have to postpone this examination. I can come back later. I—"

Dr. Webster's intake of breath expressed his shock. "You have to be joking. You've had a serious injury here, Miss Burrows. The specialist hasn't even seen your X rays."

Serious was losing a child! "I realize you don't understand—"

"I certainly do not. Now, I assure you, this is absolutely necessary. It won't take as long as you think. Please lie still."

Arguing wouldn't accomplish anything. Gritting her teeth, Candy swung her legs around. The doctor had turned aside, and she heard him murmuring to someone, his nurse, she assumed. "Valium. Quickly. She's overwrought."

In a purring about-face, Dr. Webster positioned himself so that Candy's feet struck his legs when she started to slide off the table. "I'm going to give you a little something to make you feel better, Miss Burrows. This isn't uncommon in cases where the patient has sustained a blow such as you have. Try to take deep breaths now, and remain very calm."

Even without the memory of the little white tablets that the doctor had prescribed for her in high school and the memory of herself dialing the number of the drug rehab clinic and going through the nightmare of detoxification, Candy was terrified. Every psycopathic thriller she had ever seen on television rushed back to haunt her now. She saw herself wrapped in a straitjacket, strapped to a stretcher, thrown into a padded cell by Nurse Ratched.

A hand flexed about her wrist, and in that one dazed moment Candy's body was so saturated with adrenaline, she could have torn the room apart.

Knocking the hand away, she scrambled to find the floor. The stitches were coming alive in her head now, and they took the pain of the jolt when her feet struck the tile. She immediately lost track of where their voices had been, and when she stood up, everything tilted. She teetered, arms extended and wobbly: a novice on a tightrope with no net.

"She'll hurt herself, Doctor!" cried a woman.

"Miss Burrows, are you out of your mind? Get an orderly, Nurse."

Candy's disorientation was so complete, she didn't know where the door was or where either of them were. She knew then that she was helpless, and she wished, in her misery, for the safe, comforting arms of Reuben North.

"Wait!" she cried.

Everything stopped—all sounds, all movement, all breaths. Candy could see them in her mind's eye, crouched, exchanging warnings to be ready to pounce on her before she could get through the door.

Cautiously, one step at a time, Candy began inching back to the examination table. At the first whisper of a movement, she spun around, threw out her arm.

"I'm all right." Her voice was shrill. "Just leave me alone."

But they were circling her. She had gone too far. She had broken their rule. Though it sent pain knifing across her scalp, Candy threw back her head and assumed her tall, unapproachable stance, the one that warned life to either back off or kill her because she had nothing to lose.

"I may not be able to see," she said with bluffing desperation, "but I'm in perfect possession of my senses. And if you dare put a needle in me, Dr. Webster, I'll sue this hospital and both of you for every penny you can make for the rest of your lives. And you, Nurse Whoever-you-are, are you listening to me? No injections. No sedatives. No tetanus shot, no antibiotic. *No injections*. Is that clear?"

Vernon Webster was an intern doing his stint of emergency-room duty. He was a highly competitive man and had taken up medicine as much for the prestige as the money. A patient just didn't question the deity of the physician, damn it!

"I know it's asking a lot of you to understand under these circumstances, Miss Burrows..." he began in his fatherly tone that rarely failed to bring the most difficult patient around.

"Is that a yes or a no?" Candy asked coldly. "I don't have time to waste."

Dr. Webster blinked, dropped his shoulders in astonishment. "I will not be held responsible—"

"No one's asking you to be responsible for anything."

"No sedation, Mrs. Adams," he droned out his order as if he were excruciatingly bored. "Now, if you don't mind, Miss Burrows, I'd like to get this examination over and done with. I do have other patients."

A reaction was settling upon Candy now. She could already see Victor convincing Amber's sitter to give the child over to him. She could hear him badgering an attorney to get him an emergency hearing before a judge, "But the child's mother is handicapped now. Oh, sure, I sympathize. Who wouldn't? I'd rather do anything than take a step like this, but we all have to rise above personal selfishness in a time of crisis. It's the welfare of the child at stake now. I must have equal custody, at the very least."

"It's quite likely that this blindness is only a temporary condition," Dr. Webster said as he rattled his instruments importantly.

Candy's jaw dropped. "Why didn't you tell me that at the beginning?"

"Well, you hardly gave me a chance, did you? And this is not a positive diagnosis, mind you. I will not be held to this. A specialist has been called in to go over your X rays. No one can be sure of anything until then."

"What's causing the blindness?"

"Internal swelling is my guess. Fluid. It's pressing on some nerves that go to your eyes."

To Candy, it was a straw in the hands of a drowning person. Perhaps her sight would return in a few hours, and she could follow through with her plans. In twenty-four hours she and Amber could still be on that plane for St. Paul.

Trembling, she pulled back her sticky hair from her face. "How long will it take to go away?"

"I couldn't possibly guess. Mrs. Adams will be asking you some questions to admit you to the hospital." In an aside, "Mrs. Adams, if you have any trouble..."

Mrs. Adams was wrapping a band around Candy's arm as the doctor left, and she pumped up the blood-pressure gauge. Candy made a Braillelike inspection of the rest of her body, and when the reading was taken, she slid off the table again. She would have to wear this terrible gown out into the street, she supposed, but she had to get a cab.

"Miss Barrows, you are still classed as an outpatient in this hospital," Nurse Adams reminded with stern disapproval. "We do have rules."

"Burrows," Candy said and heard a telephone being dialed.

"I'm calling the hospital administrator, Miss Burrows. We'll just see what he has to say."

Only by sheerest luck did Candy push the magic button. "Fine," she declared. "You get the administrator, Ms

Adams. And then you get the chief of staff and anyone else you can think of. You tell them all that I don't have a penny's worth of hospitalization, and I don't have any money. Now, will you please get my clothes?''

At this moment, her spirits as low as they had ever been, Candy became aware of an amazing thing. A person possessed a sort of inner radar that could home in with a great deal of accuracy when it had to. Now that her other senses had been strained to their limit, her nose picked up the scent of Nurse Adams's chewing gum. Beneath the strata of the obvious—the woman's voice, her dark sighs and moldy disapprovals—Candy could distinguish the sound of the nurse's bra scratching against her uniform. Nurse Adams was heavy. And Candy could feel the air-conditioning vent above her head chilling her scalp. Disinfectant in the corner offended her nose. The clock on a wall had a whining second hand, windows were on the west, a lawn mower hummed in the distance, traffic on the street, a jet.

''A man brought you in,'' Nurse Adams was saying with icy reproof. ''A Mr. North. I was under the impression that his insurance was going to pay for your treatment. He said that he was the...responsible party.''

Reuben North? Here? Candy's memory was a collage of half-dazed impressions and embraces. He had brought her here. He had stayed. Would he help her? ''Where is—''

''I'll get him.''

The moment the emergency-room door swung shut, every nerve in Candy's body went on alert. Like a forest creature, she tilted her head and tried to sniff out the lay of the land. The first thing to do was to find the telephone.

Feeling about in the radius of where she stood, she connected with a water pitcher and glass. The plastic glass went bouncing to the floor and scuttled away with a swish. Wincing, holding her head, she slowly begain inching around the wall.

By using her bare toes much like a cat uses his whiskers, she made her way. She stubbed them once on an IV unit and sent it crashing into the wall, but she kept doggedly on, reaching out on both sides as far as she could. She didn't really despair until she kicked the wastebasket; its clatter was enough to bring the whole nursing staff running down the hall.

Scalding tears of self-sympathy welled in her eyes. Her head was hurting murderously now. She reached with one hand to a wall and there, behind a cart, her foot found the blessed telephone outlet.

At last! Now all she had to do was follow the cord. "I'm coming, Amber," she whispered out loud because she needed frightfully to believe it. "Mommy's coming, darling."

Chapter Three

Over the years Pete Dysan had found Reuben's impressive bearing to be complimented by an extraordinary sense of balance. No more so than in today's crisis. In all the confusion—luckily, there were no injuries except the uninvited scientist—his orders were competent and delivered in the time most men would have taken to recover from the shock.

Once Stretch had called for hydraulic-powered rams to be installed, to virtually pinch the pipe shut at the wellhead, Reuben immediately notified the Coast Guard Strike Force. No, he couldn't estimate how many gallons they would lose into the bay; the well wasn't a heavy producer. The lieutenant said they were on their way. Even as Reuben commenced the delicate feat of getting Candice Burrows off the rig, a reconnaissance plane left the naval base a few miles south.

Never did Reuben appear uncertain of his own split-second expertise. Yet as Pete and he took their seats in the corridor outside the two emergency rooms at Alexander General Hospital, the accountant watched an astonishing transformation.

A long-legged man to begin with, Reuben paced. Up and down he strode, oblivious of his filth and his smell. He watched the doors, glanced repeatedly at his wristwatch, sighed, folded and unfolded his arms, stuffed his hands into his pockets, then dragged them out to look at his wristwatch again. With a rudeness astoundingly out of character, he looked more and more like an expectant father misplaced from the maternity ward.

A nurse stopped by and tactfully informed Reuben, "There's a snack bar on the second floor, sir, in case you didn't know."

Reuben glared at her. "What's going on in there? I want to know what's going on in there."

She smiled thinly and ran her gaze up and down his length, assessed the once-excellent quality of his clothes. "I'm sure everything is all right. Would you like for me to show you where the snack bar is?"

Reuben looked at her as if she had lost her mind. Over her shoulder he spied the doctor pushing through the swinging doors and left the nurse with her mouth hanging open. "Just the man I want to see," he said and started after him. "Dr. Webster!"

The last thing Vernon Webster wanted was to become any deeper involved with Candice Burrows. Since he'd already gotten a glimpse of the dramatic Mr. North, he pretended not to see his signal to wait up.

"Son of a bitch," Reuben mumbled and let his yell ricochet down the hall. *"Webster!"*

Turning, the doctor smiled evasively. "Sorry. I didn't see you, Mr. North."

Flabbergasted, Pete walked up just as Reuben was saying testily, "I *said*, I want to know about Candice Burrows."

"Are you a member of the family, Mr. North?"

"No."

"I'm sorry. I'd rather wait until her family arrives before I go into any great detail. I can assure you, she's coming along nicely."

Reuben lowered his voice a notch. "Miss Burrows was injured on property belonging to my family."

"If you'll send the proper insurance forms to the hospital, we'll see that they get processed. Now, if you'll excuse me..."

Webster took a step to pass, but Reuben placed a hand on the man's sleeve and smiled so lethally that Pete tugged the ends of his mustache in alarm.

"I'm sorry." Reuben's words were silk, and the vise of his long tanned fingers circled the doctor's wrist. "I'm afraid I can't do that, Dr. Webster."

Dr. Webster glanced down at Reuben's hand—the only clean square inch about him—and knew fear. "If you don't remove your hand, Mr. North, I shall be forced to call one of the security guards."

With an expression as sweet as an angel's, Reuben lifted toast-gold brows. "Dr. Webster, do you see that chair sitting over there?"

The doctor's eyebrows beetled together. "So?"

"If you haven't decided to tell me everything you know of Miss Burrows's injuries by the time I finish speaking, I'm going to take that chair, and I'm going to walk over to the nurses' station and put it through the screen of that ten-thousand-dollar computer."

Pete nearly strangled, and Vernon Webster's lower jaw sagged.

"Yes," Reuben said and smiled again. "I will."

Webster closed his mouth and took refuge in the duty of his profession. "It is my opinion—" he accentuated every word "—and I will not be held to this before a specialist has seen the X rays, that Miss Burrows is suffering a temporary condition resulting from fluid pressing upon the optic nerves."

"Temporary?" Relief drastically improved Reuben's temper.

"It's possible that she could even be dismissed in a day or so," Webster added. "If there are no adverse developments. But, as you may have gathered, we've incurred a slight problem about Miss Burrows's admittance."

While Dr. Webster indulged himself in a liberally colorful account of what had happened, Reuben stood pinching the center of his upper lip. No sooner had the doctor finished than the nurse stepped out of the emergency room.

When she spied Reuben, she snapped, "You, sir!"

"Ma'am?"

Dr. Webster saw his chance to escape and gladly took it, and Mrs. Adams informed Reuben that Miss Burrows would like to see him.

"If you have any influence at all—" here Mrs. Adams paused, and her look told Reuben in no uncertain terms that she knew he and Candy were living together in sin and that she heartily disapproved of that kind of loose, eighties morality "—you'd better use it."

Reuben grinned like a well-fed cat. "Yes, ma'am."

Nurse Adams's authority wavered. "And keep it short."

"Will do." He grinned again, even more wickedly.

Nurse Adams glanced down at her name pin, nervously straightened it. More mildly she said, "And don't touch anything...please."

"I promise." He held up two Boy Scout fingers and smiled.

"I also need some insurance information. She claims she doesn't have any. I mean, that's what she said, and I remember you..." She sighed.

"You got it." Reuben's thumb cheerfully directed her attention to Pete Dysan. "He'll give you anything you want."

Nurse Adams saw a man who was shorter than she was, and she was blessed with an instant recovery. Pivoting on her boxy heel, she warned that Pete should not move one inch. She would be right back with some forms.

Reuben watched her chug off toward Admissions, her ample hips churning beneath her uniform, and turned to the accountant. "While Tokyo Rose is gone," he said dryly, "you'd better call Dr. Stein. Tell him we want him on the case and have him recommend the best ophthalmogist he knows. I don't care where he has to go —next door or South Africa."

This was the Reuben that Pete was used to. He said he'd get right on it and watched Reuben saunter off in an irresistible, loose-jointed stride, then turn back.

"What about the rig, sir?"

Twisting his mouth out of shape as he pondered, Reuben said, "I haven't even told my family that I'm in town."

"You want me to?"

"Call my mother. Explain everything that's happened, but if you have to talk to Dad, lie."

"You're not going to keep the other wells shut down, are you?"

"Until that oil is cleaned up, yes. We may wind up with a full-fledged slick out of this, and I want reports."

Pete's blood pressure rocketed. "Do you have any idea what it costs to keep a well shut down?"

"Do you have any idea what accidents like this cost? In public opinion alone? The investigations? The lawsuits?"

The smaller man drooped and swiped a hand over his face. "Reuben, your father was never concerned with public opinion a day in his life. I can tell you one thing, when he finds out—and he will find out, don't kid yourself—all he's going to do is fire me and then he's going to get Stretch on the phone and start those wells pumping again anyway."

One step placed Reuben within inches of Pete. "Look, you asked me to come here and help. Well, my advice is that we don't drill another foot or pump out another barrel until all the wells are checked for worn parts and brought up to standard. The Department of the Interior is going to be crawling all over that rig." He plucked his shirt with disgust. "And get me some clothes, will you?"

Pete could already hear Benjamin's curses. "Sure."

"And a car."

"You can use mine."

"Oh, and call my office in New York and ask for Jayne. Explain what's happened and tell her to send me someone down here to help deal with the press."

Pete stood for a suspended moment, immobile with amazement, but Reuben smoothed down the ends of Pete's abused mustache and made for the doors with the red light above them. He was thinking about Candy when she'd stepped off that platform. If she genuinely insisted on leaving this hospital, he didn't know much of anything or anyone who could stop her, himself included.

Candy stood inside the emergency room, clutching the telephone as if it were a favorite tattered doll she'd just discovered in the garbage and never intended to let out of her sight again. When the operator came on the line, she scooted back to the examination table and crawled upon it to lie, winded and panting, upon her stomach. Her gown was twisted awry. Refrigerated air chased gooseflesh down her spine.

"Yes," she said between relieved breaths. "Would you get me an outside line?"

At last Candy felt herself connected to the rest of the world. Yet as she began to gather the shredded remains of her poise, fate, having never been known for its discrimination, chose to have Reuben North push open one of the swinging doors to the emergency room. Candy had no warning that someone was standing in the slivered portal between herself and the outside, much less that he waited in spellbound astonishment, his knuckles poised to give one of those perfunctory raps that announces when a person is already half in.

To his credit Reuben's refined sense of decency warned him that he was an intruder. He was looking at something that wasn't his to see and he should back out or at least make his presence known.

But he was incapable of tearing his eyes away. The hollow of Candy's back as it sloped down into delicately curved and flawlessly tanned buttocks was one of the most enchanting things he'd ever seen. She could have been an exquisite peasant girl in a Gauguin painting—perfect, from the soles of her feet up long willowy legs to the assertive prominence of bone that marked her side. Another symmetrical curve swept gracefully upward and ended in a discreet shadow of underarm and the side of one breast, small and full with a tiny, pinkly blushing nipple, all unmarked by bands of white.

She sunbathed nude, he realized, and he could imagine an afternoon of pagan languor in a place where the sun burned hot and butterflies flitted from dusty flower to dusty flower and nothing was forbidden. He felt the treachery of rising desire.

She lifted her head from the table and pressed the mouthpiece to her breast. She slid innocently off, smoothed down her gown to ensure her modesty, and, with devastatingly beautiful blind eyes, peered out at nothing.

Into the receiver she said, "Never mind. I'll try again, operator." But when she attempted to replace the receiver, she missed and the whole apparatus slid off the table with an intimidating clatter.

"Oh," she wailed and stooped to feel the floor's waxed surface. "Mrs. Adams, would you please help me find this thing?"

"Easy, easy." Reuben did the only thing he knew to do. He rapped sharply on the door and made an entrance much too formidable but face-saving. "It's me. Reuben North."

Candy came to her feet with a flush of warmth, hardly knowing whether to thank him or apologize. "I could hardly forget," she said and struggled with a smile that ended up as a grimace. "I think I remember embarrassing myself."

Reuben smiled as he replaced the telephone. "You were perfect. How are you feeling?"

"They tell me that it's supposed to be temporary. I think I'm supposed to be thankful or something." She dipped her head and halfheartedly shielded her blank eyes with her hand.

"I know." He grinned. "Dr. Webster was kind enough to explain it to me. Are you in pain?"

"Not really. A little headache. I'm okay."

"Let me help you back on the table."

Candy stepped away in a movement that was automatic for her, but she realized instantly that her conditioned reflex had insulted him. "What I mean is," she explained too quickly, "it's not necessary to help me. I'm fine. Really. I mean, I'm going to be fine. I..."

The explanation was even worse than the insult. Distressed, Candy touched her temple in a more basic honesty and sighed. "Well, actually, I was trying to find my clothes. I'm afraid I had a bit of a ..." Her brightness wound down like a toy with a dying battery. "A tiny...disagreement with the...doctor."

Turning, she leaned her head against the wall. "Oh, Jesus," she whimpered. "What am I going to do?"

Only once did Emma's ghost emerge and warn Reuben to keep his hands off Candice Burrows. People were at their weakest at times like this. Guards were down, barriers were crumbled. They did things they would never have done otherwise, and only a monster took advantage of a person at a time like this.

"Shh," he murmured and drew her into his arms. "You're not alone in this."

"It isn't fair."

"Of course it isn't."

Reuben tucked her head tenderly beneath his chin and rocked her in the cradle of his body for the time it took her to recover her composure. Presently she pulled her hands up between them so that they protected her breasts. Stepping back, she swiped at her eyes with the rough sleeve of her gown.

"I don't usually go to pieces like this." She sniffed. "Actually, I don't usually do a lot of things. What I was, was awful. The doctor threatened to give me a tranquilizer, and I started knocking things around." She turned down one side of her mouth. "The police are probably on their way here this very minute."

"I never knew a blind lady convict before," Reuben said, chuckling.

"I thought I could just leave here, but I wouldn't make it to the front doors. I'll pay you, Mr. North, if you'll just help me get out and into a cab."

Reuben knew she didn't realize how much the accident had taken out of her. She looked superimposed upon herself—ashen cheeks against that black, black hair, her lips pale and pinched.

"They're right," he urged her. "You really should stay here for the night, at least. Are you worried about money?"

A spark flashed momentarily across her features. "Of course I'm worried about money."

"Our company's insurance will take care of that."

She had lifted the back of her hand to her tear-stained cheek. With it poised in midair, as if questioning her ears, she asked sharply, "Is that your way of saying you won't help me?"

"No, of course not." Reuben guessed he'd made a mistake with her, but he wasn't sure of what it was. "Ahh," he gestured to the telephone, "you were making a call when I came in. Do you want me to make it for you, get word to someone? Your family? Your—"

Of course. He saw it now, with a stab of resentment and disappointment for his own momentary folly. *You'll never find me, Victor. You'll never take her away from me.* Candice Burrows was married.

The silence was the length of time it took a gavel to announce a bad verdict, and he said, "In the helicopter you mentioned someone named Victor. I...well, I got the idea that between you and him things were..."

"Victor isn't my husband."

Reuben waited for her to explain what "you'll never take her away from me" meant, but she didn't. He thought he could make a pretty good guess: Candice Burrows had a daughter, and Victor was probably her father. It would explain the brittle nervousness he saw in her now: the stern jaw, the chin that one saw only in fourth-generation portraits. She wasn't at all the soft, clinging woman in the helicopter, nor the proud, self-assured research analyst who had stepped off the platform to talk to Stretch. He wasn't sure, at this point, who the real Candice Burrows was.

Narrowing his eyes, he said, "So, how can I help you, Miss Burrows?"

"Not until you give me your price." She shook her head.

"Oh, hell. Will you quit saying that?"

Behind them the upper half of a body poked abruptly into the room around the door. Reuben started, swung around. A strange nurse took one look at him and melted. "Has she been dismissed?"

"There's a little delay about that," he replied with his Reuben-can-do-whatever-must-be-done smile.

When he turned back, Candy was refastening the tie at the back of her neck. He'd hurt her feelings. A scripture his mother used to quote when they were children floated about in his memory, a proverb about a person meddling in strife not belonging to him was like grabbing a passing dog by the ears.

He stepped directly in her path and sighed. "Tell me what it is that you need, Candy."

The last time Candy had asked a man for anything, she had pleaded with Victor to marry her. Never again, she had promised herself, but she hadn't counted then on the innumerable promises a mother would break for her child.

She clenched her teeth, then took a deep breath and said, "I'm not very good at asking for things. It's a failing of mine. I—"

"Candy, girl—"

"Don't call me that!" Frustrated, she brought down her fists, tightly clenched.

Well, what did she want from him, for God's sake? An angry muscle jerked in Reuben's jaw.

"Please," she said and waved the misunderstanding away. "I'm sorry. I know I'm in trouble. I do need to stay here, but—"

Reuben didn't trust himself enough to touch her. He stood watching her lift shaking fingers to her mouth, lower them. "Go on."

She took another moment, then, yielding, "I need someone to pick up my daughter at the sitter's."

"That's it? Pick up your daughter?" Surprised, Reuben let out his breath in a whistle and wiped his hand over his face.

"There's a bit more to it."

Yes, he expected there would be. There was now a good chance that the dog he'd grabbed would chew him to pieces. "I think I understand."

"I doubt it. There's a problem, besides the obvious one. Amber is only two years old." She lifted her head. "She would be scared of you."

"That's understandable."

"But if you. . ." She seemed to be gazing straight into his eyes. "If you would, you could go by the house where I live and get Agatha. Agatha's my landlady. More of a friend, really. But she's old and doesn't drive. Anyway, the two of you could go together to pick up Amber." She took a great breath and let it out in ragged fragments. "Well, would you be willing to do that?"

Reuben found himself wanting to say he was willing to do a lot of things—crazy, stupid things that he couldn't believe he was even considering. "Not for money, I wouldn't."

"Then what?" Bafflement flooded her cheeks with color and made her sightless eyes dart impotently to nowhere and back. "My body? Well, all right! It's yours. Time is running out, Reuben. It's literally a matter of hours before—"

Candy remembered enough about what happened in the helicopter to know that she had clung to Reuben as if he were the only thing between her and survival. Yet all she truly knew about the man was that he was Benjamin North's son. Benjamin North was the last person on earth she would entrust her daughter to. But what choice did she really have?

"Today is Amber's birthday," she said and wished desperately that she could see Reuben's face. "Victor is coming. He's trying very hard these days to play father. Oh, he has no legal claim on her. He justs wants her. What he wants is both of us. Or maybe he wants neither. Who knows what Victor wants? I don't know if he would hurt Amber just to get at me. He told me last time that if I didn't give him more rights, etc., he would take me to court. I was desperate. I still am desperate. I was going to..."

"Run away with her."

She closed her eyes, and Reuben thought at first that she would refuse to answer. She said, "Do you have children?"

"No."

She was lowering her forehead and bringing up her folded hands until they touched its center. "Life is so backward," she whispered, as if to herself. "Sometimes when children are conceived, you...you don't want them. You wish that...well, you wish that terrible things would happen. But nothing does, and they're born, and the moment you see them, they steal your heart away. You love them so much that..."

She lifted her head, stood perfectly still a moment, her lashes a smudge upon her cheeks, her lips sealed against further soul-bearing. A wave of compassion rolled over Reuben with such force that he nearly staggered from the impact of it. His instincts warned him that this mysterious young woman was reaching inside him somehow, touching something within the darkness that was him and which he suspected was the best, the finest part of himself.

He stretched out his hand to stroke her cheek, or touch her in any way that she would let him, but she seemed intuitively to know his intentions. Like a fine-blooded, spirited mare that had in some terrible way been mistreated and would now tolerate a person to come only so close, she took a step back.

He dropped his hand to his side. "I have to say something."

She didn't move.

"You have to know how exceptional a person you are, Candy. Now, don't go through the denials. You know it's true."

She looked at him from somewhere behind those beautiful, unseeing eyes. Reuben uncannily felt as if she were taking him apart, piece by unhappy piece.

"What I mean is—" he almost wished he hadn't started this "—I can't see you being involved with some worthless bum, Candy. Victor, whoever he is, has to be a rather special man in his own right. Are you sure you've thought of his heart? Maybe he's feeling the same thing as you."

Her anger was a volcano rumbling even before he finished speaking. She jerked with a tension that Reuben recognized as pain, and her words trembled violently. "Oh, you men really stick together, don't you?"

"It's not that—" he interrupted.

She sliced through. "Forget I asked you to do—"

"I didn't mean that—"

"I shouldn't have—"

Both of them stopped saying anything at all, and Reuben swore he could hear Candy's heart throbbing. She was shaking uncontrollably, and she lifted a finger in his direction and strained to pierce through the opaque wall separating them.

"Fifty dollars?" she blurted.

"Come off that!"

She hugged herself, her hands white-knuckled and determined. "I'm a good mother, Mr. North. I'm also a woman who pays her bills. I've paid for everything in my life, pretty high prices sometimes, but I paid every one of them. I don't owe anyone anything. Not Victor, not anyone. I appreciate your offer, but I'll find another way."

It was a long speech for Candy, one she couldn't remember ever having made before. Though every word of it was true, keeping up with life's outstanding debts took a lot out of a person. She wished she'd never asked Reuben for anything, and Reuben was unhappily regretting having grabbed ahold of the dog.

"I'm afraid you're in the wrong century," he said earnestly. "This is a credit society we live in, don't you know? Now tell me where to go to get your daughter."

Then it came to Candy, like the moon peeping out from behind darkly banked clouds—the missing ingredient that would reconcile everything, make the equation between Reuben North and herself balance perfectly.

"Ahh..." She wet her lips, hesitating. "You know, there is something I can give you in exchange for helping me."

"You don't listen very well, do you?"

"I could, I mean, I'm well within my rights to sue your father's company for what happened today. The reason I went up in the first place is because a canister of mine mysteriously disappeared. I'm not accusing anyone, understand, but I had placed it very near your rig, and..."

Something ugly slithered out into the open, and Reuben stroked his jaws, studied her as if she were a column of figures that came out differently every time he added them up. "My father's not in good health just now. I'll take responsibility for all that happened."

She thrust out a hand. "Look, I don't want to sue. I'm just saying that I could, that's all. My...my option creates a balance of powers, you see. On paper. An even trade. So to speak."

Over the tense silence a doctor was paged from out in the hall. An ambulance screamed its approach far in the distance.

"Let me make sure I've got all this," he said, frowning. "If I pick up your daughter at her sitter's and make sure she's safe with...what's her name? Yes, Agatha. If I make sure your daughter is safe with Agatha before Victor gets into town and hears all about your accident, you will agree not to sue my father for damages above what the insurance will pay. And you'll go ahead and be admitted to the hospital for treatment.''

He permitted himself the luxury of irony and suppressed a smile. ''So to speak.''

She cocked her head to one side and drew her tongue along the edge of her upper teeth, as if his words had set them on edge. ''It sounds a little raw when you say it like that.''

''That's because it is raw, sweetheart.'' Reuben couldn't help laughing, but he forced himself to stop, then heaved a sigh and wiped the corner of one eye. ''Dripping with blood.''

''Look, Reuben!'' One of her fists adamantly found the side of her hip. ''Just save it. Okay? I don't make any apologies. I learned a long time ago to do what has to be done.''

Her artless choice of words almost took Reuben's breath away. He suddenly saw himself, not in Victor's place, but in hers. If his baby daughter were being threatened, he would do the same thing, maybe worse.

''Well?'' she prompted, bristling with impatience.

Candy's jaw dropped when Reuben took her by the hand and led her back to the examination table. He picked her up at her waist as if she weighed nothing at all, touching her sides, her legs, her arms, in highly personal ways that should have been alarming but which were, considering the primitive level of their relationship, perfectly in order.

Then he deposited her upon the table and stood with his hands resting heavily upon her knees. ''Bargains are usually sealed with a kiss, aren't they?''

Before Candy could guess that he would be so outrageous, he tipped up her face with a knuckle beneath her chin. The kiss was too quick to be sensual and too light to be intimate, but it was the most dangerous thing Candy could imagine, for in those isolated seconds of wonderment something stirred beneath all the rubble of her life, like the twitch of a muscle in a body that everyone, even herself, assumes to be a corpse.

Candy swiftly jerked back, her senses swirling like shreds of confetti cast into the wind. Their rough breathing was its own kind of language, and for some seconds that was all she knew. Presently—she wasn't sure if it was Reuben who leaned forward, or she who stopped straining back—the invisible forces that pulled them together outgrew the logic that kept them apart.

Candy struggled in her mind to stop it from happening, but Reuben's lips carefully fastened to hers. He made no attempt to hold her; the only way he touched her at all was with his lips, which moved lightly upon hers. Candy didn't move, nor did she breathe. Only when Reuben dared to graze her lip with his tongue did she gasp softly, and, as if awakened out of a trance by the snap of a finger, she threw back her head.

He walked away, and the room was abruptly between them. Candy heard him turn and wait, and she dropped the shutter over her face, one that she knew defied penetration. She told him in a bland voice how to find Elsie Spenser's day nursery. Just as tonelessly, she told him how to find Agatha's beach house.

As he pushed open one of the doors Candy could hear life going on. It had nothing to do with her, she thought in a haze that she didn't understand and therefore could not accept.

"Okay," he said gently. "But after I do all that, Candice Burrows, how do I find you?"

Chapter Four

Not having been a father himself, Reuben was ignorant of just how wonderful a pushover he was. With a half dozen emergencies demanding his attention, he followed the scenario he and Candy had agreed upon to the letter. He picked up Agatha South at her house on the beach, explained what had happened, drove her into town, and escorted her up the curving sidewalk to Elsie Spenser's day nursery on Howser Street.

The instant they got out of the car the sound of a baby screaming caused a needle of apprehension to take a stitch in Reuben's stomach. His smile was sheepish as he missed his step.

"Music to your ears, Mr. North?" Agatha said with the cool amusement of one who has watched people for a long time. "I must assume that you're not a father."

"I'm not even a husband yet, Agatha. You musn't get the cart before the horse."

Agatha smiled and touched her throat where a pattern of lines crisscrossed the aging skin. "This decade has an overkill of moralities. One never knows. My own father, somewhat before your time, of course, always said that a man hasn't begun to live until he's sired five daughters."

Reuben threw back his head in a rousing laugh. "Perish that thought, Agatha. Perish it!"

Agatha South was what Reuben's mother would have called a handsome woman, one of those tall, slender, extremely well-mannered women who made people wonder if she ever got dirty or had sex. Her linen slack suit was smartly chic, as were the jet-black beads circling her neck. Her snow-white hair wasn't a helmet of hairspray but a soft, stylish fluff. From the beginning the rapport between them had been mutual.

How could they not be friends? Agatha had asked; they were points on the same compass, and they had Candice in common. Besides, Agatha added, she knew his father; Benjamin had been a classmate during World War II when the ROTC was cranking out men for the Pacific Theater.

"Your father, as I recall," she had reminisced during the drive into town, "was very handsome in uniform. I remember when he stole your mother away from Lucas Stanford and married her."

The unexpected cross-referencing of Agatha with his parents took Reuben by surprise. "No one thought Vivian Wells would actually marry a nobody's son." He laughed. "Especially Lucas Stanford."

"Benjamin had a relentless instinct for the flamboyant. Vivian couldn't resist him."

"What about you, Agatha? Is your husband still living?"

"Not all of us had husbands, Mr. North." A youthful laughter crept into her voice. "Now you're thinking that I'm a born spinster."

He flushed. "You're putting words in my mouth."

"I didn't say I'd never been in love."

The silence had been like unearthing a box of musty old pictures in the attic, and Reuben hadn't dared to brush any more of the cobwebs away. Now, as their steps clicked comfortably upon Elsie Spenser's sidewalk, Agatha resumed the conversation herself.

"It seems to me," she mused, "that you're pushing on in years still to be single and childless, Mr. North. What does your father have to say about that? I mean, the first-born and only son, not giving Benjamin an heir to the empire he has built?"

He shrugged. "I'm working on it. Actually, Dad says very little these days. The empire isn't...as strong as it used to be."

Reuben guessed that he had tactlessly reminded Agatha of her generation's passing. It was his turn to change the subject. He reared back in mock horror. "What d'you mean, I'm pushing on in years?"

She laughed. "Thirty-five is a child. Most people just get started earlier these days, Mr. North."

"Agatha, dear—" he patted the hand upon his arm "—if we're going to keep having these personal conversations, you really ought to call me Reuben."

They climbed the steps, and Reuben rapped his knuckles sharply upon Elsie's door. The screaming grew louder by the second, and Reuben lifted one sun-streaked eyebrow. "And you would wish five of those upon me? Shame on you, Agatha."

Elsie Spenser threw open her front door and let it crash back with a mute commentary that needed no interpretation from either Reuben or Agatha. Her pompadour of thick honey-colored hair had fallen to one side, her lipstick was smeared at a corner, and a large water stain spread down the length of one linen pant leg. In her arms was perched a toddler wearing a yellow one-piece jumper, the bib stained with peanut butter. One jumper leg was pushed up and a tiny drop of blood dotted the child's right knee.

Amber was such a carbon copy of Candy, right down to the mop of black curls and widely spaced, spicy blue eyes, that Reuben didn't have to ask who she was.

"If you could hold your horses a minute, mister. . ." Elsie began, then stopped. "Oh, hello, Agatha." She glanced from Agatha to the tall, striking man, then back to Agatha and narrowed her eyes. "Where's Candy? Don't tell me she's got a date."

"Candy didn't tell you about me?" Reuben asked with an absurdly innocent purse of this mouth.

Agatha looked quickly away and tucked her smile into her collar.

"Candy couldn't come," he told Elsie and bent over the child's knee, "so Agatha and I did. I'm Reuben North. Hello, Amber. Are you ready to go, or have you only made your pretty sitter ready for you to go?"

Elsie didn't know whether to detest Reuben North or fall in love with him. "Well, it so happens there's a splinter in her knee, Mr. North. Every time I touch it, she sounds like a fire siren. If you think you can do any better, be my guest."

When Elsie thrust the baby toward him, Amber gazed through her tears in wonder at the smiling man. With an inclination of his head Reuben accepted Elsie's challenge. He held out his arms to Amber.

To Elsie's and Agatha's amazement the child went to him—sniffling and watching him with her mouth turned suspiciously down at both corners.

"My goodness, Amber." Reuben could have been talking to an adult. "I don't know what you've got against knees. Let me see here. Hm, yes. What's that thing sticking in there? It's not supposed to be there. I don't have one in mine. Look."

Placing the baby down upon the front step, Reuben folded himself beside her chubby legs and proceeded to immodestly hike up the leg of his slacks to reveal a calf and his own tanned knee.

Amber didn't relinquish her suspicions, but her tears began to dry upon her rosy cheeks. She sucked in her lower lip and stared down at her small wounded knee and said, "Mine."

"You bet. Knees are great—the absolute best thing to have."

So saying, Reuben slipped a small silver knife from his pocket and opened out one of the tiniest blades. "Yes, sir, they're perfect for crawling and for putting your book on. Why, without your knees, your legs would go backward. So I think we might just..."

Before Amber could do more than whimper in surprise, Reuben had slipped the blade beneath the sliver of pine and, catching it with a thumbnail, drew it out and wiped it on the side of his leg.

"Now!" he said briskly as he tidily pulled down his trousers. "Shall we get all your things and go home? If you're very good, you get to talk to Mommy on the telephone. And that's what your pretty little ears are good for."

As Reuben reached to tug an earlobe beneath the tousle of all those shiny, sweet-smelling locks, his past suddenly yawned like a huge, arid space before him, and he saw himself standing quite apart from everything, gazing down at the scene. He saw the small baby girl with no father, the tall, lonely man with no daughter, the gentle old woman with no family, and in a hospital room some distance away a lovely, intelligent young woman who needed all three.

What was happening here? Happening so quickly that he could almost see it unfolding before his very eyes?

"Mommy," Amber said solemnly.

"Yes, darling," he replied, equally solemn but for a much more dangerous reason. "And Mommy said to go home with Agatha like a good girl. So tell the nice lady goodbye."

They collected Amber's things, and as Elsie stood on the doorstep with her arms crossed, puzzling over them, she laughingly called out, "If you're not Candy's date, whose date are you?"

The smile Reuben threw over his shoulder wasn't quite as confident as it ordinarily would have been. "Agatha's, of course."

Yet it wasn't until Reuben was turning Pete Dysan's Buick into the narrow, tree-shadowed length of Agatha's driveway that the bizarre ingredients of accident and incident truly meshed. Then he began to have an idea of just how far fate had entangled him with their lives.

He touched his foot to the brake and sat for a moment admiring the dignified two-story house that looked on one hand as if it belonged in another century and on the other as if it were a proud matriarch barely keeping up with the times and much too refined to complain. He looked for the greenhouse out back, which Agatha said Candy had converted into a small laboratory.

A brown-and-white Saint Bernard loped down the driveway at their approach and, after an inquisitive lunge to inspect all the tires and reassure himself about the passengers, plopped down on his great haunches beside the front door and barked impatiently for Amber.

Crawling over Reuben's legs, Amber pressed her face against the glass until a cloud of vapor misted around her nose and her mouth left its print. "Boun'er!" she squealed with delight as the animal shook the car with thundering barks.

Reuben looked down at the small sandaled feet pressing into the top of his thigh and felt the same need to protect her as he'd felt with Candy. He wanted to put his arms around her so tightly, nothing could get near enough to hurt.

His glance at Agatha told him that she was reading his mind. She smiled gently. "I know. She's a precious child. You can take my word for that."

A grin, almost flirtatious, found the edges of Reuben's mouth as Agatha gathered up Amber's things. When she turned to him, her arms full, he said, "Now, you wouldn't be trying to sell me something, would you, Agatha?"

One of her thin, ringless hands curved about the handle of the door. "I'm afraid I don't know you well enough for that, Mr. North."

"Come on." He chuckled. "Ever since you laid eyes on me, you've been thinking what a dandy husband I'd make for Candy."

For one moment Reuben thought Agatha would reach out and touch him, or perhaps cry, but she gazed out the window at someplace he wasn't allowed to follow. "When Candice was fourteen years old," she said in her quiet, southern way, "her mother walked out of their house one day and never came back."

Reuben blinked at the old woman as he added this piece of knowledge to what he already knew. He urged her with a look to go on.

"Not too long after that, her father packed Candice up and took her to his mother. No one knew for a long time what ever happened to him." Agatha met Reuben's eyes. "It took me a long time to find all this out. Bits and pieces, you see. Candice is an extremely private person."

"Go on."

"There was some terrible business about a doctor addicting her to Demerol after her parents deserted her. I don't know. She doesn't talk about it much, but somehow, during that time, Candice miraculously managed to find her father. In Dallas, Texas, of all places, and he had done rather well for himself. Quite well for himself. Married a great deal of money, I understand. Her grandmother was dead by that time, and Candice knew she was in terrible trouble...the addiction thing. She asked him for help, and Ronald Burrows told her that he would like very much to help, but that he had never told his present wife that he'd ever been married to Candice's mother. Or that Candice had ever been born. He said that he couldn't go to her now and tell her the truth.''

Reuben took the outrageousness of such a betrayal within his body and let his head come to rest upon Amber's head. ''My God.''

''It's even worse than that. He said he wanted to do the right thing by her and he would set up a fund so she could get a good college education.''

Anger licked along Reuben's veins. He didn't look up. A hard smile found his mouth. ''She didn't take it, did she?''

''According to what little she's told me, she admitted herself to a hospital the next day. She went on to graduate a few years later with two degrees from Texas University. To my knowledge, she has never yet touched a penny of that money.''

As they turned to join glances over Amber's head, it was as if he and Agatha had entered into some unspoken pact, Reuben thought. A slow warmth settled deep in his bones, and he smiled, nodding that he understood, though he didn't understand everything and he didn't know if he ever would.

Agatha's face creased with a lovely but guilty smile. ''Mr. North,'' she said and discreetly lowered her fading lashes, ''why don't you stay and have some birthday cake with Amber and me?''

''A slick!'' Candy exclaimed in dismay. It was three hours, two tests, one doctor and a seemingly endless string of nurses later. Candy's exaggerated report to Agatha of how well she was doing paled alongside Agatha's recounting of the evening news on television.

''And the well's still spewing?'' Candy gasped. ''Within inches of Laguna Madre's brown shrimp? Oh, Agatha.''

She suffered a sickening vision of the worst that could happen to the crabs and oysters and peregrine falcons and redhead ducks and the plankton, the life source of them all. Softly she wailed, "I've got to get out of here."

"To do what?" Agatha calmly protested. "Ladle the oil out with a tablespoon? There's nothing you could do right now, even if you could see how to. The Coast Guard is just now stringing out the booms."

"But I have to do something. My plankton babies will all be murdered. I've got canisters all over that estuary. You know that."

"The reports say they'll have the well capped before nightfall."

Candy dropped back upon her pillow and rubbed the creases out of her forehead. In the space of one day her life and TempCo Oil had both run catastrophically amok.

"Some comfort," she retorted with ironic gloom. "All we need now is for Victor to call."

The older woman's laughter drifted through the receiver. "He's undoubtedly changed his mind. Shame on you, Candice, for not telling me about that nasty business. Would you really have left without telling me?"

"Oh, I don't know." That all seemed a lifetime ago. "I do know I'd feel a lot better if you and Amber went to a hotel for the night. I've got to get out of this place!"

"To walk on the water. Yes, yes."

Candy couldn't help laughing. "That's low, Agatha. You use my own words against me? At a time like this?"

"At my age I have to take my pleasures where I can find them. Will you be coming home tomorrow?"

"If I have to crawl out a window. I really have to go now, Agatha. There're some things about the spill I have to find out. If I'd had the presence of mind to ask Reuben North when he was here..."

"Why not ask him now? He's right here."

Candy felt as if she'd found an extra step at the landing of the stairs. Reuben was at Agatha's house? After picking up her daughter and taking her home, he was *still there*?

"Ahh..." She pressed her temple, which had suddenly become a ruthless little drumhead. "As a matter of fact, I will speak to Mr. North. Why don't you put him on?"

She could just imagine Reuben's sexy, Tom Selleck stroll across Agatha's kitchen—long legs taking the distance across polished hardwood floors, capable hands grasping the telephone, a foot bracing upon a chair rung, one hip jutting as he slumped back against the wall.

She abruptly felt put upon, invaded, repossessed like a used car.

"Hello, little mother," he said. Amusement clung to his voice from something Amber had done. "Are you having a comfortable night?"

"What are you doing at my house, Mr. North?" she snapped at him.

"Eating birthday cake. Amber's curls are frosted. Literally, I'm afraid." Without a qualm he laughed merrily at his own joke.

"I only meant for you to take her home, Reuben, not take up residence."

The sound Reuben made in his throat was so maddeningly, so infuriatingly male—not a laugh and not a sigh but more of the intimate, hungry growl as when a lover rolls over in the night and nuzzles—that Candy laid the receiver in her lap and slumped.

"Do you want to talk to her?" his voice was asking from her lap.

Candy lifted the receiver to her ear in time to hear, "She's right here beside me, licking the cake off her fingers and listening on her own little birthday telephone. No, sweetheart, I don't think I care for any. Say hello to Mother. Here she is, Candy."

Candy stared at nothing. He had obliterated every feminine wile she had ever possessed.

"Candy?"

"What!" Starting, she flicked her tongue over her dry lips and shook her head.

"Are you there?"

"Yes! Yes, I'm here. And so is an oil slick, Reuben, and a hundred and forty million dollars worth of seafood industry."

"Doesn't that make the sheets awfully messy?"

Dear heaven! Thrown so far out of focus that she found herself groping for anything reasonably sane to say, Candy appalled herself by launching into a complex and highly technical explanation of what the team had been doing for the past six months. She threw in tons of scientific jargon that she was sure would boggle Reuben's mind. By the time she finished, one would have thought that a mere flick of her fingers could purify all the oceans of the world and put the most powerful magnate behind bars for spilling a teaspoon of crude oil.

With the topic exhausted, and herself as well, she took a deep breath and said with flagging energy, "I guess you find this all very boring."

He cleared his throat. "Not at all," he said with a rich, basso profundo generosity. "I thought we could discuss the Welsh National Opera next. Did you know that they performed *Fidelio* last season?"

"Reuben—"

"As a matter of fact, they're one of the most successful companies of the region. Standards at the Royal Opera House have wavered alarmingly in the past months."

"Reuben—"

"Some are predicting that even the government grants will be cut back."

"Touché, Reuben!" Candy's voice rose to a shriek, softened immediately, and ended up as a belated laugh. "Please don't be a bad winner."

"I'm not all that sure I won. Now—" his chuckle was a more flirtatious mockery "—back to the good stuff."

"Which is?"

"Your very nice offer to give me your body."

Heat flooded Candy's veins as her smile disappeared. It found the lobes of her ears, and she pressed her palms to her cheeks. "You didn't win that much, Reuben."

Before she could think up something to end the conversation altogether, however, Reuben's mood did an about-face. "I'm doing everything that's humanly possible out there, Candy." A shake of his head was implicit in his heavy sigh. "You have no idea."

He was so clearly troubled that Candy felt superimposed upon him, laid over his circumstance like one negative is laid upon another, until she could no longer tell if it were his distress or her own.

She spoke in a dazed whisper. "It's not your fault, Reuben."

"I don't find that particularly comforting right now."

"No one will blame you for what happened."

"I'm the one who'll be meeting the public. I'll be lucky if all they want to do is stone me."

"Is your father taking it hard?"

"I hope he doesn't know about it."

Did Reuben know what people said about his father? Candy wondered. Of course he did. "I'm sorry."

"He's dying."

"Oh, Reuben."

She was becoming too emphatically involved with this man. Candy twisted and slid off the bed, groping feebly through the messy gray vacuum that was herself. She found Candice Burrows the Mother and Candice Burrows, Agatha's Friend and Houseguest. But she couldn't find Candice the Woman, who was capable of reaching out and comforting a man she was attracted to. "I have to go now, Reuben. I...I can't, uh..."

"I'm sorry," he said. "My mind wandered. What did you say?"

"That I have to hang up now."

"But you can't. You haven't talked to Amber."

Unsurprisingly he had outmaneuvered her, and she went through the ridiculous maternal process of coaxing a two-year-old to talk on the phone. Ordinarily it would have delighted her; now it was a meaningless ritual, and she realized how dangerous Reuben truly was. He was an honest-to-God gentleman, and he was catching her on a technicality; he cared about her daughter.

"What's the matter?" he asked when Amber sat smiling and silent on one end of the line while Candy sat silent and shivering on the other.

"Nothing," she whispered and weaved dangerously back and forth on her feet. "I was just trying to thank you, that's all."

"Just a minute." Turning aside, Reuben murmured something with his hand over the receiver, then said, "Agatha's putting Amber to bed. She's falling asleep. Are you all right?"

"Of course I'm all right." She found the side of the bed and steadied herself. "I just wanted to thank you for standing in for me today at the birthday party, and..."

"You just did that."

"Did what?" she asked stupidly.

"Thanked me."

"Oh, yes."

"And you're very, very welcome."

Gooseflesh tortured the surface of Candy's skin. "It's just that this was such a messy domestic affair. I mean, it was a messy domestic *situation*. I didn't mean—" Oh, good grief!

He laughed out loud. "It was my pleasure. Now, back to the affair. Would you like to have one? Don't make a hasty decision, now."

At least his teasing gave her the opportunity to recover a shred of her dignity. With a semblance of her more normal aloofness, she said, "I've already tried one of those, Reuben, in case you haven't noticed. I have to hang up now."

"I'm sure you do. And since we've finally gotten down to trinity sand, suppose we quit playing games and face the truth of it?"

"Truth?"

"That I want to know everything about you, from the day you were born."

She covered her face for a moment. *I can't take it when people are nice to me!* she wanted to scream. *I give too much, I want too much.* Then, "You're making a mistake with me, Reuben. I'm no good at this. Even when I tried to be, I wasn't any good."

"But you keep running away, fair Daphne," he huskily protested. "How can I resist?"

"Apollo didn't catch Daphne, Reuben. He only wore himself out chasing."

"And that's half the fun, isn't it? The chase?"

It was, to Candy's mind, like having walked over rough terrain for a distance and seeing the tree and thinking its dangerous branch is held safely back, only to suddenly find it swinging toward your head with vicious, vicious force. Her reply was a reflex. Like dodging. The way Victor and her father and her mother and little white pills had taught her so very well to do.

"You don't have to say those nice things to me, Reuben," she said coldly. "I've already given you my word that I'm not going to sue your father."

Of course he'd been hurt. Anyone would have been hurt. Candy's regret spread out like an inkblot the next day, touching everything she did. Though she listened to all the news about the spill and conferred with the team in her usual businesslike way, making suggestions for setting up an investigation and analyzing how much effect TempCo's spill would have on the long-range scene, one question haunted her: why had she said that?

By noon, her courage had dangerously eroded. When she listened to the television news, the lead-in made her sit up in bed in a cold sweat.

"We talked with the spokesman for TempCo Oil," the anchorman said. "When asked about what the legendary magnate, Benjamin North, intended to do about the potential threat to the shrimp crop, he explained to WBRN..."

In a state of disbelief, Candy sat scraping her lip with her teeth as Reuben's voice filled the room. "Mr. North's first concern," he said with a calm, confidence-inspiring professionalism, "is for the environment, naturally."

"You fraud," she wanted to laugh. "You flimflam man."

"Above and beyond giving assistance to the Coast Guard," he went on to say, "Peterson Maritime Service has been called in. Other backup units are available if they are needed. We have experts working to determine the currents and prevailing winds. All TempCo drilling has been suspended."

"Is it true, sir, that you are Benjamin North's son?"

"I represent not only the family interests in preserving a healthy environment, but a team of highly skilled people ready to meet the demands of—"

"And is it not also true that Benjamin North's health is in serious decline?"

"I'd rather not go into that at the present time."

Another voice, a female one, asked, "We have heard talk that the Department of the Interior expects to find negligence at the root of this disaster."

"I'd hardly call this a disaster, Miss Koehn, at least not on the evidence we have at the present time."

"But there is talk, Mr. North. Are you denying that faulty equipment is the reason for the oil spill?"

"Miss Koehn, I have no way of knowing what will be found. Just as no one else can. I can promise that any failure of TempCo Oil's, should there be one, will be instantly corrected and compensated for. No more questions now, please."

"Mr. North—"

"There will be a later statement. Please excuse me."

"But if you—"

"Meanwhile," the anchorman cut in, "in a more political vein, the House of Representatives..."

Never had Candy felt so out of control. For the rest of the day she had to compel herself to bear the tests imposed upon her. But she made herself appear charmingly optimistic, so bravely free of self-pity that everyone marveled at her courage and told her how beautifully she was doing.

It was all an act. Reuben remained with her like a miserable cold in her head. She tried to despise him. She psyched herself by picturing him as disgusting. Reuben couldn't be all that great or he'd be married by now. Logic would testify to that; good men just didn't float around like lost luggage.

So, she must take a strong hold of herself before things got any worse. She absolutely must not wander off into any more useless and wasted fantasies about Reuben North. In a few days, if she persisted, thoughts of him would gradually fade. Her sight would return, and then life would go on. She would get over this...attraction, for that was all it was: an infatuation. Eventually she would congratulate herself on being so sensible. Right? Right.

She bathed and shampooed her hair for the third time and changed into a gown that Agatha had sent with Wendy. She tried to imagine that she could see the brightness of the sun when she stood before the hot window. She imagined herself hearing particles of dust when they crashed against the sill.

By the time the nurse brought the dinner tray, Candy thought she was so improved that she could eat some of it. But the faintest footstep outside her door sounded like an earthquake. She jerked up her head and held her breath until the steps died away. Then she suffered the most crushing disappointment because those footsteps hadn't belonged to Reuben, and she had to start all over again.

It was hopeless. Candy pushed the dinner tray aside without touching it. When she actually did hear the footsteps, heard the door creak open, she had the sensation of déjà vu. It was Reuben, she thought with an instant, reckless joy. He had come!

She swiped at her hair and wet her lips. She arranged her body on the bed and eagerly curled her tongue around her apology. Yet, something about the way the door hesitated was wrong.

It was the timing, she thought: the quiet steps, the pause, the whispering sweep shut. Instinctively, fearfully, she reached out her hand.

"Hello, Candy girl," Victor drawled softly. "Heard you had a little accident. I came right over to play doctor."

To Candy it seemed as if her entire future had shrunk, like a ray of light condensed by a magnifying glass, upon how well she conducted herself at this one, precise space in time. Victor was staring at the blank emptiness of her eyes, having the weapon he needed at last.

"Victor." The brittle sound of her own voice was a shock. "What a surprise."

As Amber's father moved easily into the room, fully aware of his advantage, he gave the moment adequate time to ferment. Chuckling, he stepped nearer and kissed her cheek. "Did you think I would forget what day yesterday was?"

Candy could taste his expensive cologne. She could picture that devilish charm. She felt her muscles stretching like rubber bands about to pop. "I meant that it's a surprise you came here. To the hospital."

"Yes, well, I got into town yesterday, and I called the foundation. One of the guys told me about the accident, so I drove over to Elsie's to get Amber."

"Oh?"

"She said that Agatha had already picked Amber up. I missed her by less than five minutes. Can you believe it?"

Less than five minutes? Hysteria tickled the back of Candy's throat, and she almost burst out into wild, crazy laughter.

But she swiveled on the bed and pulled the spread loose from its moorings. Drawing it around her shoulders, she sat like an Indian and flailed about for the dinner tray and pulled it over her lap. "That's too bad, Victor."

"But I'm here now. You look great, Candy. Really fabulous. Your eyes...I would never have guessed."

She nervously toyed with a straw, began peeling back the paper wrapping. "It all sounds much worse than it is. Actually, I'm going home in the morning."

"Really? Well, I wouldn't rush things if I were you."

"But you're not—" Candy could have kicked herself, but it was too late. She uncovered the tip of the straw and blew off the wrapping with what she prayed was a casual touch. "You're not me, Victor."

When he laid the back of his hand against her throat, horrible, furry wings beat inside the dark cave of Candy's head. The straw crumpled viciously in her fist.

The gods had cheated Victor of so very little in his life. Everyone had been surprised when, returning from Vietnam, he had taken a low-paying job on a Houston newspaper, but those were days of fervent idealism. Victor was concerned about the prisoner of war situation, and she had loved him for his humanitarianism and had felt that the dingy shadows of her past had surely created her for this moment.

She was the one who suggested that he go back to 'Nam and see for himself about the POWs. It was *she* who urged him to write the book when he returned, and who had done the typing and editing. Everything she did in those days was a gift to him: every thought, every dream, every labor. The week his book exploded upon the best-selling charts, she discovered that he was famous and she was pregnant.

"I'm not going to have you thrown out of the hospital, Victor," she told him and swallowed hard. "Have a seat."

Unable to bear the frenzy of immobility any longer, she pushed the tray aside and slid to the floor, waving him away when he attempted to help her. "I can do it."

But he grasped one of her hands and pressed a metal object into its palm. She leaned far away, her lips parting with misgiving. "What's this?"

"Your birthday present."

Candy closed her fingers and discovered a key. She traced its outline, drew her fingertip along the scratchy, serrated edge of it. It was Victor's way, invasion by generosity.

Shaking her head, she thrust it back at him. "I don't want a car, Victor."

His intonation was, as usual, a hundred times more effective than her own. "Now, don't say no. Look, I've never given you anything for the support of our daughter, have I? It's the key to a house, sweetheart. A place for you and Amber so you won't have to be dependent upon Agatha any longer."

Candy didn't know what to say that wouldn't betray how much he frightened her.

"Well?" he said.

"I can't take a house from you either, Victor."

A hesitation unscored his determination. "But I want you to take it. For Amber."

"I can't!"

"I'm afraid I must...insist, darlin'."

Insist? Drops of moisture collected on the backs of Candy's knees and drizzled down her calves. What would he do if she refused? Take her to court as he threatened before?

She knew perfectly well what would happen if she took the house. A week wouldn't pass before he would move in. Just for Amber's sake, he would say. Then he would trick her into doing some scrap of work on his book. Then he would press her to put his own before hers. An emergency, a deadline, all for "Amber's future." Soon she wouldn't even be able to find herself beneath the clutter of his life.

She shook her head as anger smoldered inside her.

"I don't understand you anymore," he said.

"You never did understand me, Victor."

He stepped so close that she could smell the astringency of his breath. He hadn't even been drinking. "You're cheating our daughter of her birthright if you refuse me, Candy. It's you, not me."

"Don't lay that guilt on me."

"She can't speak for herself. How do you have the right to rob her of her father?"

Oh, God! Defeated again, Candy suddenly felt old and ready to die. Because she had once loved this man, had opened herself so willingly and had taken that life-creating liquid into her body, he had the right to say these things to her. Maybe he was right. Maybe she would be making a tragic mistake if she didn't take him back for the sake of her child. She wouldn't be the first woman who'd done it.

As if he read her mind and prepared himself for the final, killing thrust, Victor grasped her face in his hands and tipped up her face. He grazed his thumbs across the ruffle of her lashes, and Candy steeled herself, told herself that she could bear this. She could bear anything!

"There's one thing you're going to believe before I leave this room, my pretty," he murmured.

Her voice was dead. "Victor, what are you trying to prove?"

His mouth was hovering over hers, and his grip became the pivotal point of her survival. His breath fanned her cheeks. "I'm not tryin' to prove anything. I'm tellin' you now of how it will be."

"How will it be, Victor?" He was physically hurting her now, and she didn't dare move so much as a muscle.

"Before this is over, you'll be beggin' me to marry you. You'll be wantin' it more than anything you've ever wanted in your life."

"Oh, I don't know so much about that, Victor," Reuben drawled as he walked into the room with a slow, easy gait that shocked Candy to the point that she twirled safely out of Victor's grasp and scooted back against the wall. "I don't think Candy will want to marry you. Not when she's promised to marry me. Hello, darling. Sorry I'm late."

Chapter Five

As a charade, it did have its moments. But though Reuben relished the shock that registered for one, thoroughly toothsome moment upon Victor's face, a glance at Candy told him that Victor Hirsch was of little importance.

She was wearing a gown of pearl gray that should have been vastly becoming with her wickedly black hair and sky-blue eyes, but she looked dreadful. Her gaunt tension had stretched her skin so tightly across her bones, she was practically transparent. Her eyes were a vacant, watery anguish, and when no one broke the silence, she drew the bedspread shiveringly up around her shoulders, as if she craved any warmth at all. She finger-combed her hair, and one hand remained extended for a moment in a terrible, empty gesture.

Reuben's heart broke for her. He walked over and placed the gift he had brought into her trembling hands, dipped his head to her ear. "I'm sorry about the other night. However you want to play this, I'm with you."

Candy's own apology was in the quivering catch of her breath, but before she could offer it, Reuben turned to Victor and extended his hand. "Hello, you must be Victor."

The seconds dripped like water from a worrisome faucet. "Victor," Candy said dully. "This is Reuben North."

It would have taken, Reuben thought, a man of vastly more character than he had not to have been intimidated by a man who looked like Victor Hirsch. He was by far the most handsome man he had ever seen, but Victor's striking appeal was more than mere appearance, mere height, mere perfection of features. Victor possessed a quality that, had he been a cobra, would have charmed the mongoose.

Reuben could understand how Candy could have fallen for him. Victor was reckless, with just the right amount of moody arrogance—an irresistible combination for a nineteen- or twenty-year-old girl who had been rejected by her parents and who had none of the roots that he'd taken for granted all his life. She wouldn't have stood a chance.

But even so, she wasn't of Victor's generation, not even of his own. She was of the generation of her grandmother who had raised her. And if that had appealed to Victor at the time, it had certainly disappointed him in the end. Candy was of the time when integrity was everything and marriage and family and endurance were the goal of every love. Her mistake had been doubly tragic.

Reuben took pains to make his smile and handshake a piece of theater. "I've been wondering if we'd meet. Candy has mentioned you."

"I'll just bet she has!" Victor's laughter exploded into the room.

Fine, strained lines appeared at the edges of Candy's mouth. As the laughter died away and left an ugly awkwardness in its wake, Reuben watched Candy's fingers pluck erratically at the gift wrapping. Her intensity seemed to grow, right before his eyes, and she dragged off the bow and tore the paper. The sound of its rending seemed to release some awful, built-up pressure inside her, and the rest of the wrapping was stripped with a series of savage jerks. When the lid toppled to the floor, she thrust roughly through the tissue as if it were her enemy.

The moment her fingers touched the silk, everything hard and angry in her seemed to dissolve. "Oh, my," she murmured and lovingly fingered the lace that edged the neckline as her hair fell about her face. "Oh, my."

The box slid to the floor and tissues floated away with gentle, murmuring rustles. In both hands she lifted the purest, finest silk that Reuben had been able to buy. She caressed her cheeks with it, laughing softly to herself: smelling it, touching it to her pinkening lips, and for long, painfully private seconds, burying her face in it.

When she straightened, her sightless eyes glistened. "It's beautiful, Reuben."

And so are you, my darling, he thought, astonished. This, he knew, with a gut feeling that was never wrong, was the real Candice Burrows. He was falling in love with her.

He circled her with an arm and drew her tenderly into his side. He wanted to hurry her, to dispense with etiquette and throw Victor out of the room.

"We got the well capped," he told her and forced himself to slow down. "Did you hear about it? The Coast Guard has the slick contained."

She was full of sparkling vitality now—the bristling scientist. Grasping his arm, she gave it an earnest shake and said, "I want to talk to you about the clean-up, Reuben. The ecosystem's fragile where you are. Now, you have to get the Coast Guard to work with you. I know they're experts at what they do, but they're just men. You can't take a bunch of heavy artillery in there around the shrimp larvae. I've talked to the team. They know what do do. Listen to them."

Reuben laughed and fell in love with her a little more. "Every time we wring out a rag, darlin'," he chuckled, "you'll know."

Suddenly shy, she stuffed her face into his collar, and Reuben let out his breath in a controlled stream. "Be kind, now," he ordered. "Give me some good news. How are the eyes? Any sign of life behind those gorgeous lashes?"

"There are times I think I can tell that it's daylight, but that's probably wishful thinking."

"Ah, yes." He tenderly stroked the back of her head and kept his hand there, filled with the springy black hair. "We all do a bit of that, don't we?"

Gently detaching herself, as if old habits weren't *that* easy to break, Candy held the gown to her waist so that its skirt fell over the one she wore. She blushingly arranged her face. "Tell me what color it is."

As Victor watched the loverlike exchange, leaning with his shoulder braced against the wall, he caught his lip between his teeth and considered how he had offered Candy a house. She hadn't shown a spark of enthusiasm. All Reuben North had to do was give her a scrap of silk and spout a few trivialities about an oil slick, and she was as rosily fetching as a girl on her first date. He decided that he had miscalculated Candy. Since he wanted so much in return—unless he could come up with a better first draft, his publisher said they could not accept his second book—he should change his tactics.

"It's champagne, Candy," he supplied dryly as he came away from the wall. "It'll match the walls of your new house."

Candy's battle to hold on to her delight for a moment longer formed a cold, hard circle in Reuben's stomach. Her smile faltered, but she doggedly struggled to sustain an artificial one. One could almost see her thoughts fluttering, being considered, being rejected.

Slowly that last smile faded too, and she was blind again. She drew the old aloofness about her like Cinderella taking back her rags. Her fingers creased pleats in the silk. Then they, too, stilled.

Reuben scraped the edges of his teeth together. She was completely inaccessible now.

"Victor wants to give Amber and me a house," she said and turned her face in a beautiful but icy profile.

"A touching generosity." Reuben wondered how much Candy had loved Victor to fear him so much. "I read your book, Victor. It was very well written. Of course—" he moved to Candy's dinner tray and poked idly around "—I wasn't in Vietnam myself, but there's no mistaking a credible piece of work. What're you doing now? Reporting again?"

Reluctance to talk about it flickered over the man's face. "I'm working on another book."

"Ah." Reuben framed his remarks with sympathetic nods. "That's the trouble with having a monumental success up front. You have to follow your own act."

"Sometimes."

"Ingmar Bergman quit making movies for the same reason, and look at him—a creative genius."

Victor walked to the window and faced it, spreading his legs like a sailor and fitting the tips of his fingers beneath the edge of his back pockets. "I don't intend to quit."

When he realized he'd neatly been dismissed, Reuben shrugged. To Candy, he said, "You haven't touched a bite of your dinner, darling. How're you going to get big and strong if you don't eat?"

Grateful for anything to do, Candy moved unerringly toward the sound of his voice. The bedspread trailed out behind her like broken butterfly wings. "I kept spilling things. The nurses hover if you spill things."

"You eat," he said and tapped her mouth with a piece of carrot until she opened it. "I'll hover."

She smiled again and obediently ate the carrot while Reuben pulled up a chair and placed it beneath the tray, and steered her toward it by the shoulder. There was a clumsy moment of intimate touches and soft, private laughter.

"Candy told me that you would probably come to Texas," Reuben presently said to Victor, as if making casual conversation while he guided Candy's hands and acquainted her with fork, glass, bread and butter.

"It's my daughter's birthday," Victor retorted as he turned around.

Reuben looked up. "Highly commendable. Some fathers don't even know their children's birthdays."

The insinuation was gelignite. Reuben didn't miss the fraction of a second when Victor's muted hazel eyes hardened to ball bearings. He could guess what Victor was thinking—the same thing he would be thinking if their places were reversed: imagining him making love to Candy, all those hastily discarded clothes, their bodies joined in a seam of bone and muscle, his mouth upon her breast, her hands in his hair, the chafing sounds of their urgency, and the gasping eclipse of fulfillment.

"Yes, well," Victor said and ran the edge of an index finger across his upper lip, "while I mull that one over, why don't you tell me when this celebrated wedding will take place."

Candy's slight choke was swiftly camouflaged by the sound of milk as Reuben poured it into a glass. "Here, sweetheart. Drink a bit of this."

While she was drinking, Reuben stole another glance; Victor was pretending to ponder his fingernails. "Actually—" Reuben drew out his words in a ridiculous, satiric drawl, even for a Texan "—we've changed the date so many times, we may scrap the whole church bit and elope. Careful, Candy. Ahh...look at you. Tsk, tsk, tsk."

The sound of Victor moving a chair across the floor was a raucous intrusion. Reuben grabbed Candy's fingers and crushed them until they stopped shaking. Victor, meanwhile, seated himself, leaned back until the chair was balanced against the wall on its two back legs. He laced his hands behind his head, and when Reuben stared, the question ricocheted between them: so, what's the point of all this?

"I suppose you'll be wanting to adopt Amber now?" Victor said and let his words settle like dust.

Ah! The line had been drawn—a most unbeautiful line, uncompromising and masculine, and having nothing whatsoever to do with Amber. Reuben, unaccustomed to such an emotion as jealousy, for he didn't yet label it that, forgot about Candy's dinner and wiped his hands with the napkin, continued wiping them unnecessarily.

He said, as if he were a skater testing the ice, "It's customary, isn't it?"

Candy pushed back the tray and stepped out into the dangerous frontier of open space, the skirt of her gown swirling like mist about her feet. She didn't intend for Reuben to fight her battles, and she tilted her head at a wary, listening angle. "Why are you doing this, Victor?"

"Doing what, love? I came to give you and Amber a house for your birthday, what else?"

"You're punishing me."

The chair slammed its front legs to the floor, and Victor sat excellently straight, a hand braced on each knee. "Candy, Candy, Candy." He shook his head. "You always jump to conclusions."

"Be careful, Victor. I won't always be blind."

"Sweetie, as much as I hate to say this, you have really gotten paranoid. You sure you haven't got a stash hidden away? Come on, share th' wealth. Hey, I've got it! We'll have a party. What d'you say?"

Reuben guessed that Candy could handle herself—just barely—if she had the complete arsenal of her senses. But she didn't, and she didn't realize just how vulnerable she was. He measured his words with a weight on each one. "I think you've said about enough, Hirsch."

Victor's laughter was like a needle scraping across a record, and Reuben's fury hurt clear down to his nerve core. *Come on!* he wanted to yell. *Do it! Give me a reason, damn you!*

Coming to his feet, the man grinned maddeningly at Reuben. "I surely have to hand it to you, North. You're an exceedingly clever fellow. Candy isn't easy. But I promise you she's worth it. Things aren't at their best right now, but give it time. Listen, if you ever need me, don't hesitate."

Pausing, Victor ran his eyes over Candy in a brazen, lewd manner and then smiled guiltily at Reuben. "Perhaps we could make a...uh, a contemporary arrangement."

The moment was ugly, hideous. Reuben wasn't shocked; he was infuriated. What angered him more than Victor's having made the suggestion so suavely, so smugly, was that he'd made it so seriously.

Like some grisly comic release, Candy stumbled backward into her dinner tray and, turning, struck it again with her hip. Strawberry gelatin and whipped cream flew over her hands and soup sloshed over the front of her gown and the spread. The glass of milk tipped and splattered whitely from waist to floor.

"I am in this room!" she cried out in dismay. "I will not be bargained for, Victor Hirsch! I will not be demeaned."

Her bravado went nowhere. Candy couldn't keep her mask in place. Swinging blindly out with her arms, she whispered miserably, "Reuben?"

Reuben grasped Candy's outstretched hands and drew her away, turning her. He picked up a napkin and began blotting her throat and arms and wiping off the worst of the whipped cream. The saturated gown clung to her breasts like a wet T-shirt and dipped into her navel and the parting of her legs. Protecting her from Victor with his back, Reuben plucked it loose and shook it several times, then brought the bedspread around beneath her arms so she could hug it to her bosom. Finding a clean corner, he blotted the tears that sparkled on her wet, spiked lashes.

"At the risk of hurting your feelings," he murmured and willed her not to cry with a fierce pressure of his fingers upon hers, "you have a lousy aim, Candy."

Candy's stomach was in absolute revolt, but she nodded gratefully. "I've got a lousy everything."

"Exactly the way I like my lousy."

"So do I," Victor said softly, as if it were his intention to be overheard.

White-hot rage poured out of Reuben. He spun around to see Victor slouching, a smirk on his face. Even the man's posture was insulting! Before he could stop himself, he had grasped Victor by the shirt and thrown every ounce of his body's weight into an upward drive, slamming him fiercely back against the wall.

The sound of Victor's body absorbing the force was an awful sound, and Reuben was as horrified by hearing it as by seeing what he was doing. He'd never manhandled another human being in his life: good ole Reuben? The lover of all that smooth-running machinery?

The attack left Victor breathless and in pain. A strange, dark excitement slithered through Reuben.

Yet, as stunned as Victor was, he smiled with maddening triumph. "Excuse me," he said in a high-pitched voice and cleared his voice.

Reuben knew he had lost the round. Embarrassed, he let Victor get his balance and then released him, stepping backward, his hands outspread and his chest heaving with fury.

Victor calmly straightened himself to a dignified height and pulled his shirt into place. After smoothing his hair and adjusting his collar, giving the impression that the barbarity of man never ceased to amaze him, he stepped into the small bathroom and inspected himself in the mirror.

"You know what I think?" he asked, as if, in his princely generosity, he forgave everything.

"I'm afraid my mind doesn't work like yours," Reuben snarled.

Laughing, Victor talked around the door facing as he combed his hair. "What I think is that you're a terrific actor, North. A little on the Indiana Jones side, but that's all right. Sorry to say, however—" he brushed both shoulders, peered down at them one final time to make sure he was tidy "—I'm not buying."

No more, Candy thought as the ghosts of her past dragged their awful chains through her head. *No more.*

She stepped into the room and, by the very haggardness of her silence, commanded it. She swallowed to keep her voice from quivering. With exaggerated precision she said, "If you...gentlemen would excuse me, I would like...to change my gown."

Victor was walking out of the bathroom, massaging his shoulder, and he met a coldness in Reuben's eyes that dampened the vivacity of his smile.

"I'm sure you wouldn't mind giving Candy a bit of privacy, would you, Vic?" Reuben said with a deadly warning of more violence.

Like the graceful courtier that he was, Victor immediately inclined his head in a nod of acquiescence. "I am rather thirsty, come to think of it." He paused with one hand on the door as he left and flashed a dazzling smile. "I won't be but a little ole minute."

In the days when the Burrows household lived under the same roof, Candy had accumulated a considerable repertoire of scenes; this was as horrible as any of them. If she could have paced, she would have done so. Instead, she threw the bedspread to the floor and held up her hands to Reuben like a traffic policeman.

"Don't say it," she snapped. "I don't know why I let him do this to me. I know everything you can ever say. I've given myself a thousand lectures and made just as many promises. I know what you're thinking."

"I doubt that," Reuben said with a wry twist of his mouth. He strolled over to the air conditioner and let it blow over the sweat-stained back of his shirt as he grimly eyed the way her wet bodice was accentuating her nipples.

"But I'm not going to go to pieces," Candy went on talking to an empty space. "It's all going to work out. Just because two grown men are behaving like a couple of street thugs is no reason to go to pieces. I'm composed. I'm in control. I'm fine."

"For a minute there—" he smirked "—I was afraid you didn't appreciate the theatrical finesse of it."

"Finesse?" Candy lifted her hands to the ceiling as if imploring the gods to have mercy. "A bulldozer has finesse, Reuben. King Kong has finesse."

"At least you're not upset." He wrenched his gaze from her breasts.

Candy found herself hard pressed to be irritated at someone who had just gone to war for her. With a surrendering sigh she said facetiously, "You've got strawberry gelatin on your shirt, Reuben."

Reuben peered down the front of himself and with solemn dignity picked up her napkin and rubbed at the spot of red.

"And," she said with a more realistic honesty, "you make a mistake when you don't take Victor seriously. He can hurt you. And he will if you push him."

"What's he going to do? Take away my American Express card?" Reuben's head came up.

No, she wanted to tell him. *If you care for me, he'll get to you through me.* She shook her head and absently tugged at a lock of hair. "I don't know what you were thinking of.

'We'll probably elope.' My goodness, Reuben, a turtle could have seen through that.''

Grinning until it dawned on him that Candy was a better actress than he had given her credit for, that her flippancy was nothing more than a convenient facade, Reuben dropped the napkin back to the tray. He took three swift steps that placed him in front of her, and he closed his hands about her shoulders, causing her to lean back in a sweeping curve of her spine.

''Then why don't you make an honest man out of me?'' he gruffly demanded and hungrily drank in the sight of her head tipping back, her long bared throat, the space plunging between her breasts.

''Reuben—''

''I know you've been through a lot, and you haven't known me very long. But you mistrust me as much as you do him. I haven't betrayed you, have I? I don't insult you, do I?''

''Let go of me.''

''And every time you pull away like that, you accuse me. Look at you, you're shaking.''

She gripped his shirt in her hands and pulled herself up. ''I didn't say—''

''I didn't say, I didn't say. What haven't you said? You lash out at me like some wild thing. You say things you know are going to hurt me. Why did you hurt me before, on the phone?'' He gave her a frustrated shake. ''Why did you need to hurt me like that?''

It was such a sweet, wonderful thing for a man to say— *Why did you hurt me?*—that Candy thought if she could somehow grab the moving hands of her life and turn them back to the beginning, she could tell him the answer.

But time was sprinting, and she could not say that life had taught her too well, and that she was too bitter and too conditioned to be what he expected. Reuben North wouldn't understand the place where people like her went, the place in the brain where numbness was welcome, where life was simply a process of staying alive minute by minute, and no friend, no child, no dream, could make it any more or any less.

Ashamed, she tried to turn her face away.

"Oh, no," he whispered as he caught her jaw in one hand. "Not on your life."

Even if she had had her sight, she knew she wouldn't be looking at him. Why didn't he let it go? She twisted away from him. "I have to survive."

"Surviving's not enough, Candy."

"For you, maybe not. I have Amber." She stamped her foot in frustration. "I have to survive!" She covered her face. "Tell me how I'm going to survive."

Reuben closed his arms about her, rocked her in the cradle of his body. "Okay, okay."

"You've come into my life at such a bad time," she mumbled wretchedly into his shirt. "Or I've come into yours...I'm vulnerable right now, can't you see that?"

"I see a lot."

"I have Victor on my back, around my ankles, everywhere. And God knows, after you said that to me the other day, about his rights, I thought about it a lot. You were right. Even an old dog has rights in this world. But I..."

"You what?"

She turned aside and leaned upon his arm so heavily that Reuben feared he would drop her. "I don't know," she whimpered. "Don't do this to me now. Wait until I can see you, and then we'll—"

Wincing because he was making her unhappy and didn't know what else to do, Reuben forced her to stand up. He took her hands and placed them upon his face. "You can see me," he said because he was desperate to have her touch him. "Look at me like you did before."

She dipped her head. "I was half out of my head then."

"You were..."

It was such an old ploy that Candy couldn't believe that she was rising to the bait. "I was so, what?"

"Irresistible."

Candy's breath was gone in the face of her memories. Oh, she was a fool if she listened. He was only a man, after all, like any other. He only wanted a warm body to hold, a mouth to kiss, a stroke to his ego by being able to make a woman have an orgasm every now and then. She could never be just that.

"Oh, Reuben," she groaned. "It won't change anything."

"Then it won't hurt you, will it?"

With pained anguish she halfheartedly moved her hands over his face. Her eyes were in the tips of her fingers as she touched different facets of him: the way his bones lay so cleanly beneath his skin, the precise way his nose was fashioned.

"Well," he said, battling to keep his breath from tearing. "What d'you think?"

"What?" Dazed, she didn't remove her hands.

"Am I handsome?" he teased and let his breath out by degrees.

Candy was too rattled to dissemble. She shook her head. "No."

Reuben closed his eyes, smiling as she learned the way his mouth was positioned beneath his nose; the way his hair brushed the tops of his ears; his Adam's apple when he growled that sensual sound as before; his clean, scratchy shirt, its buttons; the ripple of his biceps when she trailed her hands over his arms.

Stopping when she came to his wrists, Candy was aware of her own pulse throbbing. Women did that too, didn't they? Foolish, foolish women.

She slowly closed her hands into fists, but Reuben shook his head and, taking those fists, placed them in the center of his chest and flattened them out, holding her fingers outspread and sliding them down over his ribs, over the beltless waist of his slacks, his flanks.

Candy was as rigid as a sacrifice being dangled over the flaming pit. Reuben's lips brushed across the curve of one cheek and pressed her temple. "Stop thinking about him," he muttered. "I ain't him, babe."

As if spellbound, she let him guide her palms down his sides, back up the muscular tops of his thighs and over to the parting of his legs. When he closed one hand to the lifting proof of what he was really feeling, Candy jerked back.

"I saw you, Candy," he said thickly as he circled her with an arm and pulled her close, tested her lips with one wispy kiss, then another. "Before, in the emergency room, I saw you. Your back. You were beautiful. The most beautiful thing I'd ever seen. I wanted you. I do want you." He closed both arms around her. "Sweet, sweet Candy. I want you."

His confession tossed Candy too high, and she dragged her hands from between them, lifted them to his head, slid them into his thick, heavy hair and drew his face down to hers.

"Oh, Candy," he whispered and touched her lips, hesitantly, uncertainly, shifting, touching them again and feeling her yield ever so slightly and melting against him. He groaned, unable to get close enough.

Her fingers began to search him as his tongue sparred erotically with hers. She touched their clinging lips, his closed eyes, the creases deepening across his forehead.

When she surrendered fully to the kiss, Reuben reached between them for the fragile straps of her gown. They surrendered so easily, and when he filled his hands with her breasts, they seemed to leap to life, their sweetness a torment.

"I know you're hurt," he whispered into her mouth. "I can help you heal, Candy. Trust me. Believe in me."

Desperation seemed to overwhelm her, Reuben thought, as she, moaning, moved her hands convulsively up and down his back. She rained kisses upon his face, the tops of his shoulders, as she stroked his sides. Half his brain made him lift his chin in a starved invitation for her to kiss his neck, but the other was compelled to go with her mind, to try and feel what she was feeling.

Unable to loose the buttons of his shirt, she slipped her hands beneath the back of his slacks and the waist of his briefs. She buried her fingers into the trembling flesh of his buttocks—not a sexual aggression, but as if she were suddenly freezing to death, as if she must crawl inside his skin and steal the warmth from his body just to keep alive.

Reuben's past hadn't prepared him to deal with a loneliness like hers. Her pain passed from her into the depths of his own soul. An anger surged as he understood something of the way life had denied her, something of the people who had walked the paths of her life and looked the other way, people like himself who had everything and had not stopped to notice her valiant struggle.

He had a horrible presentiment of Victor walking in upon them, and he knew that if he made a mistake with Candy now, especially one involving Victor Hirsch, she would never recover enough to trust him again.

He shook his head in an effort to clear it of the heavy demands of passion. He'd been wrong in letting this happen here. Agonizing, he reached behind his neck for her arms.

"Don't let me go!" she begged and battled for his arms, placing them around her and huddling desperately against him. "Don't let me go!"

Reuben knew a moment of the most intense pleasure and the most intense regret he'd ever known, but muted voices seemed to come from everywhere. Moaning, he clasped her head hard between his hands. "Candy," he said and shook her. "We can't. Not here."

He could have slapped her. Or thrown acid in her face. Stepping back, her gown snuggling low on her hips, she blinked, as if she must view for herself the horror of her indiscretion. She filled her hands with her breasts and crushed them, and her lips began to quiver. "Oh. I'm sorry, I—"

Reuben despised himself. He tried to take her into his arms and force her to believe his need to care for her. "Sweetheart, listen to me..."

But her shoulder came up, and her one arm that was free doubled back over to shield her head as if from a blow. Victor's laugh sounded some distance away. And a woman's voice.

With instant reaction Reuben started stripping the ruined gown off her legs. "Hurry!"

She was too dazed to refuse him. To Reuben, she seemed oblivious of her nakedness, and he did no more than glance at the needle-thin scar reaching from her navel to the thick patch of black curls. He twirled the new silk gown out like a sail into the wind and pulled it down over her head.

The door opened, and the nurse walked into the room, Victor on her heels.

To all outward appearances Candy was calm and repaired and in total control. Now Reuben understood how Candy had stood before all those gawking men; she had taught herself to do this thing. She could walk and talk with perfect poise, while the sensitive parts of her were writhing in some completely different place of herself. He couldn't touch that place in her, and he felt both infuriated and cheated.

"Well," the nurse said brightly after a swift look around the room, "I see someone has brought you something pretty, Miss Burrows. Isn't that nice?"

Scooping up the fallen spread with a proficiency that was a rebuke all its own, the nurse moved to the head of the bed and pressed a button that lowered it. She threw out the spread with a skillful pop and proceeded to tuck the edges beneath the mattress. Then she began cleaning up the tray.

Reuben was still gathering up the pieces of his composure as Candy glided with lyrical grace to the bed. She stepped on the footstool and, with a brief gesture of reaching into space, slipped beneath the covers.

"Visiting hours are over, gentlemen," the nurse announced with an authority that neither of the men questioned. "Our patient must get her rest, mustn't she? Tomorrow's another day. Maybe Miss Burrows will have her eyes back and be able to see what she's missing in such handsome gentlemen callers. Won't that be nice, Miss Burrows?"

As the nurse breezed out the door the small room took on the feel of a trap, deathly still. The silence evolved into such a wasteland that Reuben thought the evening would end in tragedy if he didn't reach Candy upon some level.

He shot a quick look at Victor and saw that Amber's father had no intentions of leaving first. *We're animals,* Reuben thought unhappily. *We're wolves snarling over a bleeding doe.*

Reuben walked to Candy's bedside, grasped her hand. It was warm and faintly trembling. Turning up its soft palm, he kissed it and folded it upon itself.

He whispered as he bent over her, "The day will come, Candice Burrows, when you can't do that anymore. When it does, you remember that I told you so." Straightening, he turned. "Walk you out, Victor?"

It would have taken a psychic to interpret Victor's smile. He walked to the table beside Candy's head and opened the drawer. Keeping his back to the room, he removed a long blue envelope from his jacket and slipped it inside.

"I'll guess I'll be going too, love," he said pleasantly. "I've had a long day."

Candy pulled herself up higher on the pillows and arranged her face and smoothed back her hair. "I'll be going home tomorrow,'' she said. ''I don't want you to see Amber until I'm there.''

His shrug was beautifully nondescript. Casting a cool look at Reuben, he walked to the door, and turning back as if he had just remembered something, he opened his mouth and closed it again. Then he opened the door, and Reuben, feeling as if he were leaving part of himself in the room, walked grimly out after him.

How civilized we are, Candy thought in horror. *How very civilized. We've been talking about Amber, and it's all so civilized.*

A full five minutes passed before she stirred again. So drained was she now—her seconds in Reuben's arms could have never happened—that lifting her hands took all her strength.

Get up! she demanded of herself and dragged her body up on the pillows. *Who do you think you are, someone who can just drift off in an ocean of self-pity? You made your bed, now lie in it. And don't you dare cry. Women always cry.*

How many times had she used her willpower like this, beating herself without mercy, drawing money from her bank? Sometimes she knew she was on the verge of an overdraft, but she couldn't stop spending it. To stop was to die.

Sliding to the floor, she found the table and pulled open the drawer. She felt about inside and closed her hand upon a stiff envelope. Drawing it out, she smelled it. Tobacco, and the etherish smell of correction fluid. Reaching inside the envelope, she pulled out a thick sheaf of papers, long legal-size papers. Their stiff crackling overpowered the sound of her own racing apprehension as she ran her fingers across the top and found the stapled binding typical of legal documents.

''Oh, you bastard,'' she said, her bosom heaving with disappointment. ''You dirty bastard.''

Stumbling to the door, she swept it open and stepped out into the corridor, half expecting Victor to be skulking in the shadows. She almost hoped he would be. She wanted to rip her nails down his face. She whirled around at the sound of footsteps.

"Miss Burrows," the nurse scolded. "You shouldn't be trying to get around by yourself."

Candy thrust the papers at her. "Tell me what these are."

After a few moments of loud crackling and the flipping of pages, the nurse let out her breath in a stream. "Well, what I can make of it is this—Mr. Victor Hirsch wants you to sign an agreement."

Her heart in her throat, Candy said, "Go on."

"That Amber Grace Burrows's name be changed to Amber Grace Hirsch and that he, as the father, be given the customary paternal rights. In return, he will accept financial responsibility with all that that entails. In the case of your remarriage, he requests that said child not be adopted until she reaches the legal age of consent. Let me see...is that sixteen for a girl? I can't remember."

The floor beneath Candy's feet was suddenly freezing cold. The disinfectant smells and the stench of illness made her want to retch. What was Victor trying to do to her, push her over the brink? Did he seriously think she would agree to such a thing?

Shivering, she hugged herself. "It doesn't matter," she mumbled and reached for the papers, took them, and crushed them in her fist. "Thank you very much."

The nurse insisted on putting her to bed again, and Candy numbly let herself be tucked in like a child, maternal fears fluttering in her mind like wounded birds. "Thank you," she said numbly. "I'll be okay."

"You sure?"

When in doubt, smile. Candy drew her lips back over her teeth. "Of course. I'm fine."

"Good night, then, Miss Burrows."

Candy lost track of how long she lay with her eyes wide and unblinking. Her body felt like a piece of seaweed, but she knew if she weren't blind she would get up and dress herself and run, run, run as fast and as far as she could. But now she must depend upon her wits. What wits? Strength, then. The first step had to be a show of strength. Life must go on as normally and as smoothly as possible until Victor saw that his weapon against her was useless. Then she would leave.

Something settled inside her, cold and determined. Closing her blind eyes, she was aware of her own blood coursing through her. In the final analysis a person reverted to what they were in the beginning, which, in her case, had been a "thing" born to two people who had cast her away as if she were a dirty rag. Disposable child. Advance technology.

Fury rose up in her heart until she thought it would burst and spew the life out of her. She twisted the blanket in her hands until the circulation was cut off and pain was shooting up her arms and hurting her head, and her entire body was straining and soaked with sweat. It wasn't fair, it wasn't fair!

Burying her face in the tortured roll of linen, an animal-like scream burst out of her throat and went nowhere but into the hollow, echoing cavern of her head. She screamed and screamed and screamed, for every helpless and unwanted thing in the universe. And then, drained and exhausted, she lay back.

"Oh, Reuben," she whispered when she could croak out a broken whisper, "would it be madness to hope that you could be the answer? You do care for Amber. I can feel you caring. And you care for me. I'm not wrong about that. You're a good man, and if Amber had a father, what could Victor—"

Merciful Lord, had she stooped to that?

Candy kicked back the covers and slid off the high mattress and groped her way until she found the wall. The door to the closet wasn't far away, and without mishap she opened it, found the slacks and the top that Wendy had brought earlier in the day. She dragged them off their hangers and felt about on the floor for her shoes. Finding those, she peeled off the gown Reuben had given her and dressed herself, then folded the gown neatly and inched her way back to bed. The chair balked, but she disentangled its legs from some cords and dragged it close enough that she could sit and lean her head over onto the mattress.

At least she could control this much, she thought. A person had to control something.

Holding Reuben's gift in her lap, she closed her eyes and imagined herself settling slowly to the ribbed ocean floor. Her bubbles floated silkily upward like some mermaid's scattered jewels, and the silence was not really silence at all but a thousand voices of living things. The sunshine turned blue and shadowy, then sank with her into motionless darkness, where not even dust motes moved. Reuben...

Without realizing it, she slipped into a deep and exhausted sleep.

Chapter Six

You have as much business out in this mess as a rubber duck on the Atlantic!'' Beth Dickerson yelled at Candy with the merciless rudeness only a best friend is capable of.

Today was Friday. Candy turned from where she stood on the sand dunes of Mustang Island, relishing the two blurry double skylines of Corpus Christi. They stretched upward across the bay and concocted their petrochemicals and aluminum and glass. On her right twice the right amount of resorts in Port Aransas were raking in their tourist millions. Farther down the bay ran a matched pair of intercoastal waterways.

Candy cupped her hands around the frames of huge sunglasses and laughed as two identical images tromped toward her across the dunes in high-heeled shoes. It was good, better than good; it was *wonderful* to be able to see again, even double.

She slipped a miniature tape recorder back into the pocket of an oversize white shirt. A jet from the Naval Air Station screamed across the sky as she waved at Beth.

After it passed she shouted back, "What're you doing out here yourself, Counselor?"

"It's the only game in town!"

Beth wasn't exaggerating. The bay side of Mustang Island seethed with the activity of cleaning up TempCo's renegade oil. Jeeps spilled bivouac equipment up and down the shoreline while Coast Guard team members strode over the beach with concerned ecologists and worried fishermen. At the northern rim of the bay a Coast Guard cutter corraled the oil layer with floating, sausage-shaped booms, pulling it toward land because the slurp skimmer could only work in four feet of water.

Along the perimeter of the slick Miller worked the tiller of a small boat so that Wendy could lean over the side and take current readings. Farther south, around the Crane Islands, Tom had taken an infrared detector and discovered traces of oil headed their way. He had rushed the samples to the lab in Port Aransas, where he was putting them through the GC. It was unthinkable that anyone else should be called in to analyze the spill results; the Worthington team's reputation was blue chip.

The thermometer's mercury had peaked at one hundred and seven degrees. At five o'clock in the afternoon it was stubbornly stuck at one hundred and two. Beth paused in her trek to yank off her high heels. Laughing, Candy fit a hand in the back pocket of her baggy white pants and watched both of her.

Beth was the assistant county prosecutor for Nueces County. She was blond, six feet tall and a chain-smoker. She was also two husbands ahead of Candy, and, being a devout lover of all men, excused her promiscuity on the grounds that she was shopping for a third. Neither she nor

Candy had ever figured out why their friendship worked so well.

She peeled off clothes as she approached: her belt, which she thrust into the same hand as her shoes and her tote bag, her earrings and necklace, and finally, reaching under her great floral skirt, she wriggled out of her pantyhose, which, if they hadn't already been ruined, would have been.

Several of the Coast Guard officers shrilled whistles at her, and she brassily acknowledged them with a little tap dance in the sand.

"Lawd, it's hot, girl," she groaned as she walked up and flung everything into Miller's Jeep and cast an envious eye at Candy's cool cotton shirt and rolled-up pants. She reached over to draw the dark glasses down the bridge of Candy's nose. "Where's Amber and how much can you see?"

Candy smiled. "I can see through you, lady. And Agatha and one of her friends took Amber into town to a private swimming pool. Would you believe it? When she could have had all this natural beauty?"

"Uck! It smells bad here. Great-looking guys, though."

"It'll smell worse if any of that slick sinks."

Beth fished in her bag for a cigarette. "I see the local shellfish farmers are keeping a close watch. They've been calling the D.A.'s office all day, wanting someone to yell at. You should be home resting."

A Jeep roared past and left a cyclone of dust in its wake. Coughing, Candy waved it away. "I'm waiting for one of those giant worms to plow up out of the dunes."

"You and Frank Herbert." Beth laughed. "So, did you get an extension from your publisher until you can see again?"

"This little accident will probably cost me six months."

"Aggie told me Victor's in town. How long is the wretch going to stay this time?"

Smiling, Candy held a tight line on her feelings about Victor. "Too long," she said with deceptive flippancy. "He thinks Texas will inspire him to write the great American biography."

"Oh, it's a sex book. Wonderful." Beth leaned nearer and stared hard at Candy, as if she were a specimen under a microscope. "Speaking of sex...what's with you?"

Candy peered over the top of her sunglasses with an absurd look of innocence. "What d'you mean, what's with me?"

The sides of Beth's mouth curled chidingly. "Don't try to kid the expert on primitive biological urges. Being blinded didn't change your hormones, did it?"

"Nothing's happened to me, Counselor." Candy forced a nervous laugh over her protest; Beth always saw too much at the wrong time. "You, on the other hand, are suffering from overexposure."

"I'm never wrong about things like this."

"I thought I was doing quite nicely."

"That's just it." Beth lit her cigarette like Marlene Dietrich. "You should be depressed. On the verge of a complete breakdown."

Candy purposely gave the attorney her back and fished through the Jeep for her big straw hat. Actually, she had been prepared to be depressed when she left the hospital, as she wouldn't be able to work on her book, and she couldn't carry her weight with the team because she couldn't dive, and all she could see through the lens of a microscope was a blur.

Yet she was strangely contented. Reuben had called her only once since she'd left the hospital—a hurried but friendly call telling her that he wanted badly to see her but that all hell was breaking loose at TempCo. He was up to his waist in threatened lawsuits against his father.

She was proud of the sensible way she had come to terms with herself about Reuben. She had rationally tucked him into her past as one of the best memories she would ever have, and she refused to corrupt it with a lot of expectations that would only end up in frustration. But those hours with him had changed her; she admitted to feeling differently about herself, and she wanted to savor every drop of it. She strangely wanted to be around people again. She still viewed her life as a drastic failure. But still, the desire was there to laugh a little and dance a little and flirt a little. All day she'd been conscious of the men on the beach. Were any of them looking at her the way Reuben had looked at her?

Finding the hat, she took refuge beneath its great brim. She moved to the back of the Jeep where a microscope had been set up.

"I'm just glad to see you," she told Beth, which was perfectly true.

Beth snorted. "You can't buy me."

Laughing, Candy closed one eye and squinted into the microscope. She couldn't see a thing.

"I don't suppose you've seen today's paper," Beth said to keep the conversation going. "Sorry, forgot you can't read yet. Anyway, our local rag said that old Benjamin's son came down from New York the day the spill occurred. He's now conducting this new 'open door' policy into the incident. He has everyone wondering what his angle is."

Something white hot touched Candy's ribs at Beth's careless handling of Reuben's name. She compressed her mouth; talking to Beth about any man was suicidal. "What else did the paper say?"

"What? Oh, about Benjamin?" Beth walked to the back of the Jeep to join her. "The Natural Resources people are probably going to throw some stiff suits around. On the Coastal Zone Management for sure, for letting Benjamin get by with using substandard equipment."

"Then he did? Use substandard stuff?"

"Hell, yes, child. The well you got hurt by didn't even have storm chokes. Talk about your lawsuits."

What would Reuben do now? Candy wondered with an anxious fluttering in her stomach. She quickly changed the subject. "Tom found traces of oil down by the mouth of the estuary."

"Whose is it?"

Candy shrugged. "He's running it through the GC now."

"Well, if it's TempCo's, sweetie, your team will be called to testify against Benjamin along with everyone else in the state."

She'd tried not to dwell on it. More honestly, she'd buried her head in the sand, hoping that some miracle would happen before the case reached court. She'd always presented the team's report, but not his time. Tom would have to. Someone would have to. Anyone. But not her.

"Anyway," Beth was rattling on, "the profile in the living section was about the son. Better by a long shot than the one they did on me when I took office."

"The son?" A warning tingle rippled along the top of Candy's scalp and down her spine. She bent her head to avoid Beth's cross-examining eyes.

Beth puzzled a moment, then said, "Yes, the son, Candy love. The man who took you to the hospital. Are you sure you're all right?"

"Yes! Yes, I'm perfectly fine. You were saying?"

"About how secretive you've become, my dear. And speaking of lawsuits, have you seen a lawyer?"

"Why should I see a lawyer?" Candy straightened, her face an open target.

"Because of your own suit, dummy."

Candy waved her away. "I'm not planning to file any suit."

Before Beth could protest, Tom drove up in his Honda and screeched to a stop beside the tailgate and cut the engine. Both women started to ask what he'd found, but as he pulled off his helmet he was already telling. "It's TempCo Oil, all right. The machine doesn't lie."

Candy's shoulders rounded in a slump. "I knew it. And this water's so shallow."

"You can't be serious," Beth declared, so shocked that she threw her cigarette away, half-smoked.

Tom squinted at the attorney. "Of course I'm serious."

"I'm talking about Candy's lawsuit, you idiot." Beth brushed Tom aside. "Candy, I can't believe you're not going to sue. Of course you're going to sue."

"Believe it, Beth." Half of Candy's mind was on the future of Laguna Madre and the other half on Reuben. "Why should I sue?"

"Because, darling," Beth argued, "you're blind. You can get a fortune out of this, I promise you. A lovely, lovely fortune, and you won't have to be dependent upon Agatha anymore. I can't believe you haven't seen a lawyer, Candy. Grief, I'll take the case myself."

There were a dozen things Candy could have said but didn't dare. *You can't do that, Beth, because Reuben North came to the hospital and kissed me.* Or, *I can't stop thinking about him.* Or, *He made me feel like a woman again.*

Before Candy could do or say anything, however, Miller and Wendy returned from the bay. Wendy and Beth immediately began chattering while Tom told Miller the results of putting the samples into the GC.

Miller rubbed a hand over his wild punk hair. "Looks like the old crocodile is finally going to get made into a pair of shoes," he said with a cackle and glanced out at the TempCo rig.

"The old crocodile won't feel a thing," Beth threw in. "His son might, though. He's the one dealing with the Feds."

Yes, Candy thought. How would Reuben finesse the federal government? "You'd better go tell the Coast Guard what you found, Tom," she said quickly. "Every minute lost could cost those fishermen a lot of money."

Tom caught her arm, and before she thought, Candy smiled fondly at him. So surprised was Tom, he took an almost comical double take over his shoulder to see if someone had come up behind him. "Uh. . .you okay, Candy?"

She leaned forward to squint at him in astonishment. "Of course I'm okay. What's the matter with you?"

"Nothing, nothing." Tom grinned. Whatever was ailing her, he hoped it was permanent.

"And if there's any trouble," Candy called lamely to his back as he headed toward the beach, "come and get me."

Nodding, Tom trotted off toward the bay.

"What does this Reuben North character look like, Candy?" Beth asked while Wendy busily consulted her wristwatch and began dating a fresh supply of bottle labels.

Candy wished desperately that Beth would get off the subject of Reuben North. "What d'you mean, what does he look like?"

"Don't answer a question with a question. Reuben North, is he good-looking?"

"Not particularly. Okay, I guess. The only time I actually saw him was for a few seconds before I got hit. And that was at a distance."

"You had to see something."

Candy smirked. "He has nice hands."

Laughing, Beth shook her head, sending her blond hair swirling. "You can see why Candy's not married," she drolly observed to Wendy. "It's never dawned on her that a man has an anatomy. Or that it does such wonderful things."

Wendy giggled without looking up.

"At least I don't make a hobby of them," Candy retorted and arranged bottles that didn't need arranging.

"Even the Internal Revenue allows a person a few years of losing before they declare it's a hobby," Beth said with a reproachful sniff.

"The IRS and I have nothing in common."

"You're both asexual. This Reuben North is from New York, did you know that?"

"So you said."

"Not originally, of course. The paper was going on and on about his being a native son and said something about his engagement to some wealthy socialite from the Stanford clan. There're as many Stanfords cluttering the state as there are Chandlers in California. God only knows which one."

Candy reeled from the shock as if she'd stepped on a land mine. A specimen bottle slipped from her hands and shattered upon the frame of the Jeep. In trying to catch it, she knocked the others over, and their clattering echoed in the silence.

Engaged? Reuben? *Engaged?* Then all that business about the kiss and all the lovely intimate talk was just so much... All her stupid little daydreams were... Oh, she should have known better! It was Victor all over again! She never learned.

"That's all right, Candy. I've got it," Wendy said as she calmly picked up the pieces of broken glass. "It was Emma Stanford," she answered Beth's question. "Mother remembered her. Emma and this man have lived in sin for so long, Mother said, that everyone's kind of given up on a wedding. Anyway, I told her they lived in New York. Sin is all right in New York."

Numb, Candy stood with her hands hanging loosely at her sides, her lips parted. *Engaged?*

Beth groaned. "No one calls it sin anymore, Wendy."

For a moment Wendy seemed to ponder that. "Well, since it's common law, or whatever, d'you suppose North would have to pay Emma palimony if they split up?"

"It's not common law if she's not using his name, just…"

"Sin," Wendy said, and they both burst into gales of laughter.

The terrible mistake Candy had made lodged in her middle like a stone. She hadn't been sensible about Reuben at all, had she? Only last night she'd lain in her bed and thought, *I could offer him something. I'm smart—a scientist, a soon-to-be authoress. Reuben North could do worse than love someone like me.*

What she was was a penniless, sterile, unmarried mother and ex-addict! A failure! The only good thing she'd ever done in her whole life was to produce Amber.

Beth was rattling on. "Well, I daresay they won't stop living in…whatever it is that they're living in. Not if old Benjamin has a say. He and Lucas Stanford have been buddies ever since I was a cheerleader in high school. They came trucking over during an intramural game one day with a whole carload of football jackets. If I'm not mistaken, the North blood needed a transfusion of good old Lucas green even back then. After this fiasco, he probably needs a complete transplant. Reuben North had better bring home the bacon."

Wendy mumbled something that Candy didn't hear and didn't want to hear.

"But, Candy," Beth was teasing as she walked over to Candy's side of the Jeep, "your hero's still fair game. The ring's not on his finger yet. Supply and demand, I always say. And who wants a man that nobody else wants? Hm?"

Candy jerked up her head as if stung. "Is that all you ever think about?" she lashed out. "Honestly, Beth, do the world a favor and marry Travis Sinclair!"

Which was, of course, unforgivable. Candy wanted to disappear, to die. She tried to think of some way to repair the damage, but her throat seized and all she could do was bite her lips and curse Reuben because he hadn't left her alone when she'd first asked him to.

Beth began to cough, raspily, as she always did when her nerves outlasted her mouth. "Well," she said when she could talk again, "I didn't realize that this was such a delicate area."

Stomping around the Jeep, Candy kept her back to them. The wind promptly snatched off her big hat, and when it flapped away like a tipsy seagull, it was the ultimate insult.

Candy dropped her head and filled her hands with tousled hair. Then she knew why she liked Beth so much. Her friend returned with the hat and, as if it were something she did every day, tipped up Candy's face and put it on and gently tied the ribbon beneath her chin.

"I do think about other things besides men," she said quietly as she fashioned the bow and paused to straighten Candy's big sunglasses. "I think about my very dearest friend in all the world."

The tears would not stay unshed. In a high, strangled voice Candy said, "You always were more honest than me."

Beth closed her long arms about her, and Candy smelled the reassuring tang of cigarettes on her friend's breath and the queer sensation of being held against a woman's soft body. She hugged her back, and the hat slid low on her neck and cut off her breath.

"I'm a dumb blonde, Candy," Beth said. "That's all I am, just a dumb, tactless blonde."

"Whom I love above all other dumb, tactless blondes."

Eager to have the attention shift to something else besides herself, Candy casually detached herself and moved to the Jeep to pick up bottles and put them down again. So absorbed was she in figuring out where she'd gone wrong, the pickup came to a stop and cut its engine without being picked up by Candy's radar.

She was vaguely aware of Beth murmuring to Wendy, "Lawsy, lawsy, lawsy. There, my children, comes a man."

Wendy gave a little gasp, and Candy tried to shut out the distraction.

"It ought to be a crime." Reverence was heavy in Beth's voice. "A rear like that is an ever-lovin' crime. Drives a woman to murder."

Beth, Candy thought, *dear Beth, would you please just shut up?*

"Beth," Wendy hissed as she saw the tall, rugged man walking toward them.

He didn't move like a Texas oil man, Beth thought; he walked like a cocky, well-trained jock with his faded jeans tucked into steel-toed boots, a baseball cap crammed rakishly on the back of a gleaming brown head of hair, and a bare, tanned chest that was absorbing more sun than he was used to. His plaid shirt had been tied around his hips, but he was untying it and popping out the creases. The hair on his chest glinted and rippled in the sun, and the outsides of his arms showed a reddening hue when they flexed.

"Oh, wow," Beth groaned, enchanted. "He's looking straight at us. Those hands. A wedding ring? No. This one is it, girls. I'm in love. I swear I am. No fooling around this time. Oh, he's putting on the shirt. No, no, don't cover it up."

Wendy insisted. *"Beth!"*

But Beth was crushing out her cigarette and mumbling to herself, and when Candy heard the masculine voice, her nerves snapped to sudden attention like rubber bands. Her pulse was a drumbeat that quivered in the hot, crackling air. She was aware of drops of perspiration sliding down the insides of her legs.

"Well, well, well," Reuben chuckled as he walked up. "Look what I found."

Any normal person, Candy thought, would have done something brilliant. Even if it weren't brilliant, it would have kept the moment from dragging out into one of those grotesque silences where mutual paralysis sets in. How was she to know that Beth was preparing to launch one of her famous conquests upon Reuben North?

"Oooo," the attorney murmured and detached herself from the group. "If you'll give me a minute to throw a few things into a bag, darlin', I'll be right with you."

Laughing, Reuben stopped in the process of reaching for a button on his shirt and lost half his grin. He looked at Beth and lifted one shoulder and slipped the button into its hole. "Sorry, I don't kiss on first dates."

"There're ways around that, honey," Beth purred.

Candy would liked to have hit both of them. And then she would have screamed at them. Did it not occur to her best friend that a man might, just *might* have come to see some-one besides Beth Dickerson? Then she would have turned on Reuben: *how could you do it to me? How could you have let me find out like that?*

When he turned to stare at her, Candy summoned an edge to her voice that she knew would cut Reuben to the quick. "I'm afraid you'll have to excuse us, Mr. North. We're very busy here."

Halting dead in her tracks, Beth turned back to Candy and her voice dropped twenty frigid degrees. "*This* is the famous Mr. North?"

"Reuben," Candy announced stiffly and stubbornly kept her head turned in the direction of the team. "This is Beth Dickerson. The team, you may remember—Tom, Miller, Wendy."

Reuben knew the moment he saw Candy that she was no longer totally blind. Even so, the last place he would have expected her to be was here. None of the women he'd ever known would have been here at all, much less participating in the recovery of an oil spill. Perhaps that was the reason that he hadn't been able to get Candy out of his head. In his mind he'd married her already.

"I'm Candy's attorney, Mr. North," Beth Dickerson sliced through his musings. "I suggest that anything you have to say, you say to me from now on."

Reuben stopped daydreaming and tried to capture Candy's attention. She was behaving as if he didn't exist, and he didn't know why. Irritation burned in the pit of his stomach.

"I wasn't aware that Miss Burrows had retained counsel," he said tightly and knew by Candy's flinch that he'd touched a raw nerve. "So, you're the attorney. Well, you know what they say about lady lawyers."

"I'm sorry." Beth Dickerson's eyes were sparkling slits. "I do not."

"They never lose their appeal." He grinned and watched Beth's eyes grow even more menacing.

"Do you work at that rapier wit, Mr. North, or does it just come naturally?"

"Rapier wit?" Chuckling, Reuben stuffed his shirttail down into his jeans and shook his head. "Beam me up, Scotty," he murmured. "There is no intelligent life down here."

"The direction you're going won't be up, mister!" Chagrinned, Beth knew that she just swallowed his bait, and her shoulders slumped.

To Candy's mind dying was the only safe way out of this. Beth would be compelled to save face now. She would be unbearable. "Please," she said. "Just...stop it, you two."

Tom and Miller, of course, didn't have the slightest idea of what was going on. They exchanged disbelieving glances with Wendy, and their teammate mumbled something about how she should've prevented all this and ducked her head. She furiously began sorting through the day's samples.

Beth wasn't about to take her embarrassment without doing something. Despite Candy's protests, she grabbed her and led her back to the Jeep and planted her solidly there as if she must take root. Then she filled Candy's arms with the tape recorder and the tote bag and Candy's own faded beach bag and a spiral book of notes. After sliding into her high-heeled shoes, she threw a final withering glare at Reuben and turned toward her VW, parked meekly on the opposite side of Reuben's pickup.

"Come on, Candy," she said as she stomped off. "I'm taking you home. Cheer up, Miller, it'll save you a trip."

Reuben placed himself in the path of the two women, his legs anchored like an offended pirate who has conquered the natives and now has only one thing on his mind: plunder. His eyes were no longer teasing, and they warned Beth to back off.

Without a word Beth released Candy's hand.

"I'll save *you* a trip, Miss Dickerson." Reuben used the smile that Emma said she hated. "I'll take Candy home myself."

Beth twisted her mouth. "Are you out of your mind?"

He laughed. "There's some question about that."

Dismayed, utterly disappointed—for she'd had her own secret daydreams—Candy thought that if she had any pride at all she would simply throw Emma Stanford in Reuben's face and tell him that she would crawl home on her hands and knees before she would go anywhere with him. Then she would tell Beth that she was an absolute idiot. She would dust her hands and stomp off with a goodbye and a good riddance to both of them.

Instead, she shocked herself by grasping Beth's arm and giving it a little shake. "Will you call Agatha for me and tell her I'll be a little late? I'll call her myself later."

Beth leaned forward to peer through the lenses of Candy's glasses. "Candy Burrows, have you lost your senses?"

The flesh across Candy's cheeks tensed with uncertainty. "There are things..." She didn't know how to finish, for she could not say that she had no choice here, that she was as destined to go with Reuben as a subject was to comply with a posthypnotic suggestion.

"Insurance," she finished lamely. "What-have-you."

"Then you'll need me."

"Beth..."

Beth had always been of the opinion that Candy was not quite human; she was above making errors of the flesh like the rest of them. With a gesture that no one but a slapstick comedienne would use, she threw both hands into the air and gave up.

"Of course I'll tell her." Then, shaking her head, she dragged her tote bag from beneath Candy's load of paraphernalia and in doing so leaned close to Candy's ear. "But for pity's sake, be careful. There's something terribly untrustworthy about this man."

Candy guessed that she would wish more than once that she had listened to her friend. "I'll be okay," she lied and pressed Beth's hand. "It's nothing I can't handle."

The past seven days had been the worst week of Reuben's entire life. Aside from the nastiness of the oil slick and the worsening investigations, the only viable course that seemed left for Benjamin was to declare bankruptcy. By using a good deal of his own capital he, Reuben, could hold back the tide for a few weeks, but that was a terrible personal gamble. So he had spent the past days conferring with Federal investigators on Benjamin's behalf, and bankers, accountants and, added to that, people from his own firm in New York, a curious Emma and a near-desperate mother.

Through it all he had found himself clinging to the memory of Candy in his arms. Part of it had to do with his increasing sexual need for her, and part of it was her unique practicality that seemed at a far more advanced stage than his own. She was the only thing that represented sanity.

Now he gazed down at her, so small and so slender in her fluttering shirt and rolled-up pants, and he felt as if she'd suddenly turned on him and sunk treacherous claws into his flesh.

His words were as hard as stone. "Remind me to get your word in blood the next time we make an agreement."

She watched Beth storming out of earshot. "Don't be ridiculous."

"Then the genteel Ms Dickerson isn't your attorney?"

"Beth's gentility is none of your business, Reuben." Whirling back, one of her fists found her hip. "And remind me to get your history the next time we make an agreement."

Reuben sighed. She knew about Emma. He had a speech memorized for this exact moment, but now every single word escaped him except, "There was this woman, see..."

"Okay." He grimly finished tucking in his shirt. "So we're even. How did you find out?"

"I read the paper." She persisted in keeping her head turned away.

"Not in the past few days, unless you've got more behind those dark glasses than you're letting on." Grasping her chin, Reuben held Candy's face and pulled down the lenses enough to see the startlingly beautiful, and very alive, blue eyes.

"How much can you see?" he asked with a wicked purse of his mouth.

She moved her gaze up, down, but he had no idea of what she was thinking. She smirked. "That you need a shave."

He laughed, and she was suddenly elusive again. When he reached out to trace one of her eyebrows, she smiled timorously, looked down. "I need a lot more than that, Candy."

"You want more than that, you mean."

"I always say what I mean."

Over Candy's head Reuben saw Tom Paughteck watching them. His open, boyish stare made Reuben feel as if he had been caught standing outside a woman's room, peeping through a keyhole.

"Damn it," he muttered and grabbed Candy's hand and walked her rapidly across the sand and around to the other side of Benjamin's sleek new pickup which would probably end up being repossessed.

He pushed her gently back against the door and, in a time-honored tradition, braced an arm on the roof and pressed a knee against the side of her thigh. Back at the Jeep, Tom, seeing, sullenly flung himself around and slumped down into it.

"My engagement to Emma isn't what you think," Reuben glumly admitted to the brim of Candy's hat. "It was something that was arranged many years ago when Emma and I were both in college. There didn't seem to be anything wrong with it, so we went along. It's just dragged out for so many years now, neither of us has ended it, that's all."

Candy didn't want to ask Reuben if he had any intentions of ending it in the future. Or if he still had sex with Emma; of course he did if it suited him. The image of their clinging bodies sent a pang of jealousy burning through her.

"You mean," she said in mock amazement, "that you aren't going to marry her and save the family fortunes?"

A dark scowl marred his forehead. "Just what have you heard?"

"Nothing." Then, "Everything...I think."

"You make me sound like a scoundrel out of a lurid novel."

She laughed without the slightest shred of humor. "Only an outdated one. Unless you raped her—" here a grimace "—which, of course, makes it all legal."

Reuben found her pique to be a promising sign, and he was aware of the beach for the first time. He drew in a huge breath and let it out as he studied the Coast Guard cutter. "I hate the smell of this bay," he said.

This time Candy's laugh was genuine, and when she moved, meaning to step away from him, Reuben shifted himself so that his shoulder pressed against hers and his side was pleasantly pinning hers.

Candy fixed him with a stare. "What is that supposed to mean, Reuben? That it's body language time now? The old mating ritual? Hm?"

Reuben stepped back and hesitated for the seconds that it took for him to wonder how the suave, gracefully witted, cosmopolitan Reuben North had ever gotten into this sad state to begin with. Sighing, he mumbled an oft-used and especially satisfying obscenity.

"My thoughts exactly," she snapped. "Did you know you're spoiled, Reuben? Do you always get what you want?"

"No!" Reuben slapped at the flapping brim of her hat. "Since I had the misfortune to meet you, my dear, I haven't managed a single necessity for survival. No, I do not have what I want, or I'd have you."

With a numbing clarity snapshots from the past flashed upon the screen of Candy's memory: her mother's determined back as she got on the bus, the painful neatness of her father's office the day he'd told her he didn't want her in his life, the rain falling after Victor had walked out, the weeks she'd sat on the beach below Agatha's house and considered walking out into the gulf and never coming up.

Candy shrank into a huddle and pressed against the truck. She turned her head as far away as possible. "Please, Reuben, don't say things like that to me."

Reuben felt her breast pressing against his side. A thrill unraveled along the ends of his nerves, and he warned himself that she was tired; he was tired, but he must know one thing.

"Tell me why Emma mattered to you," he said as he stooped to dip his head beneath the big brim of her hat. "Tell me."

Every time he touched her a shock went through Candy. Something delicious inside her was opening to him. She was fluid and yearning, and the moment was clamoring to become the worst kind of heartache.

"I don't want to fight with you, Reuben," she whispered.

"You're not answering the question." His hand was moving over her ribs, spreading its fingers wide so that he almost held her whole side in the web of his hand.

Candy whispered, "Are you sure you don't love her?"

"I don't love her."

At least there was that much. "Does she know it?"

"It's never been said. She has her life, I have mine. We...don't talk much along those lines."

She dropped her head back against the window glass with a thump and kept her eyes closed. "I wasn't jealous. I'm in no position to be jealous of anyone. I simply resented not knowing before I—"

The truth was so close to the end of her tongue that Candy closed her mouth about it and shrank into the hot chamber of her mind. How foolishly she had labeled her feelings of the past days: fantasy, daydream, imagination, sensibility. Somewhere in those tangled emotions she had begun to trust Reuben North with her heart. She had made a commitment to him, one that would remain with her for the rest of her life, no matter what happened. It wasn't sex. It wasn't even knowledge. It was a sense, a deep and sure certainty that part of her would be irreparably deprived if he were not in her life. Victor would never be able to hurt her as this man could!

She was frantic to free herself, and Reuben was dazed to realize something escaping that had been, up until a few seconds ago, at least within his grasp. In his mind he circled her, grimly trying to find a crack in the wall she'd thrown up between them. And over the pickup he met Tom Paughteck's look—a knowing look, almost a sympathetic one.

"I wish I'd never met you," he said.

His words were a needle in Candy's arm, and she jerked around, revived. "That can be remedied, Reuben. Very quickly."

"No, it can't. Then I only had a pain. I didn't know there was a cure. I was happier in my ignorance."

His confession was its own kind of comfort. What woman didn't need to feel just once that she had that kind of power? She shook her head. "You don't see what I am."

"I don't see?"

"No, you don't."

He pushed her back against the truck. "That evening I spent with Agatha," he said, his voice a deep, muted rumble in his chest, "she told me about watching you from the widow's walk for all those weeks, then going down to say hello. She said you came every day with your diving things. Finally one day you told her about your parents. And, much later, after Amber was born, about Victor."

From behind her glasses Candy strained to see beneath his surface. His hair furled out from beneath his cap. A deep line was gouged between his brows. She couldn't believe the words he was saying.

"What I see when I look at you, Candy," he said, "is a scared, pregnant, abandoned girl of twenty-two, twenty-three, standing by an old woman through all her surgery, a woman who wanted only to die. Agatha said you would sit by her bed through the night. She said she would open her eyes and you'd be kneeling beside her, praying, and you'd get up and shake her and say, 'Don't you die on me, Agatha. Don't you die on me.' And I sat there in that helicopter that day, holding your unconscious body in my lap, and I felt the same thing for you as you had felt for her. Don't tell me what I see, Candy. Don't ever tell me what I see.''

If he had said that he loved her, it would have meant nothing. Candy's scars weren't programmed for ordinary words. But this? A man standing back and looking at her from a distance and seeing someone more than the mother of a fatherless child? Someone more than a girl from a deprived background? Someone to be admired?

There was no miracle, no instant rebirth. Candy waited, holding her breath and having her ear attune to the world. She wasn't sure what she heard, she was only sure of one thing: she was a real woman. She was Candice Burrows. As hacked up and as scarred up as that was, she was herself. An original.

"Come," Reuben told her with a hard crush of her fingers and pulled her along with him. "Get your things. I want to tell you everything. I'm going to marry you, Candy. You're going to be the mother of my children."

Chapter Seven

With an endearing grin that was only slightly less overwhelming than his proposal of marriage, Reuben added, "But you don't have to say anything right now."

As he stood against a backdrop of feverish activity that his father was to blame for, Candy actually opened her mouth to blurt out her confession, *Well, you see, Reuben, I have this little problem about children....*

But the seconds passed, and she looked at the way the wind caught his hair when he pulled off his cap, the way the lines crinkled at the sides of his eyes when he smiled down at her. Knowing Reuben had changed her life, parts of her would never be the same, and a deep, core-splitting anger at life burned inside her. After all the costly steps to get from point A to point B, was it going to end up like this? Disqualification on a technicality?

With trembling hands she pushed her sunglasses up into the windblown mass of her hair. Bluntly she said, ''I've already thought about it.''

''Really?''

Overhead a jet streaked across the sky. She watched its double image disappear. ''What d'you think an unmarried woman with a two-year-old daughter would think about a single man like yourself, Reuben?''

''I don't know.''

Candy shot him a half-flirtatious, half-chiding look. ''You know perfectly well.''

Balancing on one foot, she removed a shoe and poured sand out onto the beach like grains of her past. Conscious of Reuben studying her, she brushed sand from her foot. ''Everything in my whole life contradicts this moment,'' she said honestly.

''If you're talking about Emma, you mustn't—''

''It has nothing to do with Emma. It has nothing to do with feelings at all.''

Reuben dropped to one knee and, grasping her foot and pulling it up to steady it on the top of his thigh, he retied her shoelace. He held her foot between his two hands as if it were his most precious possession, then looked up.

''But if it had to do with just feelings,'' he said, ''your answer would be yes, wouldn't it?''

She didn't know who commanded the silence, only that she was the one to yield first. Her sideways glance was her reply, and she knew when he came to his feet that he was smiling.

That was the end of it. All through the tenaciously hot dusk and the bucket of chicken that they bought on the bay side of Port Aransas and walked down the beach to eat braced against each other's back while tourists roasted or languished in hotel rooms, she and Reuben went to complicated lengths to avoid the subject, almost as if it were an endurance test.

They ate until the sight of food was nauseating, then they laughed at nothing in particular and everything in general and licked each other's fingers clean and murmured a hundred silly things that they would have been embarrassed to hear two other sane adults say.

All of which meant in another language: *It's dangerous to want too much.*

Candy phoned Agatha, and she and Reuben both talked to Amber. Reuben talked to his mother. He didn't mention who he was with, Candy noted. By the time the sun was dropping into the watery bed of the gulf, Candy was so starkly aware of how much she would fail Reuben in the end that her nerves were shredded.

He lay with his head resting in the nest of her thighs as the sun stained everything red, then a darker, heavier violet. Someone up the beach turned on a portable radio with Michael McDonald at his most dreamily romantic. Behind Michael's voice the sizzling highway weaved a sultry counterpoint.

Reuben sighed whimsically into the cooling darkness. "God, I love the smell of this bay."

Candy laughed until she couldn't laugh anymore, and when she bent down to kiss the tip of his nose, he captured her neck in a trap of his arm. She watched in spellbound fascination as his fingertip opened a narrow tunnel in the front of her shirt between its buttons.

"Don't move," he murmured and languidly blew a stream of seductive warm air.

She looked down the neck of her shirt and watched the dusky shadows of her bare nipples growing taut. She blushed, but she didn't close the shirt. "Animal. You think that's a sure sign of my insatiable horniness."

"A real mean streak runs through you, girl." Growling, he pushed her down into the sand until she was inprisoned by his weight.

"Am I to gather that you weren't flattered?" she gasped.

He gently nipped her through the shirt. "You can gather that *I'm* insatiably horny."

Candy had promised herself that she wouldn't be the one to bring up the subject, yet as she felt the rising heat of Reuben's body through his clothes and knew that the ache in his bones would soon meet that of her own, she had to know if there was any hope for them. "Why do you want children, Reuben?"

As if her words triggered some dread of rejection, Reuben pulled himself up to sit. Candy chewed at her lip and watched him walk down to the water's edge and spread his legs wide, clasp his hands behind his back.

Tell him, tell him, tell him. Don't drag it out. But Candy only memorized the straightness of his back, his buttocks, which bunched and tucked so trimly perfect above his legs. She wanted to press herself to them.

Going to stand behind him, she placed her hands upon his waist and he drew her arms tightly around him. Candy leaned her cheek upon his shoulder blade and flattened her breasts to his back.

The surf was sighing as he said. "Will you take me diving someday?"

"You've never done it?"

"With a plastic snorkel I got on my tenth birthday."

"It's a little different from that." She laughed. "It's like...flying without wings. Down there you're..."

"Free?"

She smiled, then tightened her arms again. On the horizon the blackness of the gulf was interrupted occasionally with the glint of running lights and the velvety silhouette of a boat: fishing craft heading for their docks.

"More like you're not in the way, I think," she said soberly. "There's room down there."

The deep silence held.

Finally, in a tough-tender voice, he said over his shoulder, "I know what you're thinking, Candy."

Blood rushed to the lobes of Candy's ears, and she suddenly wanted to tell him that she wasn't ready yet. She needed a few more minutes. "And I thought you were just another pretty face."

"You're thinking—" he ignored her attempt to sidetrack him "—that since I'm going to disappoint my father by not marrying the Stanford millions, I feel I should compensate by giving him a grandson."

The last thing Candy expected was for Reuben to come right out and say it, but, yes, she had thought that. "I've watched you," she said almost fiercely. "I've seen you come down from New York, leave your business with other people so you could try to salvage the mess Benjamin made of his life. You give more than any man I've ever known, Reuben. Yes, you would give that much."

The purple was so heavy it was black, and the lights of Port Aransas and Corpus Christi and Ingleside were like piles of glowing embers in the night. The sky was star-studded and thirsty for rain.

"You should marry Emma," Candy said and suddenly pulled herself free and struck off down the beach. Over her shoulder, she added, "You know that's the sensible thing to do."

Reuben caught up with her. "I'm not going to marry Emma. Can you get that through your head?"

"But you haven't told her."

"It's not something I can do by phone."

The distance between them was more than his arm's length, Candy thought. She stopped and took several backward steps, watching him closely as he, too, stopped to face her.

"Do you think it's fun on my side?" He had to raise his voice to be heard over the sloughing waves. "You weren't raised to have the things I've had, Candy. You don't understand what it feels like to wake up one day and realize the futility of having done everything, or just about everything. And tasted everything and driven everything, seen everything. There's no thrill to life anymore, so you try to grab hold of something, and you start acquiring things. And then, before too long, you have everything. There's nothing left to keep you playing the game.''

Candy crossed her arms in an Ed Sullivan pose and rested her mouth against her fist. After a pause she said, ''You're right. I've never played the game.''

''Oh, you play, my darling.'' He walked closer. ''Just not that particular game. You play the survival game, Candy. The fight is so hard that it keeps you going. You hate it, but it keeps you innocent, and it keeps you driving.''

''Innocent!'' She threw up her hands. ''How can you use that word to me?''

''Just because you knew a man and had his child doesn't mean that you're not innocent. You're as green as a seedling, Candy. I know people that would give anything to go back to where you are now.''

Candy closed her eyes when he covered the distance that separated them. She let herself be pulled against the long, hard length of him, and when she didn't look up, he tipped up her face and ran his hand from her neck to her waist as if she were silk. He stroked her eyebrows, memorized the way her cheeks sloped into her jaw.

''I don't know how long it took me to crystallize my feelings about you,'' he said softly. ''I've always known in theory that it's what you leave behind in this life that matters. It's the same reason that you fight to keep the world clean, Candy. You know how important that is to you.''

He took her into his arms and whispered into her hair. ''The truth of it is, I don't want to get old and see nothing but my life of things. And I don't want to know that you're somewhere fighting just to stay alive. It would work for us. Can't you see yourself having our babies, Candy? Don't compare it to Amber. I'll make life wonderful for you. We'll make the world better because we love each other.''

Her guilty secret was pressing so heavily that Candy could hardly breath. How much easier it would have been if Reuben had wanted children to appease his father.

Detaching herself, she started walking, almost running, then she was running. The moon was a pale sliver that hardly cast a reflection on the moving surface, and far in the distance the silhouette of another couple moved. They were kissing.

Coming to a stop because where she was running to was as hopeless as what she was running from, she whirled around and called back to Reuben's shadowy height. ''What you don't understand, Reuben, is that I reached this point long before you did. But the world doesn't give a damn about how much you want to make it better. It doesn't want what you're offering, Reuben.''

''Does it have to want it?''

He was hardly more than a fuzzy shadow. That's what he would always be in her life, she thought wretchedly—a fuzzy shadow because she could not give him that immortality he wanted.

''No.'' Walking back, Candy reached for his hands and lifted them, kissed their hard knuckles. Over them she said, ''But it's like pollution, Reuben. What good is it going to do for one man to use an exhaust system on his car when a factory a block away is blowing six tons of waste into the air?''

Waves washed over Candy's feet where she stood, and she stepped out of their path and moved her eyes longingly over Reuben's face. *Memorize it, Candy girl, because one day you won't see it anymore.*

''No one cares, Reuben,'' she said more gently. ''Life is too fast now. It's too burdened with survival. You will have your children, Reuben, because you're a good man, and you will expect their understanding in return for what you give them. But they and the world will be caught up in themselves. Just like we were caught up in ourselves. And they won't even care or want to care until you're gone.''

Reuben held her against him for long, silent moments. He breathed in the fragrance of her hair, cherished the feel of her slender body, which he feared so to lose without ever having known.

"That may be true,'' he whispered. "It's more than likely true. But when you and I are old and ready to die, my darling, we will look at each other with no regrets. We will have given everything we could give. What hope does this lousy world have except its children who've been loved and therefore know how to love in return? Is there any other hope to keep it from destroying itself?''

He loved her, she knew, but he would never love just her. And that was why she'd fallen in love with him to begin with: his fine distinctions about what mattered and what didn't matter. The very things she loved best in him would destroy her in the end.

His mouth was searching through her hair for her ear. "I was wrong before.''

"What?'' she replied in a stranger's voice as she turned to liquid inside.

"I haven't done everything. I haven't made love to you.''

Candy thought she would faint as he slipped a hand beneath her floppy shirt and caressed her bare breasts. Her nipples sprang to life as well as every nerve lying beneath her skin. She turned in his arms so that he stood behind her in the darkness, and she could stare blindly out at the black water. His hand slid beneath the waist of her pants, and he spread his hand across the span of her belly, covering the scar that defeated her.

"It's not all that complicated,'' he whispered and moved lower, fashioning his hand around the triangular apex of feminine bones, crushing her. "I love you. I want to marry you. I want to make you pregnant. I've been aching for you for days, Candy. I didn't even know where you were this afternoon. I called a half dozen places. I would have found you if you'd been in Siberia, just to hear the sound of your voice. Come with me somewhere. Let's—''

She turned her face around so that his kiss could find her. *Just once,* she argued with herself. *I deserve him just once before he has to know. Don't I deserve that? Haven't I waited long enough to know it just once?*

''Do I have to say it?'' she murmured as his mouth lowered eagerly and hungrily to hers.

He kissed her endlessly and with an impatient urgency that argued and debated with her tongue. Candy kept fighting back tears—of surprise or happiness, she did not know—as his mouth moved and twisted upon hers, as their bodies strained and shifted, ever moving and seeking a deeper closeness that both of them knew could never be found with kisses.

Only when she was holding on to his shoulders just to remain standing did Candy reach to the plateau where refusing was not possible. ''Yes,'' she whispered into the sweetness of his mouth. ''Oh, yes!''

Reuben seemed to know instinctively where she would feel at ease. Hers was a simple, natural world, and he didn't upset that ecosystem for a motel or some anxious, air-conditioned assignation in one of the resort hotels. Before they reached Agatha's house, he swerved off the highway and drove along the rough, less popular part of the beach.

When he had driven as far as he could, he parked where an ellipse of flat, washed sand stretched out for half a mile. A pile of rocks erupted at the farthest point, clawing upward toward a higher terrain of dunes and beach scruff and wandering paths.

Swinging open the door, he turned on the seat to take off his boots. ''Come on,'' he said.

Candy knew this isolated part of the beach well. She could reach Agatha's on foot from here. With their arms around each other they walked to the rocks. The only sound was the gentle plowing of the waves against the sand.

She thought Reuben would never stop kissing her. He kissed her until desire was straining in every muscle of her body. She heard the knock of her conscience from behind the door she had shut, clamoring to be heard. But his lips had found the sensitive side of her throat and her head was back, and she was gasping as her back arched and her bones conformed to his straining desire.

The waves flowed and receded around their feet. She must say it now, she knew. Pulling up, she stood on the tips of her toes until her lips were pressed against his ear.

"Reuben?" She ran her shaking fingers over the strong relief of his spine beneath his shirt. "Reuben, if..."

His voice was thick with dammed passion. "What, darling?"

But she couldn't find the words. On a hot wave of failure she jerked away and finished unbuttoning her shirt. She undressed down to her panties, and, without looking back, for tears were in her eyes, she walked, trembling, out into the surf that swirled around her knees.

Reuben didn't follow her. She was driving him mad. Her hesitancies inflamed him, and he lowered himself to sit in the sand in his agony as he watched her dip beneath the foam-flecked surface. He would have taken her anywhere—to Paris, London, Vienna. He would have given her everything he had, every cent, every property, every dream.

Yet she asked nothing. And that made him want to give her even more.

Presently she came up out of the water and stood with the moonlight glistening off the runnels that streamed down her body. She was only half naked and more desirable because of it; her mystery still held true. When she reached up to sleek back her hair, the curve of her underarm was as seductive as any fantasy he had ever imagined.

Unfolding himself, Reuben came to his feet and walked deliberately out into the water, seeing himself dragging her out and throwing her to the sand and plunging into her with savage force. Instead, he drew her to him and stared down at her slender beauty between them, at her nipples so tightly budded from the chill and grazing the roughness of his shirt, and her softly rounded stomach.

Bending, he closed his mouth upon her breast and closed his teeth into the tiny cluster of pleasurable-painful nerves. A shudder passed through her, and she lay back in his arms. The white roar of the water filled Reuben's senses and he kissed the saltiness of her mouth again—honey spinning from tongue to tongue—and dragged her down onto the wet packed sand to fit himself perfectly between her acquiescent knees.

Moaning, Candy closed her eyes. She wanted him inside her. She wanted to be so close to him that no unborn child could ever come between them.

His clothes were soaked, and their bodies were a mingling of arms and legs and waves licking at their legs. Catching the flimsy top of her panties with a forefinger, Reuben drew them down on one side, only enough that he could cover her chilled belly with kisses.

"Was it hard having Amber?" he whispered and worshipfully grazed his lower lip over the line left by the surgeon's knife.

Dismay sent its own kind of knife slicing down Candy's flesh. He was looking at her and his mind was so closed to what he saw that he assumed it had been a cesarean birth, no more.

Her lie seemed an abomination. "Yes," she said feebly, shivering all over with gooseflesh. "It was hard."

He kissed the scar and drew that one hooked finger lower so that the nylon was no hindrance to his eyes, so that he could watch his own fingers begin the search through wet, night-glossed curls. In the play of the darkness Candy's sight was not so blessed; she could hardly see him.

"Reuben!" she moaned when she could no longer keep still. "Do something!"

But the moment he did, she knew that the truth had only been biding its time: a sea serpent, hidden away within the white-ribbed skeleton of a sunken ship. Reuben stripped her bare with no more than a twist of his wrist, and the touch of his tongue as he bent to her was like a teardrop upon white-hot steel. Then her desires and conscience and guilt became impossibly entangled.

"But you don't know," she gasped and tried, too late, to escape him.

"It's all right," he whispered, not understanding. "I love you, Candy."

But it wasn't all right! He wasn't listening! He was turning her, lifting her, exposing her to all heaven, touching with his mouth that golden place, deeper and deeper with his fingers, reaching clear to the center where her chain-linked complexities were exchanged with something dark and primitive—like water traced to its ultimate depths, where it cannot be stopped.

A cry buried deeply in Candy's throat as the shock sucked her up in its swift holocaust only to torment her, to release her to float like a cinder down, down, down until she finally lay in the hollowed-out sand, freed from the frenzy that had compelled her onward.

And then she was forced to face the truth in all its perfection. Reuben's enormous appeal was the combination of his hard ethical stance and his vast capacity to love. If one of these were damaged, he would become like every other man. Emma Stanford could be the other half of Reuben's coin. If not Emma, then someone. But not her. And the ultimate cruelty was that she couldn't even tell Reuben the true reason, for in doing that she would damage him even more. Then he would never let her go.

So, while she was too weak to stop herself from doing the right thing, Candy pulled herself up and took him into her arms. She was stiff with cold, and she came upon her knees and held his head clasped to her breasts.

With all the tenderness she possessed, she said, "I can't marry you, Reuben."

It was a cruel joke. It was some kind of crazy feminine test, Reuben told himself, some disjointed quirk of fancy, some need of her scarred past to be reassured. She wouldn't dare say it the second time.

"What did you say?" he asked and pulled away to look at her disheveled beauty.

She hid behind her hands. "Don't make me say it again."

As Reuben braced himself on an elbow, remaining perfectly still, feeling passion die in him and smelling the sweet, musky scent of her still on his hands, he felt the building of an unspeakable rage. Was it some special prerogative of love to hurt people? Only a beloved could make a person hurt like this.

"What?" he barked at her as if daring her to speak.

She didn't. She couldn't.

Flinging himself up, Reuben strode angrily down the beach where her clothes lay like bits of moon fallen from the sky. He wasn't used to anger like this. Nothing stalled on him like this. Nothing and no one! Damn her! Damn everything!

He picked up her clothes and restrained himself from flinging them at her when he returned. Instead, he placed them carefully down upon the drying sand and watched as she began shrugging into them without a word of explanation.

"Well," he said when she was stiffly, woundedly dressed

and hidden away behind that aloof wall of hers. "Was it something I said?"

"It would never work, Reuben," she said in a voice that denied even the most sexless of relationships. "I'm just being realistic. It simply wouldn't work."

He stared at her hands, tying her shoe laces. "You don't know whether it would work or not. We haven't even talked about it."

"I know it wouldn't."

"Is this some way you have of getting even? Because I didn't tell you about Emma from the beginning?"

Her eyes lashed out at him, and Reuben winced as she scrambled to her feet and began running down the beach with long, flashing legs and flying shirttails.

"Let her go," he whispered to himself just before he swore bitterly and started after her.

She ran like the wind. Reuben was hard pressed to overtake her. Every time his bare feet hit the sand the temperature of his anger rose, and he lunged for those mothlike shirttails, but they were just beyond his reach. His desire, which had died at her words, flooded through him, matching his anger with an equal, more dangerous fuel. He reached out again, and this time his hand connected with her fly-away hair.

Her scream broke Reuben's heart, but he spun her around and grabbed her arms. "You tell me the truth!" he shouted and jerked her nearly off her feet with an unknowing strength.

She was strong too. She twisted free of his hands and stood with her hands braced on her knees, panting hard until she could speak. When she did, her words were explosive. "I *told* you the truth! Don't you listen? It wouldn't *work*, Reuben. It wouldn't *work*, a thousand times it *wouldn't work*."

"That's so ridiculous, I won't even argue with you."

She started walking again, her black hair blending into the night, the whiteness of her clothes making her look like a spirit come to earth just to torment him.

Over her shoulder she said, "See it anyway you want to, Reuben. I can't stop you."

What had happened to all his smooth-running machinery? Reuben thought. To hell with smooth-running machinery! In a half dozen strides he was looming up in her path.

"Then you tell me something else," he snarled, his eyes dark, glittering stones. "You say the words to my face. You tell me that you don't love me."

Was it really better to have loved and lost, Candy wondered with a strange clarity of logic, than never to have loved? No. The law of innocence was a good law; what you didn't know about, you didn't miss. To miss Reuben would be the most cruel of punishments.

But to Reuben's mind Candy's hesitation was the sure sign of his rightness. Catching her to him, he kissed her in the full tempestuousness of his inner storm. He kissed her until she was whimpering. Skimming the swell of her buttocks, he slipped his hand between her legs and lifted her off her feet until she was compelled to hold on to him.

With a triumph as dark as the night he said, "Tell me."

Only once had Candy tapped an inner strength like this: when she'd stood in front of the receptionist at the abortion clinic and had seen her life stretch out before her from an unending spool of pain. Closing her eyes, she also closed her ears to the sound of her own lie.

"I don't love you, Reuben," she whispered.

On the way home neither of them spoke. Words were too killing. Candy sat miserably, listening to her body dying and the gravel spraying up against the fenders. The lights of the truck sliced through the pale starlight and snatched at the patches of rough grass poking up out of the dunes.

She hardly knew when Reuben turned into Agatha's long drive and shot down its ghostly white length. Bounder had heard them from the beach, and he scrambled up the escarpment and raced after the truck. As Reuben climbed out and shushed him, Candy, her heart numbed now, started through the shadowy canopy of the live oak trees to the front door.

The worst was over now, she told herself. It was all over. All that was left was to make a clean, final tidying up. She was great at tidying up, wasn't she?

Both of them waited so long at the front steps that the birds settled back down to rest in the trees. Bounder curled up contentedly by the steps and crossed his paws over his nose, and a whippoorwill had the gall to pick up his lament. She would never hear one without dying all over again, she thought.

When Reuben finally turned without a word and started walking back toward the truck, Candy thought she saw him brush a sleeve across his eyes. She could smell the bruised grass of his steps. She could still taste his kisses, just as she could feel, deep inside her, her one last dream folding its tiny wings in death.

The birds and crickets hushed as Reuben walked past them, and Candy had to grip the railing of the steps and will herself not to go after him, crying, "I don't want to do the right thing! I want you!"

The engine of the truck growled like a surly bear wakened from its sleep, and Candy moved into the house and turned, mechanically, throwing the lock. She waited, her head braced against the cool painted surface of the door, until the sound was gone.

The stairs were miles away, but she knew she must walk the necessary distance. Then she must climb them. She couldn't sink down into the peaceful waters of the gulf. She wouldn't die blessedly in her sleep. She would be punished for however long justice would demand of her in payment for the mistakes of her past. She would go on living.

Reuben felt as if he'd just watched someone die. He gunned the truck down the dusty road toward Port Aransas as if hell itself were after him. It was his fault. He had chosen the wrong moment, the wrong words, the wrong place. Could he have expected anything else?

The speedometer swung hard to the right, and the wind lifted his hair and skinned it back over his head. His fingers worked around and around the steering wheel because he was behaving like a demon and he knew it. Taillights zoomed up in font of him, and he whipped around them, sending a tornado of roiling, side-slung dust back behind him.

Could he have expected anything from a life that only gave him things? And Emma's uncaring arms? Life that promised him every happiness but ended up by leaving him with the acidity of disappointment in his mouth?

But it wasn't life's fault. He could have done differently: he, the gracefully witted fixer of all things; he who chose the easy way and took the money because that was expected of him. He'd done everything—almost everything—that his father had asked of him, including Emma. He'd been a shoulder for his mother to cry on. He was the reason Benjamin and Vivian's marriage hadn't ended up in the divorce courts. Was he going to come to the end of his life and sit around and recount all the things he had fixed while his own life was a ruin? *Heal thyself, physician.*

If his life was going down the tubes in one fell stroke, by God he was going to know the reason why!

Reuben was a good four miles from Agatha's house, and his foot hardly touched the brake as he wrenched the steering wheel in a savage reversal of direction. The tires skidded and clawed, sending him careering toward the ditch where the weeds scraped the underbelly, but he gave the wheel some slack and slammed his foot to the floor.

With a choking cloud of dust and spraying gravel, he dug up the side of the embankment and sped back toward the long tree-lined drive. He made no attempts to hide his midnight arrival, and Bounder protested with furious barks. Reuben muttered a throaty command to shut up as he hit the ground from the truck at a dead run.

When he twisted the handle of the front door and leaned his weight against it, he found it locked. "Damn!"

He walked around the dark house and found the back door locked too. Moving back in the trees, he gazed up at the widow's walk. At one end was a screen door which, at best, would only be hooked from the inside.

Striding to the posts that supported the porch, he jumped up to grasp a section of the sad trimwork that skirted the perimeter. He heard wood splintering and nails screeching out of their holes. He swung himself for momentum, then heaved himself up and caught a leg over the rail.

It occurred to him once that he was an idiot and was surely going to kill himself or be injured for the rest of his life. With a stupendous expenditure of effort he pulled himself up from the muscles in his stomach and hauled himself over. Breathing as if he'd just gone a round with Rocky, he walked the creaking length of the second story. As he expected, the door was hooked.

"Damnation, woman!" he muttered and took a hard grip of the handle and jerked back with all the strength he could put behind it.

The hinges ripped out of the wall, and the door tore free and crashed against the side of the house. Reuben left it where it lay, driven now like some creature of the wilds, as he stepped into a short corridor.

"Mr. North!" Agatha exclaimed, wide-eyed and alarmed and gowned in white from top to bottom as she rushed out into the hall and lifted her hands to her throat. "What is the meaning of this?"

Grasping her by her shoulders, drilling into her with eyes that were more fierce than he could possibly know, Reuben ordered, "Go to your room, Agatha. And don't come out."

In the frenzy of his passion Reuben couldn't even ask her where Candy's room was. Agatha, her lips colorless and trembling, flicked her eyes to a door on his right and obediently disappeared into her room.

When Reuben burst through Candy's door, he found her standing in the center of the room, naked, defenseless, like a victim waiting for death. Her astonished eyes flared as she held the silk gown he had given her to her bosom.

His own breaths were a harsh, ugly sound in the room. Reuben pulled his lips back over his teeth, licked them and took a step closer to her. Then the anger suddenly drained out of him as if someone had driven a stake into his hard heart and left him standing there to bleed to death.

"I don't know what I'm doing here," he groaned with a twisting and unspeakable misery.

His sorrow was more than she could bear. "Yes, you do," Candy whispered and moved to take him tenderly into her arms as the gown fell, forgotten, to the floor.

Candy's room afforded an extraordinary ocean view. At the foot of her bed, which sat upon a raised dais on a level with a wall of glass, were two picture windows flanked by sliding glass doors. A small jungle of plants grew in the room, some potted in tastefully arranged hanging baskets, some staggered against the latticework that framed the picture windows.

The last time Candy awakened was in that mauve-gray haziness between darkness and dawn. She snuggled dreamily beneath the sheet, and, finding the bed empty, flew awake and pulled herself back upon the pillow.

Reuben stood in unabashed nakedness at the side of one of the windows, watching the sea. He was such a beautiful, economically built man, she thought. He turned at the sound of her stirring and leaned back against the lattice so that he could glut himself with the sight of her so sleepily and beautifully rumpled.

She blinked and flushed, and Reuben glanced down at his unaroused state, then back to her.

"Don't make mock," he said with a twitching grin and walked back to sit down beside her. He tugged at the sheet. "And don't be shy. Not now, my sweet."

Grimacing, Candy fit the sheet more securely beneath her arms, and he leaned across her knees and braced his weight on a palm. "Are you going to tell me your secret now?" he asked. "The one last secret that I can't pry out of you?"

"Must you know everything?" She hugged herself.

"Everything."

She didn't look at him, not even when he seated himself and pulled her into the space between his legs and locked her within his arms to sit there. Finally she was forced to look up.

"No secrets anymore," he said. "Why can't you marry me?"

"I just can't."

"I don't accept that, Candy."

"That's not your right, is it?"

"It most assuredly is. I love you. And you love me."

She didn't reply.

"Don't you?"

"Yes," she murmured.

Candy dipped her head at an angle, feeling the parts of herself disconnecting like some poorly constructed robot. He was right. It was time. But to tell him was to lose him. Perhaps not this very minute, but in time.

She worried with her fingernails. "It'll be the worst thing you'll ever hear about me." She glanced up in honest misery. "How will I put the pieces of myself back together again, Reuben? I don't want to lose you. Even if I can't marry you, I don't want to lose you."

For a moment he juggled possibilities in his brain, and Candy took his hand and placed it on the flesh of her belly. She drew a single fingertip along the scar and sat very still, staring at his eyes, willing him to understand.

Truth took its time to dawn, and when Reuben finally grasped what she was telling him, he reached for her and pulled her down with him, holding her until they were more one body than two.

"Oh, my sweetest girl," he said and stroked the back of her head. "My sweetest girl."

The surgery was two years old. Candy had never wept about it, not even when she'd come out from under the anesthetic and learned what had happened to her from a doctor she didn't even know. Now her face twisted and all the tears of the ocean seemed to flow out of her.

"I'm so sorry," she grieved. "I know I'm enough to drive a man mad, but I can't help it, Reuben. I was born to be a victim. I was my parents' victim, then some quack doctor's victim. Victor's victim and then TempCo Oil's victim. I think I've gotten used to it. There's kind of a prestige in being a victim, you know—a pride you take inside yourself to be able to keep up with the nonvictims of the world, or maybe even surpass them."

His chest was wet from her tears, and she wiped a place dry for her cheek to rest upon. "And then you came along. You gave me a gift after I'd acted so awful, and you stood by me and kissed me. I knew then all the victim prestige was a sham. I was the doctor's victim because I was wallowing in self-pity. I was Victor's victim because it was an easy thing to be."

He kissed her bent head. "And now I've asked you for the one thing you can't give me."

She cried for so long, Reuben was surprised that Agatha didn't come banging on the door. Afterward, when her tears had dried and she lay spent and silent in his arms, he pulled himself back against the head of her bed and cradled her against his side and trailed his fingers over her back for a long time.

"Please don't say it's all right," she sniffed at last.

"But it is all right. I'm not asking you to give me anything. I want to give something to you."

She shook her head. "Don't confuse me, and don't ask me to marry you." When he started to protest, she peered up at him with unrelenting eyes. "I mean it, Reuben. I can't take that right now. I would always wonder if you did it because of pity."

"Oh, hell, that's so stupid—"

"You love me, and so you're sorry for me. I would be sorry for you if you were in my place. If we ever do marry, Reuben, I've got to know, in my own mind, that it's—"

"No."

"Yes!"

Reuben lay back. It all seemed so simple for him. "All right. We won't talk about it right now. Okay?"

Candy closed her eyes, content for the moment to listen to his breathing and feel secure in the closeness of his strength and the soft, gentle path of his fingertips tracing the curve of her spine.

Dawn was intruding upon the darkness now, and the day was layering across the horizon over the gulf. Candy idly stroked Reuben's lean flank, finding a scar she had only felt in the darkness, and the dusky line that twirled down the center of his flat belly, the thatch of more vulnerable, brown-black hair below his waist.

He was so beautiful, she thought, so perfect in every way, and she wanted nothing more than to please him. Turning and drawing her knees up beneath her like some pagan princess bowing in subjection to her lord, Candy moved her lips along the length of his thighs, his knees, his feet.

Every muscle in him sharpened inside his skin, and she felt his bones move beneath her hands—strong, powerful. When he skimmed his hand over the curve of her hip, she gasped. Even lower he went and deeper, seeking.

Candy whimpered half in protest, half in yearning, and he hushed her with a kiss upon the back of her heel. She held her breath as his fingers found her. He found everything, and she was hot again, burning up, and couldn't get enough, couldn't get close enough.

Flexing her spine and reaching back with her hips, she stretched like a sleek panther sunning and preening on the warm rocks. She made herself accessible and in doing so pleased him even more. The wet warmth of her mouth upon him made him pulsing and silky.

Only when the time was right did he come up from behind and pull her into the hollow of his body, taking pleasure in watching himself enter her. For the second time—or was it the third? The fourth? Or the fifth?—Candy closed her eyes and let the words he whispered fit the rhythmic pattern he was composing. When the pleasure became a more urgent and possessive work, she was aware of the dawn and its invasion of the room.

Turning, she pushed him down and seated herself upon him. She wanted to say, "Don't watch me." But he was watching, watching her as she gyrated so gracefully, yet so selfishly upon him, robbing him of any pale victory he could have claimed. At this moment Candy knew she was using him, and he knew it, and it embarrassed her, but it pleased him enormously, for there were no secrets between them anymore. He knew the best and the worst of her, and it was the business of love to be so used.

When it was over and they lay spent, and the day was growing bold, he sought her ear.

''You may not marry me,'' he said, loving her more than he had the ability to ever tell her, ''but you will always belong to me. Only to me.''

Chapter Eight

To Agatha's way of thinking, there were too few cere-
monies in the fast pace of modern life. Every Wednesday
afternoon during the summer she made lemonade. Candy
often came in from her gardening, grubby from head to toe,
to peel off her gloves and sit on the top step of the back veranda and drink iced lemonade out of Waterford crystal.

Today the TempCo Oil insurance adjuster was coming.
It was a good excuse for Agatha to bring out the silver tray
and starched pink napkins and the rosebud in its vase. Convenient enough, Candy said, for she was working at home
today, grudgingly roughing out a projection of TempCo's
damage to the ecosystem.

Candy and Agatha had never come right out and talked
about Reuben's night in the house, nor about Reuben's
having left before breakfast. But the next day Candy noted
that the door was discreetly nailed back on, and she felt as

if her guilt showed like lipstick smeared on her teeth, or a run in her stocking.

Beth and Candy has skirted the subject of "the famous Mr. North" even more ludicrously. Beth had taken off work early today and driven out to the beach house. She said it was to help Agatha in planning for her one social indulgence—a statewide drive for underprivileged children whose prestige had, over the years, evolved into *the* social event to be seen at. Candy guessed that Beth was much more interested in what was going on between Reuben and herself.

"How many days since it rained?" Beth asked as she fanned the backwash of cigarette smoke from her face.

Amber was playing on the steps, and Candy sat on the top one, studying a series of photographs she'd had Tom take: clams in the process of extending their necks from beneath the mud, trying not to suffocate. They couldn't avoid siphoning oil into their systems, however. On the next low tide the bottom was white with dead clams.

"About twenty, I think," Candy answered Beth.

The drought had parched the air and everyone. The wind smelled of sulfur and made the leaves of the trees hang straight down in the heat. In the distance mourning doves cooed, and bobwhites complained to the gulls wheeling over the gulf. Bounder paced restlessly. Everything was restless, except the fat grasshoppers that clung to the zinnias and the pampas grass, gorging themselves so cheekily that a person could almost step on them before they grudgingly buzzed off.

"May I put you down as usual, Candy?" Agatha asked from behind her long yellow pad with its list of annual donors. "You'll visit the corporate presidents in the area?"

Candy pushed her new reading glasses up on her nose. "I don't know why you want me, Agatha. You have the best salesperson in the world sitting right in front of you."

"The best men are in small business," Beth retorted with a sniff that had the ring of authority to it.

Carrying her glass to the railing of the veranda, Beth slung one tanned leg over the side, then the other, and sat sipping as her chunky shoes gently bumped the clapboard. "I did that research you wanted me to do, Candy."

With a wary glance at Amber, Candy warned Beth to keep things low-key.

"He's well within his rights," the attorney said, meaning Victor. "He'll have to go through all the paternity tests, which are inconclusive, of course, but they do rule out who the father cannot be. It depends upon the judge hearing the petition, actually, as to whether paternal rights would be granted. It's a very painful process. Personally, I'd stroke the beast a little, make him a concession about the name, and get him off my back."

"But I'm not blind anymore."

"And that was the one thing that would have lost him the sympathy of the court. He's better off with his 'generosity.'"

Victor had come out to the beach house a number of times on the pretense of seeing Amber. He'd lounged around the lab and tried to look available in his cutoffs and faded sneakers, but all he'd done was get underfoot and keep up an incessant stream of talk about his own book and how much his publisher admired him.

"I'm probably the biggest name in nonfiction today," he had bragged.

Candy had been careful not to antagonize him. She'd given him a few worthless suggestions about the new book and when that didn't make him leave, she got out her own manuscript and barraged him with seemingly innocent questions that he couldn't possibly answer.

As if troubled, she fetched her artwork and opened up the metal clipboard she kept the expensive color photographs pressed between. He watched silently as she laid some out in a sequence.

"See?" she said. "I've taken them from the plankton stage clear through. Then when man pollutes the water, I've reversed the order and gone back, showing the mutations, etc."

He looked at the photos with a peculiar light in his eyes.

"Well, what d'you think?" she asked recklessly. "They're good, aren't they?"

"Nice," he replied with a thin smile. "My photograph will be on the cover of my new book. I should get you to take it."

Screw you, Victor! she'd wanted to yell at him when he left.

So quiet did things become as she mused, Candy turned around to look at Beth and Agatha. They instantly looked somewhere else, and Candy gave a fond swat to Amber's round bottom. "Go torment Bounder for a while."

Amber was immediately off with a beguiling call for the seasoned canine, who had wisely taken refuge beneath the low branches of a wax lugustrum.

"Strange behavior for Victor," Beth observed as she absently watched the baby. "I would have bet that he'd have made a move by now."

Candy didn't remind Beth that the only thing that kept Victor from making his move was his uncertainty about Reuben. She came tiredly to her feet. From out at the lab, the radio she'd left on was playing a song she hated.

"I've got to get back," she said and yawned and stretched, showing her tanned middle where a threadbare top didn't quite reach the waist of a pair of faded old shorts. "Will you watch Amber for me, Agatha?"

The older woman smiled. "Of course."

"What are you working on?" Beth asked.

"The TempCo spill. Benjamin North's hearing is going to be in a few days. We just found out."

"You mean they're going to prosecute?" Agatha asked as she placed the pitcher down in surprise and turned around. She and Candy had never discussed it.

Beth reared back. "He's guilty as sin, Aggie. Of course they're going to prosecute."

Agatha poured the lemonade over crackling ice and glanced over at Candy. "Does Reuben know you're making the case against his father?"

Candy and Beth exchanged a look. Agatha had never made any secret about how fond she was of Reuben, but she could at least show a tiny bit of loyalty, Candy thought.

"I'm not making the case against him." Candy walked the length of the veranda to pick a languishing wisteria blossom out from under the nose of a bumblebee. "And it's the team, not me. We're only reporting what we've found. And, yes, I'm sure Reuben does know, though I haven't said anything to him myself."

The older woman let out her breath with a sigh. "It's just that I've known the family for such a long time. I hate it."

Beth could smell gossip the way a bloodhound could catch the scent of a rabbit. Her shrewd eyes narrowed at Candy. "Didn't you say you had something to do in the lab?"

Candy's grimace was only half a tease. "Have you no pride? Have you no more conscience that to talk about me behind my back?"

"Would you rather we did it to your face?" Beth blew an ambiguous stream of smoke to the ceiling. "Besides, Agatha and I are going to make plans for charity, aren't we, Aggie? You'd better go now, Candy. Your microbes will go amok, and someone will have to make a movie about the bacteria that swallowed Port Aransas."

Laughing, Candy let it go, but she wasn't sure she would ever completely forgive Beth for not liking Reuben. By the time she reached the screen door of the lab, she had already soaked up enough dejection that she jerked it open and sent it wheezing unfairly against the building, then whipping shut with a sneeze.

Only two windows had been cut into the greenhouse-turned-lab. The only object of real furniture was the desk, an old degenerate she had found at a garage sale and had refinished herself. For fifty dollars she'd bought a decrepit Smith Corona typewriter, and now it huddled beneath its dust cover beside the telephone extension as if it resented her neglect.

Now the radio drowned out the soft bubbling of the six aquariums that lined the walls, but at night when she would come in, their hazy light and peaceful hiss were like old friends inviting her in so they could whisper secrets.

"I have the secret now," she murmured to the mussel who wasn't bearing up too well under several exposures to toxic conditions. "And his name is Reuben North. And my name may someday be Mrs. Reuben North. Mr. and Mrs. Reuben North request the honor of your attendance..."

Candy made her way to the desk and pulled out the manuscript. Victor was right; she wouldn't get rich from a textbook, but it satisfied something deep within her. Lifting out the clipboard, she raised the metal flap and ran her fingertips over the glossy surfaces. No one would ever know what this work had cost her. She walked over to the cupboards where dozens of petri dishes were stored.

"Well," she murmured as she leaned forward to squint at the shelf labels. She withdrew a dish and bent over it with a magnifying glass. "Let's see if you guys are incubating or just fooling around."

She removed the top, and blinking to keep her eyes in focus, she closed her worst eye and tediously focused on a single drop of liquid as it spilled onto a slide. When she lifted her head, she smiled. The microorganism she had been feeding on a mixture of whey and molasses was one that could break down hydrocarbons and produce carbon dioxide and methane gas in return. It could do this process underground; all it needed was enough oxygen to stay alive and the nutrients to reproduce.

In several other dishes she was incubating anaerobes that she hoped could do the same thing without oxygen. They were an idea she wanted to talk to Reuben about; she had come up with a way Benjamin might recoup his losses.

The last thing Reuben expected, or wanted, was to meet Kent Gordon at the end of Agatha South's driveway. It had taken him two days of meetings with Benjamin's accountants and attorneys, plus the press and everyone else who was eager for a drop of Benjamin's blood, to get the breathing space to drive out. Now that he was here, Benjamin's insurance adjuster had just turned in from the west as he was turning in from the east.

"Well, hell," Reuben muttered under his breath and touched his foot to the brake when he saw Kent's Seville ease to a stop in front of his bumper. "What did I do to deserve this?"

Kent Gordon leaned out the window of his car. "Talk about luck, Rube," he yelled, "I've been needin' to see you. Pull over an' park. We can talk while we walk up to the house."

After a glance to make sure he wouldn't be in the way, Reuben grudgingly parked a good quarter-mile from the house. After strolling over, Kent brushed the dust from his white shoes.

Straightening, he extended the same hand to Reuben and said, "How's everything goin', Rube? Heard you'd come down from New York."

Reuben arranged a smile. "Yeah."

"Pete called me right after the accident." Kent assumed an appropriate gravity. "Say, I heard about your father, too, Rube. I trust his health'll see him through all this mess. Give Ben my best, you hear?"

It occurred to Reuben that he spent a good deal of his time talking with men exactly like Kent Gordon, men whose confidence was international, though the only time they ever left the county was to attend a sales convention in Lake Charles or when their wife's sister had another baby. And he would have much preferred not to arrive with Kent; it gave the mistaken appearance that they had come to Agatha's together.

"Sorry I didn't make it out here sooner," Kent was saying. "Pete told me you wanted a rush put on this one. Tell me, now, when are you an' that pretty lady of yours goin' to put a rush on and tie th' knot?"

His smile intact, Reuben kept his eyes on the widow's walk of Agatha's house. "It'll be awhile yet, Kent. You know women."

"Not like you do, eh?" He nudged Reuben in the ribs with an elbow. "Hey, why rush, though? Things are pretty convenient like they are. Be a shame to mess things up."

"Things are never that convenient." Reuben gestured to the house. "Look, we'd better get in gear."

The seconds scattered out like the dry leaves that crunched beneath their feet.

"Some house," Kent said as he dragged out a handkerchief from the pocket of his silk suit and blotted at the furrows spanning his forehead. "It don't look to me like this Burrows woman needs anything."

"Miss Burrows only lives here," Reuben explained. "This place belongs to Agatha South. She told me that it had been given to her."

"A gift?"

"An old friend, I think."

"Some friend," Kent said and chuckled. "If you get my drift."

Reuben shot Kent a sharp warning that he was out of line. Agatha's house had come from her lover? The man who returned from the war but didn't marry her? Fascinating.

"These old women will surprise you, Rube."

Good taste forbade Reuben to reply.

"God, d'you suppose it'll ever rain?" Removing his suit coat and draping it over his shoulder, Kent allowed himself a glance at a small notebook. "How did you happen t'know this Miss..."

"Burrows. She's one of the regulars who keep track of pollution levels around here. She works out of the Worthington Foundation."

"Yes, yes. Of course."

A lock of gleaming hair blew across Reuben's forehead, and he threw it back with a twist of his head. At the same time he leveled his look upon the insurance man. "Look, Kent, for Dad's sake and Miss Burrows's sake, I want this insurance thing settled as quickly as possible. Miss Burrows has considerable compensation coming, and I'm sure she can use it."

"Hey, Rube." Kent threw an arm around Reuben's shoulders. "Leave the insurance business to me. Why, I was takin' care of your daddy when y'all were learnin' the ABCs."

Reuben thought if the man called him "Rube" one more time, he'd smash his fist into his round, grinning face.

"Just keep it cool," he said and brusquely picked up his pace. "And Benjamin's not handling this one, Kent. I am."

Candy had risen and walked to the sink to wash her hands when she heard the masculine laughter floating across the back lawn from the veranda like a breeze. The insurance man, she thought, sighing and bringing her wristwatch up to her eyes. She'd worked longer than she intended to. Well, he'd just have to give her time to freshen up and change clothes.

"It's good to see you again, Agatha," Reuben said with a hearty laugh. "Amber, my girl. You look as if you just woke up from your nap. How's the knee? Better? I don't mind telling you, I was really worried. How about a hug?"

Electrical sparks made connection with Candy's nerves as the baby squealed with delight. Reuben! His rich laughter tripped impulses deep inside her, much the way that Amber's newborn cry had brought milk to her breasts.

She touched her tousled hair, gazed down at the old, too-big shorts. Her top was a disgrace, and her thongs were run over at the heels. It never failed, did it?

Hurrying, she felt around in a desk drawer. Darn it, she knew she'd put a comb in there. Finding it, she dragged it swiftly through her stubborn hair, then felt her head and decided that she hadn't helped much. She rushed to the sink to throw cold water on her face, then blotted her face on a paper towel and gave a quick scrub under her arms. Why didn't the man give some warning?

She hesitated at the screen door. If she let Reuben come out here after her, they would at least have a few stolen minutes alone.

"I'll be damned," Beth's voice was carrying clearly. "If it's not the ever-popular Mr. North."

"Beth," Agatha gently scolded. "Remember the baby."

Then a totally unfamiliar male voice that introduced itself as Kent Gordon, "Tri-City Insurance, ma'am. I'm here to see Miss Burrows."

"Ah, yes, Mr. Gordon. We've been expecting someone to come. Do have a seat." Agatha's hospitality was equal to any situation. "Candy just walked out to her laboratory.

Why don't you pour the gentlemen some lemonade, Beth, while I find her?''

"Stay where you are, Agatha," Reuben quickly said. "The lab's over there?"

"Her little home away from home," Beth purred caustically. "Tell me, Mr. Gordon, how does your wife like being married to an important insurance executive like yourself?"

Kent Gordon's laughter covered the sound of Reuben's leap down the back steps. "I'm afraid I wouldn't know, Ms Dickerson. I'm not married."

"Oh? Is that a fact? May I call you Kent?"

Candy arranged herself, then nervously reconsidered and walked swiftly to her desk and exchanged her glasses for a pair of large smoke-tinted sunglasses. She had hardly gotten them in place when Reuben's voice murmured huskily from the doorway.

"Don't let me startle you," he said as the threshold creaked beneath his foot.

Candy felt as if her whole body had suddenly become weightless. Just turning took forever, and she drank in the sight of him standing there so clean and tall in the weakened sunlight—his snow-white tennis shirt open at the neck, his pleated slacks with pockets everywhere, the wisps of sun-streaked hair on his arms. She could taste the fresh saltiness of his skin and the wind in his hair.

"The sun god," she murmured.

He smiled, not understanding, and she leaned weakly back against her desk. She shook her head. "I'm not startled. I heard you when you came."

"And you waited for me out here? This grows interesting."

She could feel him considering her coolness, which was nothing more than a facade to hide the impact of her memories. Moving closer, he moved his eyes over her as only an intimate lover can do. Reaching forward, he removed her glasses, placed them on the desk. "You don't mind, do you?"

"Would it matter if I did?"

He considered her for a moment, then chuckled. "Everything about you matters. Aren't you going to kiss me?"

She wanted nothing more than to do that, but somehow the pacing had established itself, and she gave him a smiling shrug that only made it slow down even more. They would play a sensual waiting game, then.

Reuben walked around her and thought it was as if they had not spent a whole night together, as if there were yet another Candice Burrows he must seek out and seduce.

Smiling, he inspected the shelves and her microscope, paused to flip through a small stack of hand drawings of cells in various stages of toxidity. When he turned and caught her watching him with an unguarded hunger, he grinned, and she pressed back against the desk until its edge cut a groove across the back of her hips.

"I've missed you," he said with a restraint in his moves.

Now they were circling each other. She smiled and immediately dipped her head. "How's your father?"

"Not good, but he's managing."

"It isn't..." She'd been about to say that things hadn't gone all that well on her side of the bay, either. She faced him squarely. "It's good that you're...managing."

"The deeper I dig into his affairs and the farther back I go, I begin to understand why he did some of the things he did."

"Like what?"

Reuben plucked at a twist of cotton on his shirt. "Nothing that I can really prove. It's just that Lucas Stanford seems to have come out well in almost everything. People have always cracked jokes about my father taking Lucas's girl, and how remarkable it was that the two men remained friends over the years. Business partners, even.''

''You think he got even?''

He laughed and shook his head. ''He didn't cheat my dad. But things are tight. He presently has forty-eight percent of the partnerships with Benjamin.''

''And your father?''

''Forty-seven. Tell me, do you sleep naked?''

The charade ended with her gasp, and Candy laughed at herself blushing and pressed her palms to her cheeks. ''I hate it when I do that.''

He chuckled, and she moved to the counter, bent automatically to the eyepiece of the microscope. When he stepped up behind her and pressed into her hips, she closed her eyes and let her head fall back in relief so that her temple lay against his jaw.

''Oh,'' she breathed and fit herself perfectly to him.

''What's all that?'' he asked, though neither of them were the slightest concerned with the microscope.

''Some MEOR specimens.''

''I don't know MEOR.'' Stooping, he swept his hands all the way up from her knees to her waist and let out his breath in tattered fragments.

''It's a field test for depletted. . .oil resesrves,'' she managed to say.

''And?''

''You inject these microbes down into the well. Sometimes you can. . .'' Candy gripped the edge of the sink. ''Oh, Reuben. . .''

He was pulsing against her hips in a slow, earthy pattern, and as she shivered he spread his hands wide across the span of her belly and held her tightly back against him.

''Go on,'' he whispered thickly. ''I'm listening.''

''I—''

''I really am listening.''

"Sometimes..." She wet her lips. "Sometimes we can find oil. Almost always gas. It can increase production up to a hundred percent. I was thinking about...some of those old closed-off leases of your father's you told me about."

"A wonderful idea," he murmured, strewing a chain of kisses over the line of her jaw. "Turn around."

When she did, Reuben settled himself back against her desk and drew her into the V of his legs. They held each other tightly for long, long moments, and when she finally placed a kiss upon the side of his throat, Reuben sighed in the first contented moment he'd known since he'd left her.

"Nothing in the world feels as good as you do," he muttered. "The days have been so long."

She leaned her weight against him. "Tell me everything. What have you done? How is everything? Really?"

"The Feds have been very polite."

"But firm."

"Yes. Indisputedly firm." He was exploring the bones of her back. "I flew back to New York for a day to touch base with my office."

"And a night?" Candy had no intentions of asking such a question, but Emma had been much on her mind of late. She knew the moment she lifted her head and the seismic tremor passed between them that she made a blunder.

"Yes." His hand stilled as it came to rest upon the top of her hip and lay heavily. "And a night."

Candy replaced her cheek to his jaw so he couldn't see her eyes.

"Aren't you going to ask me if I spent it with her?" he said. "That's what you wanted to ask, isn't it?"

"Greater love hath no man than he lay down his life for a millionairess."

Straightening, he held her at arm's length. "You still don't believe me, do you?"

Candy pushed away from him. The electric clock clicked its tiny minute hand jump, and she jumped with it. "Do I believe that you'd rather have me?" she asked, feeling a silent scream in her throat. "Gutted and sterile—"

"Hush!" He took her into his arms, his apology in the way he wrapped around her.

"Don't ever stop reassuring me," she begged. "I'm sorry. I just need to hear it, over and over. I'm so afraid something will happen, and it'll all be a dream."

His gentle push placed her against the wall, and Candy let herself be sandwiched between the wall at her back and the wall of his body in the front.

He crushed his face into the hair covering her ear and whispered, "You don't think that I walk around like a sleepwalker because of you? Seeing myself doing things and hearing myself talking to all those investigators and accountants when all I can think of is how I want to be with you? I don't care about my business, I don't care about anything except being here. Doing this. Holding you. Wanting you."

Candy squeezed her eyes tightly shut. "I don't want to cry. Don't make me cry."

"Say you'll marry me." He threaded his big hands roughly through her hair and turned up her face, kissed her eyes and her cheeks. "Don't be honorable. Don't do the right thing. I don't care about children anymore."

"You will care." Her whole body was aching. "The rush levels out, Reuben, you know that. When the edge wears off, then you'll want them."

"Amber will be my daughter."

"I need to talk to you about that. Victor says—"

"I don't give a rip what Victor says. He can't do anything but throw a temper tantrum."

Candy couldn't protest because he was kissing her again, and his tongue was so hungry, so terribly, terribly hungry, that her own need gnawed at her belly. The years of the future stretched out before her, intolerable because she saw now a chance that she wouldn't live through it alone. Before, when there had been no chance, she could bear it, but now...

"Reuben," she moaned into his kiss, "we shouldn't be doing this. Someone will come out here."

"I don't care." He was pulling up her top, filling his hands with her breasts, making quick work of arousing them.

"I care." She shook her head, holding to him because her legs had finally rebelled. "You can't do this. It's dangerous."

"It won't be if you'll help me. Let's be kids again, Candy, and steal it in the cloakroom."

"Reuben..." She was lost in the crimson assault of his mouth, his wicked hands, which sent the ache deep into her groin. "Agatha...Beth..."

"Help me." He ravaged the sensitive shell of her ear. "Unzip me."

The very risk of it catapulted them back to the years when any conquest at all was an anathema. The excitement was so violent that Candy's fingers shook as she searched for the elusive metal tab. The ritual that was usually clumsy and awkward was now dizzying and inflaming. Candy saw herself from a distance, how much he wanted her, how his fingers were invading the loose leg of her shorts, pulling it aside, pushing it up until the silky wetness put the lie to anything she could say.

"Damnation, girl," he groaned and took her mouth and made promises with his tongue.

She did try to hurry, but to be so in command and still have no command was funny and infuriating and uninhibiting. "Ohh," she wailed because she couldn't manage it. "Hurry, hurry."

Yet when it was accomplished—the twist of fabric, the shifting, the arranging, the joining, the battle for each other's eyes to celebrate the fact that they had done it and were still undiscovered—Candy wanted to laugh and say that she loved him deliriously. But Reuben was fighting a losing battle with himself, and it was no longer a game. Candy knew she would do what every woman does who loves her man. She closed about him so tightly that it was unbearable and lifted herself up to him with a temptation as potent as Eve's.

"Oh, Christ," he groaned and buried his face in the sweet fragrance of her throat as he came, spilling, into her. "I'm sorry."

Candy held him very tightly and kissed his fiercely closed eyes and savagely clenched jaw. Her pleasure found the tenderness of her coos and kisses and strokings.

"I love you," she whispered and cradled his head. "I love you, Reuben North."

"It's all your fault," he said when he could talk.

"Me?" she teasingly bridled. "A li'l ole snow bunny like me?"

"You should've been born with a face like a road runner and a disposition like an armadillo."

She adored him with her laughter. But it was, after all, only stolen laughter, and the voice of Kent Gordon drifted through the trees and intruded into their secret.

"Hey, Rube!" he yelled. "I don't have all day, son. Where are you, boy?"

Reuben swore under his breath, and kissed Candy almost savagely. "Candice Burrows, you aren't making a fool out of me, are you?"

She smiled and kissed his face, his lips. "There are better ways of making a man pay than sex."

Reuben grimly watched as Candy made a few deft repairs of herself, knowing what every man has known before him and would know after him, that it was, after all, a woman's game if they only knew. Was there ever a man who, loving a woman, didn't become a slave to his own body and a fool whose greatest joy was to destroy himself at her feet?

"Hey, Rube!"

"Coming, Gordon," Reuben called back in exasperation as he zipped his trousers and brushed back the sides of his hair and met Candy's dancing blue eyes with a grin. "Miss Burrows is finishing up here."

Candy thought she and Reuben must have given themselves away a dozen different times as they rejoined everyone on the veranda. For all his hurrying, Kent Gordon was deep in conversation with Beth, and Agatha smiled at Candy in a most unsettling way.

Agatha knew, of course, Candy thought and wanted to die. Grateful for Amber, she lifted her up and moved around the table to take the empty chair next to Beth.

Beth measured Reuben with a stare that had lost none of its face-saving antagonism of before. She leaned toward Candy. "Have you two been quarreling?"

"Nothing is the matter," Candy protested, blushing.

"Well, you look like the devil."

"I always look this way."

Kent Gordon was placing a small stack of papers in front of Candy, and she focused her attention on them, leaning back in an attempt to see. She felt about on her head. Damn! "I—I left my glasses in the lab."

"I'll get them," Reuben said and vaulted easily over the veranda railing.

"This won't take long, Miss Burrows," Kent declared with a sweaty smile as he tugged at his wilted collar. "These are just routine forms for you to fill out at your leisure. I have just one or two questions, for my own benefit, you understand. I hope you don't mind my asking them."

Candy could hardly keep her mind on what Gordon was saying. When Reuben returned with her glasses, her fingers brushed his, and the contact jolted her. She started to smile, but he looked away too quickly.

''Of course,'' she said absently.

''First off, I was wondering what you were doing on the rig.''

For a moment Candy heard only the hot wind ruffling the papers. Something was very wrong here. She knew it the way she sometimes knew when a shark was near where she was diving, but to not know why was even more unnerving. Why had Reuben come here with this man?

She wet her lips and shifted Amber on her lap. The child squirmed and slipped off her lap to go to Reuben. Watching Kent Gordon's small, infuriating smile, she said, ''You did come here to make a settlement, didn't you?''

''If it's in order to do so, of course.''

Beth was shoving back from the table. ''What're you getting at? What are you trying to say?''

''Just a minute, Beth.'' Candy waved her away. ''I've told this before, Mr. Gordon. I had placed an experimental canister near the rig. It had been there for four, maybe five months. Then it disappeared. I went up to ask about it.''

''You think someone on the drilling rig took it?''

Intuition made the hair tighten on Candy's arms. ''I'm not accusing anyone of anything. I'm simply saying that the canister disappeared.''

Reuben, who had balanced himself upon the railing of the veranda, straightened out his legs and lifted Amber to his lap. Everyone was suddenly intensely absorbed in watching the baby, and Reuben was smiling but not smiling.

''What are you getting at, Kent?'' Reuben repeated Beth's question.

Beth literally snarled under her breath at Reuben. ''As if you didn't know.''

''I'm just trying to reconstruct the accident,'' Kent replied and looked at Candy with a shrewd and unabashedly superior stare. ''Now, according to what I understand, Miss Burrows, you called up to the rig and asked permission to come up. Is that correct?''

''Yes,'' Candy had the satisfaction of making him wait several seconds before she replied.

''Once on deck, what did you do?''

Candy lifted her palms. ''The rig's driller, Mr. McPherson, came over and introduced himself. He conducted me on a short tour of the rig.''

''Did you at any time put on a safety helmet, Miss Burrows?''

Now the silence had a shape and form. It was a vulture circling high over their heads in the hot, sulfured sky. Candy visualized several thousands of dollars in medical bills, and she hoped she could answer without her voice squeaking.

''No, I did not put on a safety helmet.''

''The bottom line is, Miss Burrows,'' Kent said and popped his handkerchief as if it were silk and tucked it efficiently into his pocket, ''that my insurance company isn't liable in any way, shape, form, or fashion for your accident. I'm sorry, but you went at your own risk. It's your baby, as it were.''

With that, he removed three Polaroid snapshots from his briefcase. All of them were of the same thing, so he passed them around: a sign posted upon one of the supports of the derrick. SAFETY HELMET REQUIRED AT ALL TIMES: THIS MEANS YOU, DUMMY.

When no one spoke, Agatha and Beth exchanged stunned glances. Candy touched the corner of a snapshot to her lips and flicked her eyes to Reuben and down. He knew. He had known out in the lab what Kent Gordon had planned to do.

Reuben was coming to his feet and placing Amber on the floor. "Look—"

Beth vaulted to her feet. "Oh, cut the crap, Mr. North! We know that you and Gordon here are the Bobbsey twins. You came here together and you're protecting Benjamin North as you've done from the very beginning of this disgrace. How's it arranged, Mr. Gordon? A kickback? Well, gentlemen, I suggest that no more be said here today."

"Look, lady, I don't know who you are," Kent began, his brows working furiously.

"I'm Miss Burrows's attorney. Any further communication, Mr. Gordon, will be between your legal department and myself."

Tipping back his head, Kent laughed, then said, "Oh, brother John. Well, Ms Attorney, why don't you just give me your price, and we can settle this matter one-two-three. Okay?"

Kent Gordon leaned far back in his chair until his stomach bulged on equal sides of his belt. Beth, smiling until she was sure she had his attention, leaned forward so much that she could have pushed his chair over with a forefinger. "Oh, about a million, I think."

Kent's neck turned purple and he tumbled forward with a crash. "Dollars?"

"I ain't talkin' pesos, pardner," Beth drawled and wiggled her whole body in victory.

Agatha cleared her throat and rose to frantically begin pouring lemonade. Whimpering, Amber crawled halfway up Candy's leg in alarm.

But it was Reuben who absorbed all of Candy's attention. He took the two steps necessary to place him at the table, and when Amber looked up at him and said his name, he didn't even hear. He leaned over the table toward Candy until only the two of them remained alive in the universe. His weight was braced on his fingertips. His neck was a dull crimson, his cheekbones granite.

"You're suing, after all?"

With those four words, Candy thought he destroyed everything. Neither of them had the reserves on hand to fight this kind of war—no repertoire of trusts stored up over a period of years. How could he ask a question like that after what had just passed between them? *How could he?*

Beth's laughter rippled in a delicious purr. "Well, actually, Mr. North, honey," she wickedly took her vengeance, "it's not quite as simple as that. But, yes, basically, Candy will be suing. The fact is, Candy did not refuse a hard hat. She was not offered a hard hat. It was your responsibility to supply her with one."

Reuben didn't even acknowledge the attorney's existence. Candy was suddenly aware of the sun cutting through the roof like a laser, and into her skull. Her eyes blurred. This was all wrong. How did things get so messed up like this?

"For a million dollars?" Reuben's voice was like the slice of a knife now.

Candy did the only thing that she had the experience to do. She did as life had taught her to do, and she lifted her chin as she had lifted it that day when she stood in her father's office and listened to him telling her that there was no place in his life for her.

Nothing showed on her face. When she came to her feet, her chair crashed to the floor, but she didn't flinch or turn her head. "Come with mother, darling," she said to Amber.

"I'll take her, Candy," Agatha said on a sad breath.

Kent Gordon was already snapping his case shut and talking to Beth at the same time. "Not a cent," he declared. *Click, click.* Then to her, "You won't get a cent, Miss Burrows, and if you listen to Ms Dickerson here, you'll end up payin' the court cost on somethin' that won't do you a pin's worth of good.''

Agatha's height was a queen's authority. She inclined her head to the insurance man as a reminder that he was partaking of her hospitality. Even Beth drew in her claws, but Reuben heard Candy's words ringing in his ears. *"There are better ways to make a man pay.''* He thought of Emma. His stomach burned. Why didn't Candy do something or say something? Why didn't she deny it?

He came within inches of throwing Agatha's table across the veranda. ''Well,'' he said, his Reuben-can-come-through-in-a-pinch control knotting in his throat. ''This is what you want, Candy?''

Turning, she looked at him with the same eyes she'd looked at Victor with. Something priceless shattered inside Reuben. *And Humpty Dumpty and all the king's men...*

''You want a million dollars, Candy? Hm?'' With shaking hands, Reuben felt his pockets, and dug into the left rear one. *Don't do this, North,* some strange, unwanted voice called to him. *You will never stop regretting this.*

Breathing hard, he drew out his checkbook and flipped through the stubs that were considerably nearer depletion since the helicopter had put him down on Mustang Island. ''Well, then, you got it, babe.''

Stepping to the table, he scribbled furiously across the paper and ripped it out and threw it at Beth. It skimmed over the starched pink cloth with a sound that Candy found deafening, and when it fluttered to the timbered floor, it was as if a mighty oak had been felled.

Beth scooped up the paper, but Candy didn't need to look at it to know that six zeros were on that check. She moved stiffly to the back screen door. The paint was wearing around the handle. She must repaint it before it started to peel. And if the back door needed painting, the window-sills probably needed attention too.

Placing her hand upon the curved brass, she glanced up at the sky. Maybe it would rain soon. After the rain, she would paint the house.

Candy never saw the horrible look that passed between Reuben and Agatha. One small shake of that old graying head as she stood holding the baby, and Reuben saw his folly like blood on his hands. He had just joined the ranks of Maxine Burrows and Ronald Burrows and Victor Hirsch. It wouldn't do any good to go after Candy now.

Chapter Nine

At twilight, clad only in her pink ruffled training panties, Amber cavorted about in the lawn sprinkler like a frisky young pup and squealed, "Rain, Mama, rain!"

"Twenty-five days without rain," Agatha mused as she fondly watched the child from a rocking chair on the veranda. She blotted her mouth after a sip of iced tea and sighed. "Sorry. When it gets hot like this, I just sigh. I can't help it. I just sigh and sigh."

The sky, which for days had been ruthlessly cruel, was now enormous and incandescent. It filled the whole west with a sullen, bilious cast. When the sun had fallen through it at dusk, it seemed to burn its way down and suck up all the oxygen so that even the dusty sparrows lined up in rows on the power lines and took themselves a rest.

"After it rains," Candy said, as depressed as the sparrows, "you'll rest better."

"It wasn't the heat that kept me awake last night." Presently, in a parody of martyrdom, Agatha added, "Several times in the night I would have sworn I heard crying. Old age, no doubt, affecting my hearing."

"Everybody gets a little crazy when it stays this hot."

Inside, the clothes dryer cut off, and Candy stepped in to unload it. When she returned with an overflowing basket, she said, "Heat brings out the beast. Original sin or something."

Agatha laughed.

Candy hadn't laughed in days. One towel, three towels, a dozen towels. Presently she slumped over her folding, all pretense discarded. "I'm sorry you heard, Agatha. I didn't want you to know I was crying."

"I would have known even if I hadn't heard you."

But she would have, Candy thought as she folded and stacked, stacked and folded. She and Agatha had lived together so long now, they were almost an extension of each other. She paused to idly finger the edge of a washcloth. "You know, I never thought I would hear myself saying it again."

Agatha looked up, and Candy answered her unmasked query with another one. "How could I have fallen in love with Reuben? It's like I don't care about anything anymore. I want to just...devour him, fill up something inside me that won't ever fill up."

"Why don't you call him, Candice? Get rid of this misunderstanding between you."

Silence, except for the miller moths that had found the lamp behind the screen and were battering themselves senseless: the story of her life, Candy mused.

"I want to call," she whispered. "She would call."

"Emma?"

"The incumbent."

"She's not in his life anymore."

"Well, she's not out of it."

"Neither is Victor out of yours. He'll never be out of it."

Candy's shoulders slumped. "I thought love was supposed to make you happy. I'm more miserable than I've ever been in my life."

The rocker stopped creaking, and Agatha's steps on the pine planks were as silent as the clouds that banked higher and higher. When Candy felt the thin hands touching the ends of her hair, some pent-up pressure that had built for days seemed to roar over the dam inside her.

"Oh, Agatha," she said and wrapped her arms around the woman's tired, old legs and hung on for all she was worth. "It's going to kill me."

"No, no," Agatha cooed and stroked her head. "you'll wish it would. Many times. But it won't kill you."

When the tears were finally over, Candy wiped her face with the washcloth.

"I loved a man once," Agatha said as she remained standing by Candy's side, looking out at Amber.

Candy stopped blotting her eyes and gazed up at her.

The old woman smiled. "Oh, I was capable in those days. I was more than capable. He was married."

"You were the other woman?"

"Our affair lasted for nearly twenty years."

Dumbstruck, not because she hadn't known about a man in Agatha's past but that she had so easily accepted the image Agatha projected of herself, Candy got up and leaned back against the banister of the steps.

"I've shocked you," Agatha said.

Candy turned up a palm. "People get conceptions of other people, that's all. And they hold true."

"People thought what I wanted them to think, what it was necessary for them to think. I gave them a performance, and they believed it."

"To protect him?"

"I had to."

Still amazed, Candy picked up a dishcloth and absently folded it into a square as small as her fist. "Is he alive?"

"Oh, yes, very alive, very troubled. He had...faults, a lot of problems."

"Children?"

"Yes."

"And his wife knows?"

"She knows there was someone, but I'm sure she didn't know who it was. I did my homework well." Agatha made a grim sound that was akin to a wry laugh. "It was so easy. Agatha South? Have an affair with a married man? Never."

Candy arranged the linens in the basket. Agatha pondered for a moment, then smiled sadly. "I never though it would last."

"Because you saw the bad things in him?" Candy shrugged. "The honeymoon ends, Agatha. Sometimes it never gets started."

"There were too many strikes against us. As it ended up, his wife and I together gave him what he should have had in one woman. It wasn't a happy arrangement. We were more willing to sacrifice to a moral code in those days."

Amber had grown tired, and she crawled up the steps and lifted her arms to be held. Candy pressed her face into her curls. "It's over, then?"

"Occasionally he calls me. We chat rather awkwardly, and then we're both glad when he says he must go. It's just not worth the pain anymore."

From far in the distance drifted the rumble of thunder. The wind had picked up, and the smell of rain was deep in Candy's nostrils. So softly she almost didn't hear herself, she said, "Reuben made love to me, Agatha. That day he was here."

"I know."

"I've got that silly check up in my room, and I can't even throw it in his face, which is what he wanted me to do. I could give Reuben a lot, Agatha, but I can't give him everything. I can't have another baby. And there're other things. We come from such different worlds. I don't do well with people. I'm too shy. I get paranoid. I'm a mess."

Stooping, Agatha lifted Amber in her arms to take her in the house and change her into her nightie. She gripped Candy's shoulder and pressed the strong network of bones. "Perfection wears a very high price, doesn't it, dear?"

Yes, it did. And that was what she craved to be, wasn't it? Perfect, as if to prove how unfair her parents were by deserting her, and how she didn't deserve to be made the victim of some quack doctor who was in a worse condition than she was.

The temperature had dropped drastically in the past ten minutes. The thunder was insistent now, hardly seeming to stop from one crotchety complaint to another. Starting to call out, Candy heard Amber and Agatha in the back of the house, talking their own charming little language. She walked down the back steps and around the house and struck out across the lawn beneath the live oak trees. The wind caught in her hair and teased the hem of her shorts. A single drop struck her cheek, and she smiled.

"Come on, baby," she said to the blackening sky. "You can do it."

As she turned, her mind vaguely in transition between the promise of rain and wondering if she could get up the courage to call Reuben, the first jagged white streak cut across the sky with the clarity of acid.

Candy stopped in her tracks, and her brain took the milliseconds to interpret what had happened. She had seen the lightning perfectly—no fuzziness this time, no guessing. She pulled off her glasses and rubbed her eyes. How many times before had she thought this? Do it again!

The wind had caught the tops of the trees now, making them groan. At least the worst of the oil slick was vacuumed up, she thought, but now the storm would disperse hundreds and hundreds of ribbons of oil into the water, millions of scattered droplets that never really went away. The winds would wash them into shore, and once again Texas tourists would track tar balls on the bottom of their feet.

Candy headed back to the house, and the rain, no longer isolated needles but hard, stinging bullets, began striking the top of her head and her back. She started to run, but before she reached the driveway the driving sheet of it rushed in off the gulf and hissed its way up the escarpment and across the lawn.

She dashed around the side of the house, her head bent.

"Here!" Agatha called from the doorway. "You'll drown!"

As her foot touched the bottom step a fearful crash of thunder threatened to tear the veranda off the house, and Candy whirled around to receive the battering force of it as lightning struck in a series of explosive flashes like heavy artillery in a far-off Asian jungle.

With her glasses in her hand, Candy saw the trees silhouetted sharply against the black and orange and yellow-white sky. She saw the tendrils of ivy flinging themselves suicidally against the outside of the lab. Pampas grass bowed in subjugation with one reckless grasshopper clinging to a spire for all his tiny worth. She saw everything.

Laughing, Candy ran up the steps.

"Goodness gracious, child, have you gone mad?" Agatha cried out, holding the door as Candy stamped her way in.

"I saw it, Agatha," she cried and twirled around in a silly, girlish dance. "Like a thunderbolt from the hand of Zeus."

"You what?"

"I can see. I can see again!" Candy thrust her glasses into Agatha's hand and snatched up a wide-eyed Amber, who stood with her nose pressed against a windowpane.

"Amber, I can finish my book! I'm going to take you to Six Flags!"

"Give me that baby," Agatha scolded. "You'll make her mildew. Now, go change your clothes and mind you don't fall down on the stairs. They're slick as glass when they're wet."

Candy kissed Amber again and headed for the stairs. As she was going out she turned back. The happy words stuck to the tip of her tongue, and she realized she'd been about to say that she was going to call Reuben and tell him the good news. At least one of her imperfections was out of the way.

With a half-smile, Agatha waited.

Sobering, Candy brushed away the thought with a wave of her hand. "Nothing."

She slipped around the door, up the stairs, and into her room, freezing now. Dragging out the telephone directory, hardly noticing the blessed clarity of the letters, her fingertip raced down the column of Norths until she found "Benjamin L."

Memorizing the number, she dialed. "Oh, yes," she said when a soft southern voice answered on the third ring, "could I speak to Reuben, please."

"I'm sorry. Reuben's in New York. He won't be back for a couple of days yet. Could I take a message?"

The pause was a mixture of defeat and a promise of future failure. He had gone back to Emma was Candy's first thought. What a loser she was.

Candy let her head come down until it almost touched her knees. "Oh, uh...no, thank you. That's all right. I'll...I'll try again later."

Losing track of everything except the wailing wind and rain outside, Candy finally looked around at the plants she could see perfectly. Rising, she walked to the bathroom and peeled off her wet clothes and stared at herself in the mirror, at her small round breasts, at her waist, her navel, the scar, which slashed to the curls as sooty black as the hair on her head, all of which she could see perfectly. Touching herself with absent familiarity, she flushed to recall Reuben's hands upon her. How enchanted he'd been with every part of her body. She had nagged him into admitting to having known many women, yet he had also admitted having to try, in time, to desire them. With her, he teased, it was a battle just to control his lust. Delighted, she had flaunted herself shamelessly before him.

Didn't that mean anything? Yes. It meant that she had too carelessly let a good thing slip through her fingers. Many people had sex and a few had love; Reuben and she had the rare privilege of finding both in one person. She had let pride trip her up once too often.

She looked at her reflection with disgust.

Benjamin North's hearing was to be conducted in one of the sterile new offices on the same floor of the courthouse as Beth's office. It would not, Beth promised, be a complicated affair. Present would be Benjamin's attorney, Al Kenazi, and Pete Dysan and another junior accountant from TempCo Oil. Representing the Coast Alliance would be Harold Jennings, plus Meredith Darling from the Natural Resources Defense Council. Also, a representative from the National Advisory Committee on Oceans and Atmosphere. The predictable press, of course.

And Reuben.

Seeing Reuben was something Candy had pondered for days. She wanted to see him; she could hardly think of anything else, but if he looked at her with coldness, or even with regret, she didn't know how she would bear it.

Though she figured that Tom guessed the reason why, Candy didn't tell him why she wanted him to present the findings of the team on behalf of the Defense Council. He agreed to, and the statistics and analyses were gone over with a fine-tooth comb. Candy didn't want any mistakes, especially on this case. With everything arranged as well as a potential disaster could be arranged, she walked into the hearing room, swept over it for Tom.

He wasn't there. Well, she thought with an apprehensive glance at her wristwatch, she was early. Taking one of the rear seats, she crossed her legs and waited.

A representative of the Environmental Protection Agency also walked in and sat down. "Nice day," he said.

Smiling, Candy agreed that it was.

Up front, a long table stretched nearly the width of the room. In the center was the only chair with arms: the judge's throne; no one would get by with anything in this room, it announced.

Candy had worn the one truly nice summer suit that she owned, a bone-colored silk with a softly shaped jacket. It wasn't great, but she wasn't ashamed of it. It matched her inexpensive bone pumps, which were newly reheeled and smartly buffed. The amethyst printed shell she had made herself, but she was an excellent seamstress and no one could buy it in a store for much less than a hundred dollars. Her makeup was tastefully understated, and she had miraculously compelled her hair to behave. Her only jewelry was a set of marble stone earrings trimmed with gold that caught the amethyst of her blouse.

Glancing at her wristwatch again, Candy sighed and rose to her feet. She had just started for the glass doors when one of them opened and a secretary poked in her head.

"Who are you?" she asked.

Candy smiled thinly. "Candice Burrows."

"A phone call for you. You can take it in my office."

Following her outside and into the judge's outer office, Candy picked up the receiver lying innocently on the desk and slipped off her earring. "This is Candice Burrows."

"Candy?"

"Tom?" Candy's pulse took a leap. "Where are you? You're going to be late."

A cough, a voice aside, vague sounds she had heard before, the ominous clatter of metal. "I'm at the doctor's office."

"What!"

"I borrowed by mother's car and slammed the door on my hand. Broke two of my fingers, tore a nail off."

"Tom!"

"You're going to have to go on without me. I'm sorry."

The sunlight was angling through the venetian blinds of the office and into Candy's eyes as if it were saying, "Don't look at me, I'm only doing my job." What now? Candy wondered. She couldn't present the case against Reuben's father. She just couldn't! It would be hideous of anyone to expect her to.

Miller? He was at A & M today. Wendy. . .she didn't know where Wendy was. "But I don't have any of the material, Tom," she protested with a wail.

"I had it sent by messenger. It should be there any minute."

Candy's natural instinct was to fall back into her old pattern of mechanically doing what was necessary and not letting it touch her on an emotional level. Her love for Reuben made that impossible.

"I'll come over when I'm finished here," Tom was saying. "Maybe there'll be something I can do to help."

Trapped, Candy leaned back against the desk and tried to think. But fate, now that it had her in its capricious clutches, seemed bent on making the most of it. She lifted her head to see Reuben walking down the corridor, flanked by a tall, striking man and, slightly behind, by a slender blondish woman.

Her heart nearly jumped out of her body. She envisioned herself dashing out of the office and hurling herself into his arms, telling him that she took the blame for everything and would take the blame forever if they could just begin again. But she was Candice Burrows, the oil-spill researcher and analyst now. She was about to hand Benjamin North his head on a platter.

She turned quickly so that only her back was visible from the outside and slumped.

"Candy?"

"Everything's all right, Tom," she said hastily. "Get your hand fixed and don't worry. I have to go now. I think I see the messenger."

"I'll get over there as soon as I can."

Hardly aware of herself hanging up the telephone, Candy smiled sadly at the secretary and stepped out into the hallway, which was now filling with people. Reuben had taken his parents inside, and a man with a short, flapped jacket with Acme Express stitched on a pocket caught her signal. He walked over to present her with an envelope and a cash ticket.

Fumbling through her bag, Candy found some money and paid him. Clipping her earring back on, she dazedly made her way into the hearing room. Some of the principals had already taken their seats around the table. Reuben was seating his parents on one of the rear benches.

Candy had never seen Benjamin North before, but she guessed she would have known who he was if she'd seen him a thousand miles from this place—his face made handsome by its fatigue and a courtly, uncompromising carriage. An old crocodile, people had called him, and the ferocity was undoubtedly there, hidden behind those icy brown eyes that were the most alive thing about him. But something else was there that she had difficulty defining.

Vivian North's beauty was as much in her bearing as in her face. Some women were born that way, Candy thought with a pang. Agatha had some of that queenliness about her. Emma would have it. She herself would never have it.

Candy hung back, wanting desperately to catch Reuben's eye. How was she going to tell him that her status on the defense had changed? She had no time to, for Reuben, glancing up, found her as truly as a needle swinging to the pole, and he immediately began weaving his way through the people who separated them.

Before he could reach her, Meredith Darling, the counsel for the defense, whom Candy had worked with before, naturally assumed that Candy would be presenting the report. "Any of those seats on the right," she said.

Candy nodded without looking at her. She'd never seen Reuben in a business suit before. She had once told him that he wasn't handsome, but she'd been influenced by Victor's beauty. Handsomeness didn't have all that much to do with physical characteristics, she now realized. Reuben's carriage was so assured, his breeding so distinguished, that his total was a remarkable, extraordinary dignity. He was extremely handsome. She loved him more than she thought possible.

"Hello," he said when he reached her, his smile reaching the brown of his eyes. He studied her with such frankness that Candy glanced around to see if anyone was watching. "You can see again."

"How do you know that?" she retorted and shyly risked a smile.

"Is there anything about you I don't know?"

Yes! But she couldn't stop smiling. Wasn't it ridiculous? She was about to ask their love to bear an impossible test, and she was smiling.

She said, "The book's nearly done."

"Ah, you've been making up for lost time."

She watched him moisten his lips, and a longing stirred inside her. In a small voice she said, "There's something I have to explain."

"That you've been as miserable as I've been?"

Her pulse quickened, but she spoke coolly. "Misery comes easily to me."

"I've made love to you a thousand times since I saw you," he said and chuckled. "I think it's some kind of record."

Candy was fighting a small civil war in her head now, but he didn't seem to notice how agitated she was. He persisted in undressing her with his eyes, and the sides of his mouth kept reminding her of deeply private intimacies.

"Reuben, there's something I have to tell you."

He hooked his little finger though hers. "Me first. I just got back from New York."

"I know."

"You checked up?" He was delighted.

"I called your house." Candy's laugh was more of a gasp. What did this man do to her senses? "To tell you I was considering entering a convent. No, to tell you that my eyes fixed themselves."

Al Kenazi touched Reuben's elbow, and Reuben halfheartedly leaned his head back. "You should bring Benjamin up to the table now," he said. "The judge has arrived."

All three of them looked around to see the federal official walking into the room, wearing a business suit. As Al walked away Reuben moved to follow him, but he leaned into Candy as he turned.

"I told her," he murmured.

Emma? Candy thought with a riveting start. Emma the millionairess? Emma the mother of children? Emma of the white, white skin and hair that never rebelled?

"How did it go?" she heard herself asking on a gasp.

"Everything's all right. No sweat."

No sweat. What male optimism, she thought. Well, perhaps it was true. Maybe it was an omen. Maybe this day wouldn't be a disaster, after all Reuben was a professional; she was a professional.

She reached out for the cuff of Reuben's sleeve. When he looked back, a lingering caress in the eagerness of his eyes, she whispered, "I'm having to do it, Reuben."

His frown was hardly more than a flicker over his face, and he blinked once. A terrible exhaustion washed over her. She had no idea what he was thinking in those seconds, and she didn't dare ask.

"Tom was going to present our findings," she hurried to explain, as if words would make it better. "He had an accident this morning. I'm sorry, Reuben. I know this complicates things terribly, but there's no one else to do it, and I—"

"I understand."

He was lying; it was all over him: his hurt, his anger. Candy's first thought was to beg him to at least defend her to his parents so their love could have some kind of future, but she could no more have asked him that than she could have taken Ronald Burrows's money.

What an awful miscalculation she'd made. Candy watched Benjamin coming forward to take his place at the table and Vivian gathering her handbag and gloves and moving up to sit directly behind him. Her own folly was unbelievable—a blow to her groin.

Because she couldn't do anything else, Candy took her own place beside Meredith Darling.

Benjamin North took the chair Al Kenazi held out for him and wondered just how many rooms like this he'd been in during his lifetime. Too many. It hadn't been an easy task, migrating from the peaceful existence of a ranch hand's son to being one of the most resented men in the state of Texas. But he was sick now, and he was dying. Nothing gave a man objectivity like dying.

If he had one regret more outstanding than the rest, he supposed that it was remaining married to Vivian. From the beginning he'd known better, but he'd been so fearless and cocky in those days, and he'd hated the way people like Lucas Stanford looked down upon him. So, because he could, he'd stolen Lucas's sweetheart. What a mistake.

But then, his whole life seemed to be one big mistake, one giant game of chess with Lucas. Every time he'd thought he was gaining a little, Lucas made a move that caught him up short. Lucas, with all his pedigrees, was much too fine to make a clean kill and get it done with. Instead, he'd become his business partner and quietly, stealthily, and with meticulous integrity, took his vengeance.

Not until he was fifty had he seen just how complete Lucas's vengeance was. Not only was it complete, it was perpetual. Lucas had passed the reins down to his daughter. Emma Stanford had controlling interest in every business transaction that he and Lucas had ever entered into and had since she was twenty-one.

Actually, it was laughable. Benjamin North, controlled by his son's fiancée! Not even Reuben knew because Emma was more skilled at the game than her father had ever been.

Still, he could take his seat today almost without bitterness. While the evidence was presented against him, he remained silent, for he had one back-up play that Lucas hadn't counted on. Two days ago—and the irony of it was that Emma had told her father and Lucas had told him— Reuben had broken off with Emma. Not only had his son unwittingly weakened Lucas's position, he had had the good sense to fall in love with the very young woman sitting across the table from him, from whose lips were coming words that would cost Benjamin more money than he would ever see again.

Benjamin didn't care. To him it had the hilarity of an off-color joke. Was it possible that this lovely young woman could bring him down with one hand and redeem him with the other? When he looked at her he saw strength, a tough strain of character that one seldom saw these days.

Then he looked at Reuben and saw pain on his son's face, and he wanted to get up and walk back to him and tell him not to be sad, that this was one of the best days he'd had in many years. But he wouldn't, he knew; those kinds of words had never passed between Reuben and himself. Besides, some things you just couldn't put into words; you kind of had to be there.

The hearing lasted slightly less than an hour, just as Beth had said, and when it was done and Candy sat staring at her hands, folded upon the papers in front of her, she felt as if there were blood on them. She sat rigidly while Benjamin North received a fine of seventy-five thousand dollars, plus all costs of cleaning up the oil slick and any restorative measures to be recommended by the Advisory Committee. She heard Vivian North's gasp and the stirring murmur of the observers.

Several times during the hearing Candy had searched for Reuben's eyes, but he was deliberately avoiding her. He was immersed in his cloud of resentment, and the desire to punish her was in the angle of his chin. Though she loved him, she didn't think she would ever forgive him for that.

After the judge had declared his verdict, Candy came to her feet in a quick surge of righteousness. She scooped up her papers and her clutch bag and shouldered her way through the confusion near the doors. In doing so, she walked past Vivian North. The woman's look was neither cold nor angry. It was nothing: a look that went through Candy, through all the flesh and bones and dark interior as if she didn't exist.

Emma would never have tolerated such a look, Candy thought. Emma would have had that breeding that the very rich come by naturally, and she would have shriveled Vivian with a mere lift of her brows.

Enough! Candy moved past Benjamin North and almost stepped on his feet. Forced to glance up, she was astonished to find the old man gazing urgently down at her. Even as Candy saw his expression, she didn't believe it—the unmistakable comprehension in Benjamin's vital brown eyes, as if he knew everything that had ever passed between Reuben and herself and understood where Candy had come from and the forces that had combined to make her what she was. Forces, he seemed to be telling her, that Reuben would never understand.

Wetting her lips, not knowing if she should speak or not, she responded with a smile that never reached her mouth but one that she guessed Benjamin recognized. Then she slipped out of the room and walked to the elevator. Part of her listened in the hope that she might hear Reuben's voice calling for her to wait.

No one called. Was there anything as pathetic as waiting for your name to be called?

Without a backward glance Candy swiftly chose the stairs. Her heels clattered on the echoing tile. *He said he'd come. He won't come. You're a fool if you wait for him to come.*

She hurried toward the outer doors by way of the tax collector's office. Shoving open the doors against a brisk, early fall wind that sent a shower of fallen leaves scuttling across the street, she lifted her head. The last thing she expected to see was Agatha coming up the courthouse steps.

"How did you know how much I needed you?" she blurted and rushed to her, grabbing her hands and turning her around. "Let's go somewhere. Tell me everything will be all right."

Chapter Ten

It was one of the most awful nights of her entire life. Sometime around one o'clock in the morning Candy finally accepted the truth: she was a fool. Reuben wasn't coming. He would never come. She'd ruined everything with her duty-before-all attitude. Or he had ruined it. What did it matter? It was ruined.

Hot-cheeked and insulted, she pushed through the front door and strode out onto the veranda, where the wind could cool her blazing face. She tried to breathe deeply and calm herself.

If she hadn't been wearing old Levi's and a faded shirt, she could've been the heroine of *The Heiress*. Except that she wasn't really Olivia de Havilland, and there was no auntie in the wings to help her pick up the pieces. Nor had she inherited a fortune so she could take a delicious and well-deserved revenge upon Montgomery Clift.

"Ohh!" she fumed. "Damn you, Reuben North. Why didn't you leave me alone? I knew you would break my heart."

Which was the bald truth of it. Some hearts were doomed to be broken. She was the victim again. But with a difference; she had been loved. Oh, yes, she had been loved most splendidly, and nothing Reuben could ever do could change that. So? So, the point of it all was: she was Candice Burrows, the victim. Again. But at least she didn't want to be a victim this time. Dadgummit, she was tired of reacting. For once in her life she wanted to do the acting.

Well, all she had to do was start. Except that she wasn't sure how to turn things around. How did one change the self-concepts and habits of a lifetime?

"Come on, Bounder," she said and struck off across the lawn to scramble down the escarpment.

For miles she stomped along the beach with the faithful animal plodding sympathetically at her heels. When she reached the jetty far up the coast, she turned around. It was nearly dawn, and she still didn't have the answers.

Oh, Reuben. She threaded her fingers into her hair and pulled it back until it brought tears to her eyes. *I don't wish I'd never seen you. I love you. I wish I were in your arms right now.*

When Candy returned to the beach house, the day had risen up out of the gulf like a strange man-of-war on the horizon. She drearily climbed the back steps and smelled coffee brewing. Agatha was making breakfast. The radio was on.

The back screen door creaked as Candy walked through it, and the masculine voice said in precise, rounded tones, "...died early this morning in Spahn Hospital after a series of worsening strokes that began early this year. Mr. North was sixty-seven years old and owner of several local businesses, one of which is the TempCo Oil Corporation, recently in the headline as..."

Time floated aimlessly around with no center. In disbelief, Candy watched Agatha turning from the sink, the wet cloth dropping from her hands as her fading eyes stared wide and unseeing. Then Candy grasped the horror of it.

With an irrational, ghoulish relief, she thought, *Reuben didn't stand me up. His father died.*

"...Yesterday in a federal hearing, after receiving combined penalties by the National Advisory Committee on Oceans and Atmosphere..."

Candy groped behind herself for something to lean against, anything to steady the swirling room. Benjamin North was dead. Dead! And she had helped deal the blow that had killed him.

The newsman was droning out the announcement of where funeral services would he held, then he launched breezily into the next item of news. Candy stumbled across the room, needing Agatha more than she had ever needed any human being in her life.

"Agatha?" she gasped.

But the woman was staring at something Candy couldn't see. "Benjamin is dead."

Now, Candy thought. Now was the time to turn it around. She could comfort when she needed to be comforted. She circled Agatha's waist and pulled her to a chair.

"Benjamin's been sick for a long time," she said inadequately. "You know that. That's why Reuben came down from New York."

"We're dying. We're all dying."

"Do you want me to get you something?"

Agatha looked at Candy as if she were surprised that she had come into the room. She sat down. "I'm all right. It was such a shock. Death is..."

"So close," Candy said on a dwindling breath.

"Yes."

"I'll get you some coffee."

"Yes."

Candy hurried to the counter, thinking with every heart-beat, *I killed him, I killed him.*

She searched through a cupboard and found some brandy and sloshed some into the cup, pressed it into Agatha's hands. "Drink this."

"Poor Vivian," Agatha whispered and sat holding the cup.

Candy urged the drink to her mouth, and the telephone rang almost immediately. Candy lurched forward. Oh, Reuben! she thought when she heard his voice, wanting to reach through the telephone and embrace him. Terrible pressure was in his voice. Reuben, too, needed her strength.

Do you need me to come? she wanted to ask. He said that he was making all the arrangements. He said that he loved her. He said that he needed her desperately, but he didn't ask her to come.

"Everyone is looking to me to give them something I don't have," he said as his humanity lay very heavily upon him.

Yes, she said, understanding now. Vivian North blamed her for Benjamin's death. It would be..."un-right" for her to be with Reuben now.

The day of Benjamin's funeral it rained. St. Luke's church was so overflowing with people that many had to stand, and the air conditioner strained to cope with the bodies and added humidity. For a man who was disliked, Candy thought, the old crocodile had many people showing respect at his passing. She wondered if any of them had ever seen beneath the husk of the man. Somehow she doubted it. But she had, and that pleased her. Very much.

Still, except for Agatha, Candy wouldn't have come to the funeral. She sat tucked discreetly away in the back with Agatha and Beth and hugged Amber close. Beyond her, on the right of the ebony-shrouded bier, Reuben sat beside his mother and his sisters, his arm draped protectively around Vivian's shoulders. Candy stared at the way his hair furled beautifully upon the top of his collar, the backs of his ears, which were still slightly sunburned, the contrast of the snowy cuff upon his tanned hand as it curved around Vivian's back.

Behind the North family sat the Lucas Stanfords. With them was one of the most stunningly lovely women Candy had ever seen; even from the back—the creamy blush of her cheek just visible beneath the brim of her hat—Candy knew who she was.

It was only natural that Emma should be at Reuben's side during this time, Candy told herself. The Stanfords had been friends of the North family for more years than Candy had been on earth. Emma belonged here. Still, a deep bitterness smoldered inside her. *She* wanted to belong here.

When everyone emerged from the church, sunlight shone over the freshly rinsed city. The wet concrete of the streets and sidewalks threw back gold, pooled reflections, and patrolmen directed the attendants out onto the highway, tires hissing and swishing. Candy slumped against the back seat with Agatha as Beth pulled her car out into the long, snaking procession to the cemetery.

"He shouldn't have died," Agatha said. "Someone should have been able to do something."

"He's resting now, Agatha." Candy absently stroked the thin arm. "We can't begrudge him that."

Sighing, Agatha didn't reply.

The graveside service was blessedly brief. Only a few more minutes, Candy told herself, and her dealings with Benjamin North would be ended. She and Agatha had stood on the fringes of the mourners, and the moment the final prayer was said, she grasped Agatha's arm and began walking her back to the car. They had just cleared the granite markers and had moved across the expanse of clipped emerald lawn when the woman's voice rang over the cemetery as if it were amplified.

"You, Miss Burrows!"

Candy thought that some small part of her must have been waiting for such a voice—the part that had vowed to never be a victim again. Else, why did she feel no surprise when she turned to find Vivian North looking at her with repulsion? Slowly releasing Agatha's elbow, Candy started toward Reuben's mother, meaning to take the first step. She smiled.

Resentment blazed over Vivian's face. "How do you have the nerve to show your face here?" she yelled with such vehemence that strangers turned their heads and tried to pretend they weren't gawking.

A pain began to spread through Candy's chest. She shook her head. "Mrs. North—"

"Murderess!" Vivian cut her off. "You and the rest like you." She stopped and turned away, as if it were over as suddenly as it had begun. Then she spun back and pointed a finger. With low roughness she said, "Get out of my son's life. And stay out. You don't belong there."

It felt, to Candy, like topping the crest on a roller coaster. You knew that the body had to throw itself in reverse because the drop was coming, but you were never ready for it. *Just let it come. What's one blow, more or less?*

But Reuben, viewing the incident from a distance, cursed himself for not having second-guessed his mother. Moments earlier he'd seen Candy as the limousines had been pulling away from the curb at the church. She'd been descending the steps, one of the last to come out, and a premonition of disaster had riddled through him then. He'd wanted to stop the car and go to her.

Now he struck out across the lawn with a quick, hot fury that turned heads more swiftly than Vivian's outcry. Askance, he saw Lucas Stanford doing the same thing.

He reached Vivian first and brought his hand down upon her shoulder. No one treated Candy this way, not while he was alive. "Mother—" he said and flicked an apologetic glance at Candy.

But Vivian threw Reuben off with surprising strength. "She took years off his life!" she cried. "She and the others in this town. He didn't deserve that, Reuben!"

Rushing up, Lucas muttered something to Reuben about how sorry he was and took Vivian by the arm. "Come to the car, Vivian. My dear, please. This won't help."

Other women hurried over and huddled around, and Candy guessed they were Reuben's sisters and aunts. "Get your hands off me, Lucas!" Vivian was screaming. Then she turned on Reuben. "And you remember who you are, Reuben North. I am your mother. That man lying in the ground over there is your father, and she helped put him there!"

Dissolving into hysterical tears, Vivian finally allowed herself to be led away.

One of the funeral attendants hurried up to apologize to Reuben. Another stepped to Candy and said with a hush, "Are you all right, ma'am? Could I walk you to your car?"

Candy didn't know how to answer the man. She was swimming in pain now. When Reuben pushed past the attendant and caught her in a swift, crushing embrace, shielding her from Vivian's ravings, which still carried across the rain-sweet grounds, she gratefully accepted his greater strength.

"Don't listen," he whispered and kissed her ear, kissed her temple, her cheek. "She doesn't know what she's saying."

Though Candy craved any comfort from Reuben, they had gone too far to tolerate such a pretense. Pulling back, she peered up at his ravaged face. "Yes, she does. She means every word of it."

A pain seemed to shudder through his body, and his shoulders drooped with surrender. "I wish it were going to be easy to love me."

His strength was greater, she knew, but her endurance would always exceed his. She stepped back from him, stared at him for long moments before cupping his jaw in her hand. "You know, Reuben, when I was a girl and my parents were still at home, there were terrible fights. I mean, real fist fights. But there was also a lot of kissing when it was over and gushy words and lavish promises. And I thought about how loved I was. Then they left me, and I found out the hard way that when you're talking about love, all the dressing up doesn't count. All the syrupy words, all the kisses—they don't count, Reuben. They're frills, icing on the cake. This is love, what passes between two people. The desire to give and want nothing back. I would take all your pain if I could. I even love you enough to let you go if I have to. Your mother can't hurt me, Reuben. Only you can do that."

He held her in one those wordless embraces that transcends anything else on earth. "Thank God for you, Candice Burrows." He walked them to Beth's car, and Candy felt the first peace in days.

"Miss Dickerson?" he said and smiled regretfully as he stooped to peer in at Beth.

"I forgive you, Mr. North," Beth offered generously, and they all had to smile at her cocky brashness. "For everything."

"Well, that's a relief," he retorted with an almost equal cockiness. "Since we're all going to be seeing a lot of each other, I think first names are in order, don't you?"

Laughing, Beth swiveled in the seat to open the back door. "What I think," she said as Agatha climbed in first, "is that you should tell Scotty that you've had second thoughts about leaving earth. Stay down here with us mortals. You might find that you like it."

Reuben looped an arm around Candy's neck and pulled her against his side. "Hey," he said and lightly nuzzled the side of her neck, "I like it already."

If Candy hadn't turned her face up to be kissed, she guessed she wouldn't have seen Emma first, but over Reuben's shoulder she caught sight of that stunningly graceful walk, the gorgeous black dress, the splendid crownless hat. She stiffened in Reuben's arms.

Reuben looked back. "Oh, hell," he mumbled and sighed.

This one, Candy thought, *you can handle yourself, Reuben.*

She slid across the seat beside Agatha and held herself in a pose that was a little on the ridiculous side, but no more than Emma's as she moved languidly up beside Reuben like a wife coming to bid her departing guests goodbye.

Emma stepped to the car door and gently closed it, then bent in a swoop so that her frothy black skirt swept the glistening grass. Her courtesy included everyone in the car. "We're so glad you came. I hope you don't let what happened with Vivian disturb you, Miss Burrows. She's absolutely grief-stricken. And you, Miss South, Vivian just told me that you were an old friend of the family. Do come to the reception. My parents are giving it at the town house. In fact—" here a gracious smile "—you're welcome to ride in the limousine with us if you like."

Candy felt sweat moistening her palms. Were men stupid, or were women smart? How could Reuben possibly have deceived himself that anything was over with Emma Stanford? Emma was just getting started.

Making her reply match Emma's for politeness, Candy said, "Agatha's very tired, Miss Stanford."

"Oh, please call me Emma."

"Thank you very much, Emma." The whole exchange was incredible. "We really should be going."

With an unexpected movement Emma leaned very near, and then Candy could see the fine lines edging her eyes. Yet her skin was as smooth as a baby's and her perfume the most exquisite delicacy.

"Oh, what an adorable baby," she cooed at Amber.

Candy hoped that her color hadn't risen. "I'm very proud of her."

"She the spitting image of you, Candice. May I call you Candice?" Emma's green eyes twinkled. "That's such a grotesque expression, isn't it? The spitting image? What could be nice about spitting?"

If you don't get away from this car, Candy thought with a viciousness that shocked her, *I'm going to lean over and spit in one of those beautiful green eyes.*

But of course she wouldn't do that. Candy knew she would sit exactly where she was and be aware of Beth's struggle with her laughter and see Emma pat Amber's hand. *See? Emma's finished talking. She's straightening, looking as if she knows something no one else does. See her touching my hand?*

Candy gazed down at the diamond on Emma's finger, saw the stone catch the light in a flash of breathtaking fire. With a jolt Candy realized what she was looking at: the engagement ring.

"Are you sure there's nothing I can say to change your mind?" Emma purred sweetly.

Now Candy saw how complicated Emma really was; Emma had no intentions of losing Reuben. It was a matter of pride, and pride was capable of doing terrible things. Anger licked along Candy's veins. Was having Reuben worth all this?

She peered up at the fierceness of Reuben's scowl and his folded arms. She remembered him holding her in the helicopter. She remembered hearing him coax Amber to talk on the telephone. She saw herself burying her face in the silk gown he'd brought after she'd treated him so terribly, the way he'd cleaned her up and defended her against Victor's insults, his tearing the door off the house because he needed so badly to be with her.

Reuben was worth anything, and for the first time in her life Candy challenged another woman. With precise clarity she said, "There is nothing you can say to change my mind."

How was that for acting instead of reacting?

Emma paused, understanding. She laughed, a silver, musical mirth. "I didn't think so."

A dull flush was staining Reuben's cheekbones, and Candy didn't know how much he grasped by intuition. Men weren't mean enough to understand the total of women's ways with each other. Reuben's face was drawn with a bleak harshness, but Emma, if she saw Reuben's anger, seemed unconcerned. With a husky laugh she nestled possessively close to his side.

Score one for Emma, Candy thought.

Slumping, Candy took Agatha's hand in hers and was grateful that Beth had the good sense to get them out of the cemetery and back onto the highway as soon as possible. For long moments, while Beth chattered aimlessly to Amber, Candy sat patting Agatha's hand.

She looked over at the older woman. Agatha seemed more calm now. Smiling, Candy pulled her hand free, but Agatha gripped her with an almost inhuman tenacity. The tighter Candy pulled back, the tighter Agatha held.

A pain shot up into Candy's arm, and she sucked in her breath. Agatha didn't blink an eyelash. Flashing a look in the rearview mirror, Candy failed to get Beth's attention. "Agatha?" she whispered.

Nothing.

Candy bore the pain, and when they finally reached home, as if she had just awakened from some grisly dream, Agatha released Candy's hand and smiled over at her.

Dumbfounded, Candy gazed from her bruised hand back to Agatha climbing the veranda steps with her usual erect posture, her customary gracefulness, her poise. For some moments Candy worked her fingers.

Beth called her from the steps. "Are you coming?"

"Yes," Candy said and crawled thoughtfully out of the car. She thought she understood now why Agatha's lover had a wife and children; why Agatha had turned up at the courthouse on the day Benjamin had had to appear; why Agatha had been devastated at news of Benjamin's death, at his funeral.

How silly to think that Agatha had come to the courthouse because she thought Candy might need her. She'd come because she had loved Benjamin North for twenty years. She'd come because she couldn't stay away. Benjamin North was Agatha's lover!

In the kitchen, Candy paused for a moment to hold her hand under running water. She looked around herself at the walls of the old house, the acreage. If she were a betting person, she would wager good money that Benjamin had given this house to Agatha too.

Agatha was standing before the front door when Candy walked into the living room, staring out at the distant horizon. Presently she turned and smiled. Her pale, gentle eyes were overburdened with memories.

"I think," Candy whispered and took her place beside her old friend, "that he stole a little of my heart too, Agatha."

Outside, the freshly rinsed lawn had the pungent smell of seasonal change. The rose bushes beside the front walk had started foolishly to bloom again. "He was always giving things to me," Agatha said so softly that Candy had to lean nearer to hear. "I was never able to give him anything back."

Out of respect for Agatha's dignity, Candy didn't look at her. What was there about these North men that could make you go a little crazy?

"That's the way of love, Agatha," she said quietly. "It never comes out even. Pray God, it always comes out right."

Candy wasn't sure what awakened her. She had drifted off to sleep from where she lay curled up in a chair, waiting for Reuben. When she moved, her neck was stiff, and she stretched and rubbed the soreness. Blinking until she could focus on the small red digits of the clock on the table, she saw that it was after midnight. The house had taken on that quiet, womblike safety, and Candy automatically listened for Amber's cry.

Nothing, and Candy lifted the skirt of her silk gown and lightly climbed the stairs. She peeped inside to hear the peaceful, even breathing of her daughter. Going to Agatha's room, she cracked the door—the same quiet breathing, punctuated occasionally by a low moan, as if the dreams were disturbing.

Were they of Benjamin? Candy wondered and tested the soreness that had set up in her hand.

Going back downstairs, she sat down in the chair. But something wasn't right, and she rose again and checked the back door, then the front. There, in the misty shadows of the drive, sat Reuben's pickup. Then, as her eyes traveled along the length of the porch, she saw him fitted between two of the posts like a man would stretch himself into a hammock. In his exhaustion, he had fallen asleep, and his chin rested uncomfortably on his chest.

Oh, my darling man! The front door groaned as Candy opened it, and she flew to him on bare feet, the silk trailing out behind her so that she looked like a spirit of the netherworld. Kneeling, her heart swelling with love until she feared it would burst, she adored him for a moment.

How could Benjamin ever be disappointed in this man? How could he ever think Reuben was not strong? What man could bear as much so patiently? What man could give as much and ask for so little in return?

Candy touched his forehead and gently smoothed back a fallen lock of hair. ''Sweetheart?'' she whispered.

His head came up with a snap, and he blinked himself awake, then grinned wearily. He hadn't shaved after the funeral and his stubble was scratchy. His eyes were red-rimmed and puffy, and he smelled slightly of liquor. But he was here, and he was the most beautiful sight she'd ever seen.

He closed his arms about her as if he were home at last. ''I love you,'' he muttered hoarsely and tried to swallow down tears that had fought to surface time and time again for the past twenty-four hours and had cruelly been pushed back.

Trembling, he stuffed his face into the curve of Candy's throat. ''I've needed you so much.''

''I know,'' Candy said, feeling his deep, heartbreaking grief as if it were her own. ''I'm here.''

She held him until he got it all out.

Chapter Eleven

Marriage," Candy said succinctly. "A ten-letter word spelled i-m-p-o-s-s-i-b-l-e."

Reuben leaned on the top of his rake, his face a conflict of emotions. They were cleaning up the leaves in Agatha's front yard, and they'd been at it all morning. "It's emotional blackmail," he declared. "I'm not going to let Emma get by with that."

Candy mildly continued raking. She looked like a farmer in her old jeans and a plaid shirt, flapping in the brisk November breeze, her hair a tossing riot of black.

"Men never understand the fury of a woman scorned," she said blandly. "After centuries, they still think they can outwit it."

"Bull."

She threw him a sidelong glance. "You're used to equalities, Reuben, things being fair. You're talking to an expert on inequalities. You can't win against Emma by fighting back. You win by outliving her.''

''We'll get married and outlive her together.''

''If we get married, we'll seal your mother's fate.''

''Emma already knows I love you. She has to know that we're having a love affair.''

''Yes, but you haven't made it legal. Or public. We have to be patient. Very patient.''

''How did you get to be such an expert on patience?''

She gave him a look that Reuben thought was more deliberate than fanciful. ''I was taught by masters.''

When he growled, she flicked her rake and sent a spray of yellow leaves showering over him. Then she wrapped both hands around the top of her rake and wickedly mimicked his grumpy posture.

At the reception following Benjamin's burial, Emma had made her grand announcement to Reuben. She was in possession of the controlling interest in the corporations Lucas and Benjamin had formed, and had been—technically speaking—for years. She now intended to exercise her rights. It was time she did something constructive, she said. She would become the female executive. She would be chairman of the board, and Reuben could take over Benjamin's place as senior vice-president.

Reuben's greatest shock wasn't that Emma would do such a thing; Emma was spoiled and her pride had been damaged. It was surprise that Benjamin would have sat still for a thing like that. Or that Lucas, a man whom he'd admired, would slowly squeeze the life out of his father. The Stanford millions would never miss a few corporations; they'd be a handy tax write-off.

It was no wonder that his father had been driven to terrible lengths to survive. Emma came by her vindictiveness naturally, didn't she?

''I'm right, Reuben,'' Candy said and looked him straight in the eyes. ''With your father's estate in virtual bankruptcy, all Emma has to do is lie back and do nothing, let all the partnerships go down the tubes, and your mother winds up with nothing for the rest of her life. I suspect that Emma lies back very well.''

Angry and frustrated, Reuben stomped over to a different part of the lawn and started a new pile of leaves. When Candy walked over to help him, he paused, looked up.

''How can you think of my mother,'' he asked, ''after what she did to you?''

Behind them, Amber and Bounder were dutifully romping through the leaf pile, scattering them everywhere. Reuben glanced around and yelled, ''Hey, you two! Cut that out.''

Amber stopped and obediently dropped the leaves from her chubby hands. With her Windbreaker hood tied around her round face, she looked like an adorable cherub. Bounder wagged his tail and continued to race around her in delirious circles.

Laughing, Reuben tossed down his rake and went to pick up the baby and throw her high into the air. Catching her, he fell with her into the leaves and disappeared.

The sight of their happy play was a balm to Candy's heart. With a fine mistrust of anything so perfect, however, she abandoned her rake and dug her way through the leaves to rescue her daughter. No sooner had she done so than she found herself dragged down into the ocean of leaves by a stealthy arm.

''Now's your chance to get even with Vivian,'' Reuben insisted as he wound up on top and spat debris from his mouth, then gazed down at her while Amber scrambled away and crowed her triumph. ''All you have to do is marry me.''

''I know that,'' she said and reached up to smooth his hair down around his ears.

He picked leaves from her hair. ''No one in the world would blame you. She has it coming.''

"Yes, she does."

For long, wondering moments, he studied her. "Then, why don't you?"

"Because you love her," she said simply. "If we wait to get married and give her some time, maybe she'll mellow."

Reuben shook his head in amazement. "Vivian's not known for her mellowing, my darling."

"Then I want to wait because it's the right thing to do, Reuben. Agree with thine adversary quickly. You know?"

"Girl, you never cease to amaze me. I have never known anyone with the capacity to give like you give."

He rolled off her, and Candy lay back with only her head poking out of the leaves and gazed up at the clouds scudding across the sky. Stretching out beside her, Reuben braced himself on an elbow while Amber grew bored and went off on a search with Bounder for bigger and better things.

They enjoyed the mutual peace of just being together. Without looking at her, he asked, "Are you afraid?"

Candy popped up like a jack-in-the-box. She ruffled her hair and smiled down at him. "Isn't it strange? Everything's hanging by a mere thread—Emma's threat, Victor's threat, your mother's situation, your father having died. But all I think about is that I've got the manuscript finished, and that it's proofing better than I'd hoped. I've got my eyes back. Amber is healthy and safe. Agatha opens her heart and her home to us. And—" she licked her finger and drew a line in the sky "—I've got you. Chalk one up for me."

Reuben pushed her down beneath him and kissed her. Candy loved the promises he made with his tongue and the tiny nibbles of her lips, her chin. Finally she whispered, "Yes, I'm afraid. I don't want to lose any of this."

His eyes glowed with his love for her. "But what's a little fear here and there, eh?"

He slipped his hand beneath her old shirt and found her breast, and Candy smiled at his familiar caress. Their lovemaking was assuming the comfortable play of lovers at ease with themselves.

"Fear keeps you young," she retorted and giggled as she slipped her hands into his back pockets.

He nipped the tip of her nose. "Fear makes you hot."

"Silly. Impure thoughts make you hot."

"You make me have impure thoughts."

She laughed. "And you make me."

"That I do. A vicious circle, isn't it?"

"Shut up and kiss me."

Two days before Thanksgiving, a festive banner stretched between the two chandeliers of the Regency ballroom: OUR YOUTH ARE OUR FUTURE. For weeks Agatha had worked at her charity. Her ladies had met with businessmen all over south Texas. They has spoken to women's groups, had sold tickets to the annual hundred-dollar-a-plate dinner.

Members of the symphony in Corpus Christi were donating time to play for the gala event. Agatha and Beth had slaved over the menu—Agatha to have the best quality possible, Beth to make a profit. They had decided on sliced artichokes and lobster meat arranged around red-tip lettuce and bathed in butter sauce, plus dense hot bread. And for dessert a wafer-thin, delicate apple tart.

Candy planned to wear a black velvet skirt and a white evening sweater. Simplicity plus, she thought, but she could splurge on accessories. Then Agatha had solved that problem by insisting on lending Candy her Petochi pearl choker.

"I couldn't," Candy protested as her jaw slackened at the sight of it. She inwardly wondered if the jewelry was a gift from Benjamin. "Really, I just couldn't."

"They'll be perfect with the sweater. Benjamin would have wanted you to wear them." Candy's brows lifted, and Agatha lifted a guilty palm. "I was a typical mistress, I'm afraid. I could never turn him down."

So, with the pearls clasped stunningly around her throat, Candy and Beth arrived at the Regency Hotel late, having taken more time than they planned to put Amber safely to bed and settle Wendy in to sit with her. The festivities were well under way. Dancing had already begun. Some people were being served dinner.

"We deserve this," Beth gaily announced as she threw off her stole and tossed it to the hat-check girl. "I worked my buns off getting my quota this year."

Candy hid a smile. "As long as that's all you worked off, darling."

"You're so smart. Just because you've got a thing going."

"I wasn't sure you'd noticed."

"Reuben's not used to me yet. He still has fantasies, I think, of pawning me off on one of his out-of-state friends."

"You'll be my maid of honor," Candy protested with a laugh. "He has no choice but to like you."

"As long as this best man he's got in New York is single, I'll put up with him."

Beth immediately spotted a more likely candidate than some unknown from New York and told Candy she would see her later. Smiling at the predictability of her friend, Candy gave the maître d' her name and watched as he moved his stubby finger down the list.

"Has Mr. Reuben North arrived yet?" she asked.

The man twitched his mustache and flicked her a glance that said Mr. North was a fortunate man, whoever he was. "I don't believe so, mademoiselle. Shall I ask around?"

"No, no. That's all right."

White-coated waiters rushed everywhere as Candy trudged off behind the waiter, their trays held high above their heads. Voices called out over the music, flashbulbs and strobe lights twinkled like stars, silk brushed against linen in a soft sibilance.

Since learning about Benjamin, Candy guessed that much of Agatha's phenomenal success with her charity was due in part to strings that he'd pulled behind the scenes. Countless Texas publications would be represented by reporters cruising around the Regency ballroom tonight.

So engrossed was she in scanning the room for Vivian and Emma, Candy didn't realize until she was nearly to her table that it wasn't empty. Calmly sipping a vodka and tonic sat Victor.

Drat! Sighing, she was hard pressed to remember her own good advice to Reuben about having patience. But she took a grip on herself and waved Victor back down to his chair. "I've been doing this for years, Victor. Don't exert yourself."

"Must you needle me tonight?" he complained with an agreeable chuckle as she settled her skirt and crossed her legs. "You'll give me a complex."

Victor always did more for a tuxedo than it could ever do for him. Candy grudgingly had to admit that he was stunning in the same way he'd been stunning four years before. His smile was attracting every woman's eye within viewing range, and he was well aware of it.

"Chablis for the lady," he said to the waiter.

Candy caught the waiter's arm before he could write it down. "Make that a Bloody Mary."

"You just couldn't resist, could you?" he said.

"No."

Irritation curled his lip, but he hid it with a smile. "Well, you're extraordinarily beautiful tonight, my dear. How's life been treating you?"

She inclined her head. "Why are you here, Victor?"

"Tsk, tsk," he said and pursed his beautiful mouth so that becoming grooves appeared beneath his cheekbones. "Can't I want to see you without having a hidden motive?"

The waiter returned with her drink, and Candy twirled the straw and sipped before replying. *Don't blow it by being nasty, Candy.* A photographer passed by their table and, sensing an uneven tension, took pictures at the next table.

"Are you enjoying the house?" she asked him.

He gave a faint shrug. "I'd enjoy it better if you were living in it."

"Victor—"

"Okay, okay." He leaned forward, his hazel eyes growing smaller with intensity. "Candy, are you really serious about what's-his-name?"

Candy's intuitions tried vigorously to hold back the quickness of her tongue, but she'd suffered too much because of Victor not to avail herself of the satisfaction of letting him know she hadn't forgotten anything.

She unconsciously touched the choker at her throat. "I'm as serious about him as I once was about you, Victor."

Victor regarded her for a moment without betraying his thoughts, but when he smiled, his face was rigid with determination. "Where is he tonight?"

"He's meeting me here."

"Ah. There's time, then."

Now it was Candy's turn to stiffen. "Time to what?"

"Talk about our daughter."

She had taken his silence during the summer to mean that things were holding steady. The cold glass suddenly hurt her fingers, but she didn't want to put it down. She took a long pull on the straw. "Amber's fine."

"Not that kind of talk."

"What, then?" She knew what he was going to say. There was nothing she could do to stop him.

"I've waited as long as I can for you to make up your mind," he said as easily as if he were remarking about the weather. "I'm having my lawyer file the suit, Candy."

His intentions touched Candy like a cold breath. He wasn't joking; he wasn't bluffing. So harshly did she lunge to her feet, she tipped over his drink.

Vodka sloshed onto someone at a neighboring table, and there was an embarrassing flurry of napkins and a number of scathing looks. Candy tried to hold on to some modicum of dignity and leaned over the table, her hands clutching her bag until they were numb.

"Stay away from her," she said through gritted teeth.

He ignored her outburst and stepped toward her as if he had every intention of taking her into his arms. "Have this dance with me, darling."

"I don't want to dance with you, you—"

His fingers were nearly breaking her wrist. "But I've been looking forward to it."

She jerked away with such force, she stepped into a man seated behind her. Color flooded her face as she turned with a sick half-glance. Warning herself that she was making the same mistake with Victor that Reuben had wanted to make with Emma, she nonetheless forced his hand.

"You know what you've been looking forward to, Victor?" Her fist found her hip. "Well, I'll tell you. It's just come to you that you're a fraud. You pretend to be a writer, but you're not. You never were. You want me to do it again for you."

Her mind was molten, her body strung tightly from her toes to her head. "Well, find the talent yourself, Victor," she cried when he stared blankly at her. "I don't have time to fool with you anymore!"

There was nothing like burning bridges, was there? As Candy whirled away from Victor and tried to shoulder her way through the wall-to-wall crowd, she knew he was stalking her. Victor would never let a woman get by with something like that.

They had passed the last of the dinner tables, and he caught her by an arm and nearly jerked her off her feet. He bent over her with such seething fury, Candy wouldn't have been surprised if he'd hit her. "You're making a mistake."

She met him, look for burning look. "It couldn't possibly match the one I've already made."

Victor's face was waxen. His eyes were cruelly slitted. Muscles twitched convulsively beneath his skin, and Candy knew he was pushed as close to the edge of the precipice as it was possible to get.

"Ah, yes," he said when he saw her comprehension. "You do well to be afraid."

She whirled around, her hands aching from clenching. "I'm not afraid of you."

When she'd gone a dozen steps, he called out to her. "Hey, Candy?"

She had to turn. He made a movement of his head when she did, almost as if he were throwing her a kiss. A flash of white teeth, the twitch of a smile smothering itself. "Watch your back, Candy."

"You monster," she said, but he had already left her standing there.

Candy wasn't sure if she should laugh or cry. She was abruptly tired and wanted nothing more than to get away from people. A hundred eyes seemed to be watching her as she threaded her way through the human mass to the women's room. Actually, she was only sure of four eyes: Emma's and Vivian's, some distance away, seeing everything.

"Oh, great," she mumbled angrily to herself. "You've really done it this time, Candice Burrows."

People were still pouring through the front doors into the huge lobby, some of them to see, some of them to be seen, very few concerned about the youth of Texas on this particular evening but all having given many dollars.

More photographers and more reporters, Candy thought as she searched and searched for Reuben. She spied him just as he walked across the end of the lobby and prepared to enter the ballroom. Reaching him would be impossible, and Candy waited near the potted ferns and literally willed him to look her way.

His eyes came to life as they casually passed over her, then jerked back. He smiled, and she turned down one side of her mouth in a grim commentary. Understanding at once, he made a motion to stay by the telephones. She nodded gratefully. Everything would be all right now. Reuben was here.

"You're going the wrong way," he said, laughing as he walked up. "The tables are that way."

"That's what you think," she said on a whimper. "I just came from there, and there's not enough money to pay me to go back."

"Victor?"

"Yes."

"Where?" Reuben took two backward steps and craned his neck for the handsome Georgian, but Victor was nowhere to be seen. Returning to Candy, he stared hungrily down the neckline of her sweater. "Well," he growled, "what suggestions do you have, my pretty? I don't want any of that to go to waste."

She wanted to tell him about Victor's threat. She wanted to say that she was more frightened for Amber than she'd ever been in her whole life, but she caught the front of his tuxedo in her hands.

"Do you really want to get married?" she asked.

He laughed.

"I'm serious," she insisted. "Right now. This week. As soon as we can get the license—the wedding, the honeymoon, the adoption. The whole bit, Vivian or no Vivian."

He glanced at his watch and into her eyes, his own darkening with gravity. "I don't think I can be ready in less than ten minutes."

His arms closing around her seemed to make everything better. She laid her head on the wonderful pillow of his shoulder. "Just take me out of here."

As Reuben held her, wondering what had brought her to this crisis point, he made a quick sweep of the room for Emma. Hardly a dozen words had passed between them since the day of Benjamin's funeral. As he guessed, he found her watching their embrace with bitterness marring her lovely face, and he telegraphed her a warning over the distance.

Then he dipped his head to Candy. "I'll do better than that." His voice was hard. "Do you have your things?"

"My coat's checked."

He crushed her fingers, detaining her. "You know," he warned, "that once we walk across the lobby and out the doors, everyone will have us pegged. It'll be only a matter of time."

She smiled unhappily. "I'm counting on it."

Neither of them had exaggerated the stir they would cause as they made their way against the flow of traffic through the lobby. They made an impressive couple, and leaving just as the festivities were beginning could only mean one of two things, and anyone could look at them and tell they hadn't quarreled.

Reuben drew Candy close and protected her with his back. Several men he knew grinned at him as if to say they didn't blame him one bit. He called for Candy's coat, and as he was helping her on with it, a reporter stepped up, signaling a photographer, who snapped several shots of them. He said he was from the *Tribune*.

Reuben smiled down at him, glanced at his name tag. "You want a scoop, Mr. Hillman?"

Hillman thumped a cigarette from a pack. "Have you got one?"

"We're leaving. We're going to get married."

The reporter gave him a suspicious sidelong look. "Who's we?"

Reuben's brows were a devil's brows. "That's for you to find out."

The cigarettes went back into his suit coat. "Hey, come on, man. Gimme a break."

Laughing, Candy slipped her arms into the coat Reuben held for her, and, hand in hand, they dashed down to the lower level that opened onto the front doors, leaving a string of gaping mouths behind them.

Emma Stanford moved against the tuxedoed traffic more slowly than Candy or Reuben. Several times she thought she had lost sight of the man Reuben had spoken to, but she discovered him near the hat-check booth, smoking.

Sidling up to him and waiting until he grew aware of her and turned, she was amused that he had the predictable reaction to her. "Yes, ma'am," he drawled as he came hopefully to life, "what can I do for you?"

She slipped a folded bill into his hand. The man didn't flinch as he palmed it. "What did that gentleman say to you?"

The reporter hesitated, then grinned. "He said he was getting married. Big deal!"

The green of Emma's eyes always darkened when she was intense; now it was emerald. "Not so big."

With a shift of her hip, she threw back her sparkling skirt behind her and let her clicking heels carry her across the lobby to the ladies' lounge. Glancing around to see who else was there, she proceeded to open her evening bag and lean toward the mirror. In the periphery of her vision she saw the young, pouting girl slouching against the wall in a jet-black uniform.

The girl stared at her for so long that Emma started to snap at her. Instead, she fished out a fifty-dollar bill and folded it, tapping it against her tooth. She crooked her finger in a sultry command to come nearer.

"You want this?" she murmured.

The girl didn't say anything. Her hungry look told it all.

"Come with me." Emma took the girl to the edge of the huge ballroom and searched over it until she found the blond gentleman that Candy had danced with. Then she proceeded to point him out to the girl.

"You go to that man and find out his name for me, and I'll give you this. If you get him to come over and talk to me, I'll give you two of them."

The girl drew her lips into a lipsticked circle and considered for a moment. Then she smiled. "Yes, ma'am," she said knowingly and threw her own hip as she walked out across the floor.

The arrangements were very simple. Reuben drove Candy home, where they talked to Wendy—Miller had just happened to "drop by," but Candy was secretly pleased to know that a man was at the house—and paid her an exorbitant amount to stay the night. Miller wasn't expected to stay the night, Candy dryly reminded him.

He raked through his terrible hair and grinned his Rod Stewart grin. "I'd do it for free, boss lady."

Candy wrote a rather hysterical note to Agatha and promised her that their wedding would take place at any point in time after tonight. Tonight was to be spent on Benjamin's yacht before the creditors came and hauled it away. They would call her.

"Bundle up," Reuben ordered Candy with a rough kiss, "and pack all the food you can carry and meet me at the jetty."

"Are you sure you know about yachts?"

Reuben flexed his biceps and demanded that she feel one. "You ask me that? A man born and bred in Corpus Christi? Lord, girl, what nerve."

The stache of food turned out to be everything that Candy could cram into a backpack: dried fruit and some flatbread, cheese and a melon. Agatha had some bittersweet chocolate wafers, so Candy threw them in with a promise to replace them. In a baggie she stuffed two kinds of grapes and apples. One last trip to the refrigerator yielded sliced lamb. Topping that off, she took two bottles of Cabernet Sauvignon. Those she would have to carry, a bottle in each hand.

As an afterthought, she filched one of Agatha's starched pink tablecloths and two crisp napkins. Then she gave Amber a final kiss in her sleep and took a deep breath of exhilaration. With one last warning to Miller to behave himself, Candy slipped out the back door.

"You're just what I need, old friend." She laughed as Bounder loped up and took several hopeful sniffs of her backpack. "On second thought, you're not what I need. Get down."

He ignored the advice and ran ahead of her, barking as she slid down the escarpment and struggled to protect the precious bottles of Cabernet at the same time.

"Some guard dog you are," she murmured as the beach stretched out in a ghostly white strip beyond her, and Bounder dashed out of sight.

Either she was too caught up in her own dreams of her romantic tryst, or the person out on the beach was extraordinarily quiet. When Candy first heard the voice, she was practically on top of him. Her first thought was that Reuben had reached the jetty first, had anchored the yacht and walked down to meet her. But she could see the jetty, and no boat was there.

Shrugging it off, Candy started to call for Bounder when another voice made her heart kick in surprise. Waiting with her head bent, she listened and heard at least three distinct voices. Teenagers? Having a party? Possibly, except that there was no music, only the hushed murmurs of their conversation. And it was too chilly for a night out on the beach. Not many people wandered down this far.

Candy glanced down at her snug jeans and waterproof boots, which reached to her knees, at the sturdy, lined Windbreaker zipped up to her chin. She was too weighed down with the backpack to run. Anyway, what was she so alarmed about? Victor's nasty threat, she grimly answered her own question.

"Hello," a strange man's voice called out to her, and Candy swallowed her gasp.

With a quick recovery she said, "Hello."

"Is this your beach?"

Accompanying footsteps came nearer, then stopped. At least one of them belonged to a woman. Candy could smell her perfume before she saw her. "Only the property above is private."

The man came closer. "We're just out wandering around. Don't mean anybody any harm. This is John and his girl, Dotty. I'm Hank. Hank Thomas."

He thrust out his hand, and Candy lifted the two bottles of wine, as if she couldn't possibly put one of them down. "Well, Mr. Thomas, as long as you don't climb the escarpment, you'll be all right. Be careful of the dog. He doesn't like strangers."

That should dampen their inquisitiveness, she thought, but several beers had bolstered Hank's courage. "Glad to meet you, Miss...uh..."

"Look, Mr. Thomas..."

"Want a beer, honey?" the woman offered.

Dotty was the artificially fingernailed, hard-to-dislike kind of woman whom Candy imagined would think nothing of going to a topless bar with two men at once. Candy smiled lamely at her. "No, thanks."

"Where're you headed?" Hank inquired. "Looks like you're ready for a party." He nodded to the wine bottles.

"I'm meeting someone."

"Yeah," Hank protested with a laugh, "but he ain't here, and we are. Say, we got a Jeep parked a way back. Wanna go for a drive?"

He actually had the nerve to move closer and slip his arm about her waist. Candy tried to get a fix on her equilibrium, but paralysis seemed to have claimed her limbs.

"We can drive back into town and go dancin' if you want to," he said. "I'll bet you're a great dancer." He leaned into her, squeezed her side. "What d'you say? We can pick up a little grass, maybe have ourselves a real party."

"I'm sorry," she said and came to life enough to try and pull away. "I'm afraid not."

"Hey, lady..."

"Don't touch me!" Candy cried out and jerked back. She practically fell on top of the woman, and she found herself smothered by a soft body and full, perfumed arms.

"Hey, honey," the woman purred, "are you okay? Listen if you want to come, don't mind these jokers. They're harmless."

Before Candy could stop the world from exploding, she heard Bounder's bark as he raced back along the foamy surf. Worthless animal!

Flinging herself free of all the reaching hands and dropping one of the bottles and throwing the other into the sand, she clapped for the dog. "Here, Bounder!" she cried. "Here boy, here boy."

He nearly bowled her over with his happy, worthless body, and she dropped to her knees in the sand, looped her arms around his dear old neck. "Where have you been, you miserable wretch?"

The intruders, uncertain if the dog was all she'd intimated that he was, kept a prudent distance. The sudden sound in the distance of an approaching motor stopped any second thoughts they might have cherished.

"Listen," the woman said and hushed them.

Bounder dropped to his haunches, and Candy, holding to his collar as if her fingers were welded to it, could feel the two men coming to attention and peering apprehensively out over the dark water.

"It's my date," she said brightly. "He'll be here in just a minute."

Far in the distance, the white slip of the big boat veered in the moonlight, and swung gently alongside the jetty. Candy started for it at a vigorous trot and was surprised when the trio fell in behind her at a slower pace. As the great dual engines cut and were followed by the sound of Reuben tossing out a line and dropping onto the jetty, Candy heard one of her escorts say, "She really was meeting someone."

"Maybe we ought not to—"

"Shut up."

When Candy could make out Reuben striding down the beach, wearing boots too, with his jeans tucked into their tops, his light jacket zipped and a buff-colored toboggan perched jauntily on the back of his head, she thought he looked like a Viking coming from the mother ship. She ran gratefully to meet him.

"Candy?"

Bounder came to life at the sound of Reuben's voice and also plunged to welcome him. "Hey, hey," Reuben laughed when he caught Candy. "Where are you flying in such a hurry, Mrs. North?"

"Just to you, Mr. North," she said on a breath of relief and pressed herself to him. "Just to you."

Reuben hesitated when he saw the people walking up behind her. Under his breath, he muttered, "Who's this?"

"Someone wandering around on the beach," she whispered. "Are you ready to go?"

"Hey lady," Hand said as he got within calling distance. "You forgot your bottles."

The look Candy and Reuben exchanged was brimming with unvoiced questions and answers. Reuben lifted a brow and stepped forward to accept the two bottles of wine. Without smiling, he thanked the man, smelled the strong fumes on his breath. "Thanks."

"Think nothing of it," said Hank. "We're just looking things over."

"Yes, well..." Reuben felt Candy's shiver and hugged her close. "Thanks again. We'd better be going. Are you all on your way out?"

"Yes," the woman said quickly.

Candy shifted her backpack higher up on her shoulders. "Let's go, Reuben."

But Reuben caught the inside of his jaw between his teeth and hesitated. He didn't want them lingering. "We can give you a lift up the beach, if you want," he told Hank.

Hank shook his head, threaded his fingers through his hair. "No problem. We got a Jeep. We were just leaving."

"Good idea," Reuben said. "It's private property up the escarpment."

"Yeah, that's what she said."

Once they were miles from Port Aransas and the engines of the big yacht were throbbing reassuringly beneath them, Candy felt stupid for having been afraid. Presently she relaxed enough to look around her at all the gleaming steel and sleek mahogany. In the wheelhouse, where Reuben steered them out into the gulf, were stretched instrument panels and sophisticated radio equipment. Reuben was immersed in his admiralty and periodically consulted his map.

She placed her hands into her back pockets. ''I had visions of those people spiriting me away in the night,'' she said. ''I saw them shooting me up and selling me into white slavery or something.''

He chuckled, but Candy guessed he didn't find it all that funny. There was a distance about him now that made her vaguely uneasy.

For some time they moved along at a snail's pace, neither feeling the need to break the silence. Then Reuben cut the engines and dropped anchor. With the generator keeping the exterior and interior lights working, he satisfied himself that they were safe and turned to her with a raffish doff of his toboggan.

She cocked her head. ''Nice place you got here, Reuben.''

''My father never did anything in moderation. Shall we head for the galley, ma'am.''

She had already spread out their midnight feast in the well-equipped galley: the pink cloth in place on the little table, the wine chilling, cheese and sliced melon spilling out of a brass bowl, grapes and sliced lamb arranged on a tray.

''You may be Tom Jones or the Sheik of Araby,'' she said with a lavish gesture at the food.

Reuben unzipped his jacket and shrugged out of it, pulled his sweater down around his waist. ''Since I'm neither Rudolph Valentino nor Albert Finney, I'm in trouble. Who might you be?''

He was restless, she thought. Even though he was pretending not to be, he had something bothersome on his mind. Candy picked up a wine bottle and handed it to him, along with the corkscrew. Taking her seat on the floor, she began pulling off her boots.

With more honesty than she intended, she said, "I'm no one, Reuben."

His breath came in a rough sigh. "Please don't."

Candy wrenched up her head, and he placed the bottle down without having opened it. He pressed his spread fingers to his abdomen as if he hurt inside.

With dismay Candy felt her face reddening. Her remark had offended him, and he saw, in turn, that his offense had grieved her.

He looked down, then away, and his thoughtful pose made him look very young. Candy had a glimpse of him as a boy, being caught in the middle of his parents, and she wondered if his experience was all that much better than her own. At least she hadn't expected anything.

Unable to bear his unhappiness, Candy came to her feet and put her arms around him. "Why are you sad?" she whispered and moved her hands over the strong, torqued leverage of his arms.

His shoulders drooped. "I don't know."

She didn't believe him, but she didn't dispute him. She pulled away and bent over the portable radio. The dial spat static, then music, and when she turned back Reuben was pinching the bridge of his nose.

A combination of frustration and irritation swept over her, and a grief settled into her stomach. Her steps were quick and to the point as she confronted him. "Is it the marriage thing? I wouldn't have asked you, but you'd asked me so many times that I thought—"

His brows lifted in bewilderment. "It's not—"

"Then what?"

Something flashed in his expression, something Candy couldn't analyze. His whole attitude was tense and guarded, and she sagged with disheartenment. She'd done it all wrong again.

"Do you want the truth?" he asked her with more brusqueness than anxiety.

She glared her answer at him.

He wiped his face, and the shadows that played over him accentuated his gauntness. He took a deep breath. "It is the marriage thing. But—" He cut off her interruption before she could make it. "But not for the reason you think. I had in my mind this scenario, you see, of being the perfect husband, giving everything to you, making your life wonderful. I even said I'd do that, didn't I?"

In a turmoil Candy stood staring at him, her hands helpless. How should she answer him?

"I'm just a man, Candy," he said with a very human sigh. "Just a flesh-and-blood man, and I'm scared. I'm scared that I can't make it all work. I'm coming into this marriage with a dozen millstones tied around my neck, and it's not fair to ask you to share that. After I left you to get the yacht, it hit me—like the pretentiousness of this damned boat. I'm not sure I can make anything better, for my own family or for you."

"Is that it?" Candy had to hold herself rigid to keep from going to him, taking him into her arms.

"*Is that it?*" His nostrils flared and his legs tensed. "Of course that's it. Isn't it enough?"

Candy couldn't bear the distance between them, and if she had ever feared to take the lead with him, that fear was dissolved in her new and wild need to be the other half of his coin. She wanted to be everything for him. She wanted him to flourish and do impossible things. She wanted him to be the best and the finest and the most admirable. Perhaps that was selfish; then everyone would look at her and think how very exceptional she was to have caught him.

She went to him, rose up on the tips of her toes, and kissed him. Reuben was both thrilled and horrified at her initiative, for he needed her comfort more than anything in his life, but he didn't think he could be aroused for all the riches in the world. He just wanted to curl up in her arms and lie with his face against her breast. He just wanted to be safe.

He started going through the motions with her, kissing her back and so honestly grateful for the sweetness of her mouth that he was tearing apart inside. He caressed her breasts through her sweater, and when she reached for the bottom of the soft knit and drew it over her head, standing there before him in the soft light with all that sensual food and drink and music behind her, offering him her beauty, he lowered his head and took her nipple into his mouth.

"I love you," he felt compelled to tell her because it was true.

His words didn't seem to affect her one way or another, and Reuben kissed her hair and drew her into his arms, taking her fragrance down into his lungs. There had been times when just picturing her could bring an awful ache into him. Or smelling her. Now he kept thinking of his mother and Emma and the tens of thousands of dollars that he'd been pushed into spending on his family when he'd wanted to use it for Candy and himself. He was in a trap and he didn't know how to get out.

Candy placed her hand upon the placket of his jeans as he often teased her into doing, and he froze inside, hardly able to look at her. Now she knew.

"It's all right," she whispered and began doing the thing that he'd dreamed she would do: taking the control out of his hands and into her skillful ones, which knew how to work his jeans free and push up his sweater, how to kiss his waist with such tenderness and passion that he slumped back against the wall and closed his eyes. The things that she did to him made him want to die, and that only added to the avalanche that was sliding down upon him.

His hands shook as he threaded them through her hair and tipped up her face. "Candy..."

As if to somehow make amends, he bent to kiss her, but she moved easily away from him and, without making a move to replace her sweater, handed him the wine bottle again.

He was grateful for something to do with his hands, but her serenity stirred a volatile self-disgust inside him. The cork popped, and the sound of wine pouring into the glasses made her crinkle her nose and laugh. She had picked up a piece of lamb, and she smilingly bit off a huge piece as he watched, licking her thumb and reaching for the glass as she chewed. She drank the whole thing without stopping, and Reuben had to laugh, despite his gloom, when she ran her tongue over her upper lip and grinned.

"I think I'm over dressed," he said wryly and set down the bottle to drag his own sweater over his head.

As he tossed it across the galley, she picked up a slice of melon and bit off a chunk. Juice trickled from the corner of her mouth, and she wiped it away with a flick of her tongue. Reuben sloshed some wine into a glass and, lifting it in salute to her tempting eroticism, drank it down.

She peered down at another drop of melon juice that dripped to her breast and slid fascinatingly over the round curve to the tip. She lazily touched her fingertip to it, then licked her finger.

Reuben didn't quite recognize the sound of his own breath. Without bothering to even rebutton his jeans or finish pulling up the zipper, he picked up the food, removed the pink tablecloth, and spread it on the floor and piled everything back on top of it. He bent to unlace one boot, then the other. Without looking to see where they fell, he dropped them behind him and met her eyes with a double-edge challenge.

"Let's get down to some serious eating," he said hoarsely and folded himself to the floor.

They ate and drank, and the more they ate and drank, the slower the night seemed to move. They touched a lot, and by the time they had started on the second bottle of wine and had smeared cheese over the flatbread and topped it off with grapes and apples, they were both a little drunk.

Candy pulled off her socks in a ritual as fascinating as a striptease and grew engrossed with her toes. The longer Reuben watched her, the more the pressure of the past weeks seemed to drift away like fog in the sunshine, and he grew as engrossed with her toes as she was. More engrossed.

When only one piece of the lamb remained, she leaned over his lap to reach it and, tearing it in two, reached up to poke a piece into his mouth.

"What we have to do, Reuben," she said as her throat and her breasts pinkened rosily, "is to sit down and pool all our liabilities and attack them in order of priority. What do you think is pressing us the worst?"

Reuben hesitated to say what was pressing him the worst. She was driving him crazy. And when she slid down into the space between his legs and propped her head on his knee, continuing to talk with her mouth full and reach around him for her glass, he knew that he was being systematically seduced.

Warm energy slid into his body as he watched her delicious wantonness. When she made a production of twisting around to refill their glasses, he caught the tab of her zipper and, with a deft twist of his own, grabbed a hold of the legs of her jeans and stripped them off her, leaving her in only her panties.

Laughter gurgled up from her throat. "You're so subtle, Reuben."

"You've got nerve."

He laughed and caught a leg of her panties with a toe and toyed with it. Where before he'd been unable, he now feared he would be uncontrollable. Pulling her on top of him as he dragged off the wispy panties, he clasped her buttocks and pulled her up higher, kissing her for what seemed an eternity.

The music grew into a hazy blur. The light turned to gold. Everything seemed touched with a breathless excitement, and the confines were warm and filled with rich smells and their own desire.

Not quite certain how he ridded himself of his jeans, Reuben wanted to sigh with relief at the tautness and length of himself, but she was as unabashedly interested in that as he was. He watched her touch him, thrilled to the way she made the slightest sensation increase until it was intolerable. The sheen of moisture that glistened on her body drugged him and made him reckless.

He touched her everywhere, fingers urgent and delving. She moaned. Every touch was its own unique fantasy, and when he finally entered her, every movement seemed lethal. She touched where their bodies joined, unashamedly enhancing her own pleasure, and then he touched her, first fiercely, then gently, then sublimely until her groans sounded as if they were being torn from her by force.

Still he couldn't let her rest. He withdrew and satisfied her over and over, it didn't matter how, until she was pleading with him to end it. She clung to him when he took her and made terrible demands of him. She raked her nails down his back, and when he thought he couldn't last another second, she compelled him to. The release was a blinding pain, but he never wanted it to stop as, gasping, he strained to pour the essence of his whole being into her.

Time ceased to mean anything. Reuben thought it was dawn when they lay spent, having never made it to one of the luxurious cabins. He was just slipping into a drugged slumber when he felt soft hands running over him.

He would have sworn there was not a drop of life left in him. He couldn't even open his eyes, but she found response with her insatiable mouth and her hands and her soft, throaty sounds. He didn't even try to stop it from happening.

Love was as much a gift of receiving as giving, and when she kissed him and curled happily into the hollow of his side and laid her head upon his chest, she whispered, ''You're not alone, Reuben North. You'll never be alone again.''

Chapter Twelve

When Emma arrived in downtown Corpus Christi by limousine the next day and walked into the North-Stanford offices, she saw little point in having herself announced.

She asked aloofly if Reuben was there, and the surprised receptionist informed her that Mr. North and Mr. McPherson were having a meeting in one of the conference rooms. Smiling, Emma thanked her and walked to the door and opened it without knocking.

Reuben's breath made an ugly sound in his throat, and Candy thought, as she and Stretch lifted their heads to see Emma posing in the doorway, that they all must look like burglars with stolen goods in their hands. They were studying the possibilities of recovering some of Benjamin's closed-off oil leases through the process of MEOR.

Reuben placed his fist upon the thick sheaf of geological surveys that were spread over the surface of one table, and

Emma laughed. "Go on, Reuben, dear. Don't let me interrupt."

All of them were roughly dressed. They had planned to drive up to Refugio County and walk over one of the leases afterward.

Reuben pushed up his sleeves. His jaw was granite. "What are you doing here, Emma?"

"I work here." Without acknowledging Candy or Stretch at all, Emma gestured to the paperwork cluttering the desks. "What's this?"

"Stretch," Reuben said wryly, "d'you want to explain to Miss Stanford what we're doing?"

But Stretch gladly passed the explanation of MEOR to Candy. It was the last thing Candy had expected, but she took a quick breath and, grimacing, asked, "Are you familiar with MEOR, Miss Stanford?"

The Stanford heiress fondled her heavy ivory-and-silver necklace and smiled. "You're going to tell me."

Candy ignored the velvet sarcasm. "Well, what MEOR would actually involve is to reopen old wells and inject microbes into them. This is a molasses mixture with a culture in it, and it would be injected right into the borehole. Then the well would be sealed up—anywhere from two weeks to twelve weeks. On the lease we were just looking at, I would suggest ten."

Emma was wearing slacks, and she perched upon the edge of a table and crossed her long, lovely legs. Candy waited for her to settle before she continued. Reuben, she thought, was approaching detonation.

"How much would this cost if you weren't doing the injecting yourself?" Emma sweetly inquired.

Candy smiled. "About five thousand dollars a well."

"You work cheap, Miss Burrows." Emma flashed a smile at Reuben. "What do you think, darling?"

Reuben thought if he said what he thought, he'd be arrested. Never once had he known Emma Stanford to be interested in anything substantial, and every instinct he possessed—they had proved to be excellent instincts—warned him that this was some kind of malicious game with her.

He wet his lips. "I'm all for it," he said aridly.

Knowing that Reuben couldn't make a move without her approval, Emma played out the tension until the last possible second. No one said a word as she slid sensuously off the desk and ran her hands down her sides to straighten her blouse.

"I don't know, Reuben," she drawled as if debating the matter. "It's such a time-consuming thing."

She stood tapping her jaw with her long, lacquered nails, and Reuben felt as if he were tied to the tail of a kite. She reeled him out; she wound him in. "Damn it, Emma."

Her laughter rang out over the big room. "Naughty, naughty, Reuben. As for the microbes, Miss Burrows, I think we'll pass. I'm sure you understand. Maybe next time."

Emma walked to the door, and Candy and Reuben looked at each other in amazement. As she stopped in the doorway Emma blew Reuben a kiss. "Oh, by the way, tell Vivian hello for me."

Chalk another one up for Emma, Candy thought. She'd never seen Reuben so angry. His chest was heaving, and his dark eyes were burning with rage. After a few incoherent attempts at speech, he suddenly swung back his hand and sent the surveys flying all over the room. Then, in an eruption of absolute fury, he slammed the same fist into the wall.

Candy flew to him, caught his arm, clung to it. "Reuben, listen to me."

"She's going to bring us all down just to get at me," he stormed as he nursed his throbbing hand. "Well, I won't sit back and let her do it, by God. I—"

"Can't you buy her out?"

Reuben's laughter was bitter. "Sweetheart, be sensible."

But you told me you only have one percent less than she does. That's almost an equal voice."

"Almost equal doth not controlling interest make, my love."

"Then buy the other five percent."

He threaded his hands impotently through his hair and dropped them. Discouragement was settling upon him like silt. "You find it, babe, and I'll buy it."

Candy stared blankly at him. Why *couldn't* he find the stock after searching for it? Perhaps Lucas had hidden it away. More likely, Benjamin. It didn't make sense. It wasn't even consistent.

Or was it? Candy lifted her hand, hesitated. Benjamin North had been a strange man, leading two lives as he had—presenting one calloused face to the world while, behind the scenes, he planned for and provided for a mistress to whom he gave Petochi pearls and a house...and...

Candy whirled around so quickly that both men started. The smile on her face felt cockeyed, and she laughed out loud, breathily, wonderingly. "Reuben?"

Deep furrows spanned Reuben's brows. "What?"

She turned up her palms and said one wonderful, all-encompassing, self-explanatory word. "Agatha!"

The night after Benjamin's funeral she had told Reuben about his father's deep love affair with Agatha. It had comforted him to know that Benjamin had found a little of life's happiness, however off-beat and forbidden. Now, as Reuben stared into Candy's excited blue eyes, it took him two seconds to make the connection.

He covered the distance between them and swept her up and twirled her high into the air. He kissed her very hard on the mouth, then he threw back his head and laughed uproarously.

"Well, shiver our timbers, girl," he crowed and thought the smartest thing he'd ever done was to fall in love with her. "Chalk one up for our side. At last!"

In the moonlight, the battery-operated device looked like some child's erector toy. Hank Thomas made one last inspection of it as he trekked to the beach where he'd unexpectedly run into the woman the night before.

Then he'd only been looking the place over; tonight he was working. Satisfying himself that everything was in order, he replaced the device beneath his parka and zipped it up. After poking the flashlight back into his hip pocket, he set off down the beach at a good clip. The device bumped against his chest.

At least he knew not to try and climb the escarpment. That much he'd found out last night. He trotted past and found the path leading up to the house at a point farther down the beach. Once on the higher level, he waited for the dog he knew he would find. When the animal came, he called it by name.

"Come on, Bounder," he coaxed and reached into his other pocket for some meat treated with a strong knockout solution. "Come on, boy. Come on, Bounder."

Nor until the animal was quite unable to move did Hank attempt to go any closer to the house. He waited patiently for a light to come on in the house, but it was nearly eleven o'clock and the house remained dark.

Crossing a small cobblestone bridge, he came to the ivy-covered outbuilding that had been described to him. Once he located the door, he stepped inside and waited. The beam of his light moved cautiously over the desk, the bookshelves, the aquariums and double sinks. Then he found the desk and ever-so-quietly opened one of the side drawers. After removing a box, checking it to make sure it was full of typewritten papers, he opened the drawer below it. A metal clipboard was the only item there. Photographs and drawings were inside. Taking it, he glanced at his wristwatch again and removed the device from his parka and set a timer on it.

In a matter of seconds he had put the confiscated items into his jacket and had stepped out onto the grounds again. He returned to the beach without incident. Once he reached the approximate place where the woman had turned up the night before, he sat down on one of the dunes and burrowed deeply into the chilly sand. Slipping a pill into his mouth he guessed that he was good for another ten or twelve hours without sleep. Now all he had to do was wait.

Candy never heard the explosion, only felt the shuddering aftermath that shook the whole house. Reuben's feet slammed to the floor before she could even jerk up in the bed.

"What was that?" she gasped and groped in the darkness.

When he didn't reply, she tumbled out of bed and located the light switch. Reuben was jerking on his pants as he hopped and skipped to the door. Candy's first thought was for Amber, and she darted out after him only to collide with Agatha in the hallway.

The older woman stood staring at her as if she were disoriented. She blinked and said with heart-stopping simplicity, "The laboratory's on fire."

The laboratory? It was a dream, Candy thought. It was impossible. The laboratory was where she worked, where she...

Amber's cry jarred Candy to life and she flew into the baby's room. From the window she could see the sky lighting up, a brilliant crimson color. Flames were already jerking up over the trees—orange and killing gold against the shadows that lurched back and forth. The heat surged upward and made the windowpanes crack, and the sound filled the yard with a tremendous roar.

Dazed, Candy scooped up Amber and some blankets and hurried out of the room and toward the stairs. "Agatha, get—"

Then the appalling reality struck her. *The laboratory was on fire!* Dear God! With her arms filled with Amber and Agatha hurrying behind her, her arms also loaded with blankets, Candy wheeled around and stared in crazed desperation at the old woman.

"My manuscript!" she screamed.

Candy didn't feel herself running down the stairs. Amber was wailing, and the roar of the fire was deafening. She saw Reuben hanging up the telephone from calling the fire department, and she started to run to the kitchen, but Agatha caught her and snatched the baby from her arms. "Get out of the house!" she cried.

Past logical thinking, Candy gave her the child and darted through the kitchen door, flew to the screen, and out onto the veranda. Someone up the beach had seen the flames and was pulling into the driveway, their horn blaring.

Candy started down the back steps, and Reuben caught her by the tail of her gown. "My manuscript!" she shrieked and struck at him with hysterical super-strength. "My pictures, my pictures!"

"No, darling. No, no."

He was dragging her back across the veranda and around to the side of the house where the heat wasn't so hellish, and he shoved her back against the wall so hard that sparks of red flew before Candy's eyes.

"Listen to me!" he shouted. "I've got to hook up the hoses until the fire trucks get here. The back of the house must be kept wet. Can you hear me?"

She beat at his chest. "My life is burning up in there! Oh, God, oh, God, it's burning!"

"Candy!"

Candy collapsed back against the wall and started sliding down to the floor. Only Reuben's inhuman yell at her brought her around. *"For God's sake, help me!"*

She was trembling uncontrollably, but she nodded her head. "Yes," she choked and began to weep. "What do I do?"

The next hours were a nightmare of such horrible proportions that Candy lost all track of time. No until the gray sky was streaked with dawn and the fire was extinguished, not until the firemen were winding up their hoses, did Candy look around to search for Reuben.

She found him near the ruins, his back hunched and his fists crammed into his pockets. When he saw her, he took her wordlessly into his arms. Candy hurt all over. Her hands were scraped and sore, her bare feet ruined. Her lungs felt as if they'd been scraped with a knife, and the most unreal fatigue was claiming her whole body. She stood lifelessly in his arms.

"What will I do?" she asked in a dead, hopeless voice.

"Didn't you have a copy?" he said.

"Of the book but not of the artwork. What'll I do, Reuben?"

Reuben knew that she must be told, though he wasn't sure yet what it all meant. Taking her by the shoulders, he tried to infuse her with enough strength to accept it. "Candy, darling, I want you to listen to me."

She couldn't imagine herself doing anything else. She was too exhausted. She coughed. "What?"

"It was set, Candy. The fire was set. There's a device in the rubble. One of the firemen spotted it."

"Set?" she echoed numbly. What was happening to their lives? What terrible, uncontrollable evil was beating them and beating them?

Reuben walked her to the place the fireman had showed him. The rubble was white with ash now, and the steam curled up into the cold morning air with an almost peaceful, lacy grace.

"There." He pointed. "Beside the broken glass of the aquarium. Do you see it? The cylinder?"

The human mind could only take so much. During the fighting of the fire, even when Bounder's unconscious body had been discovered by one of the neighbors, Candy had been charged with a wild, exhilarating terror. Now, as the truth registered, of how truly tragic the whole episode could have been, her brain reciprocated by shutting off.

She stared at Reuben as if she couldn't keep awake. "Who could have done such a thing?"

Which was precisely the question Lieutenant Timothy Guthridge asked them at five o' clock the next afternoon.

After a sleep that left them all feeling jet-lagged and depleted, the man's questions had a way of snapping things into focus. Did anyone they knew bear a grudge? Had anyone made a threat? Was anyone behaving in an irrational manner?

Reuben kept a steady eye on Candy as she absorbed the man's questions. She was wearing a long shell-pink cotton robe, looking fragile and delicate and lovely. She wore just a blush of lipstick but no other makeup. Her hair was freshly washed and shining, but she was so pale that her cheekbones gleamed like porcelain.

No one in the house had speculated about how the fire had been set, though it was all they had thought about. When the lieutenant asked the question, Reuben thought Candy might keel over. He softly prodded her. "Candy?"

She didn't look at him. Her hands rested motionless, and she studied them for long moments. Then she said to her lap, "Victor wouldn't do it, Reuben. I know he threatened me, but he would never do anything that would jeopardize Amber. He wouldn't do it."

The heavyset officer shot Reuben a suspicious look. As he fished out his small notebook he said, "The arsonist wasn't a murderer, Miss Burrows. He wanted to destroy property. Why the laboratory?''

For the dozenth time Candy traced back over the evening when Victor had behaved so badly. She recalled how she had packed the food in her backpack. She remembered her trek up the beach to meet Reuben, her collision with...

She snapped up her head so sharply that she found Guthridge and Reuben scowling at her. ''There was someone else,'' she said bluntly.

Guthridge started to say something, but Candy asked Reuben in a flare of concentration that seemed to consume her, waving her hand, ''What was his name? The man on the beach? The man and his friends who wanted me to go into town with them?''

''Hank Thomas,'' Reuben said and sighed.

When he had finished writing down everything they could remember about the incident on the beach, Lieutenant Guthridge smiled his bland, official smile. ''I'd like for you to come into town and look at some mug shots.''

Finding Hank Thomas's picture was the easy part. Under questioning the next day, Hank even admitted that he had set the fire. He was promptly arrested and booked, but he mutinously refused to confess who had hired him. Victor was a prime suspect; he was swiftly picked up for questioning.

Candy supposed she wasn't too surprised when Victor turned up on Agatha's doorstep the next evening—out on bail, pale and haggard, his eyes heavily shadowed so that his beauty took on a rather striking fragility.

''I've got to talk to you,'' he said without preamble and stepped into the house only to realize in dismay that Reuben North and Beth Dickerson were seated there, talking to Agatha.

But he was already in, and Candy, with a quiet passion that she hadn't expected to feel when she next laid eyes on him, said before he could even be asked to sit down, "Why did you do it, Victor?"

The sides of Victor's mouth twisted. He took a step forward, glanced at Reuben coming to his feet, and warily stopped. "Candy, listen to me." He swallowed hard. Then, "They're going to indict me, for Christ's sake. You must help me!"

Candy had never believed Victor capable of such villainy as hiring someone to commit arson, but neither did she believe Victor capable of great innocence. At this moment she wanted to despise him and yell that he had every bit of this coming to him for the way he had caused her to suffer. She wanted to make him pay for his egotism and his callous disregard for human pain. She wanted to do to him what he had done to her.

Darkness was falling outside. Agatha, always the hostess, was turning on lamps, and Beth was dividing her time between intimidating Victor with her persecuting looks and entertaining Amber with a puppet.

Having stayed out of things to this point, Reuben placed a hand upon Candy's waist. "You knew about the lab, Victor. You'd been there. You'd seen the manuscript and the artwork."

Victor kept his balance with an effort. "It wasn't—"

"You wanted to hurt Candy, and you knew that her manuscript was there."

"All right, *all right!*" Victor ran his tongue over his lips and took a defeated breath. Not having the courage to face them anymore, he looked at his feet. "I did know where everything was. But you're after the wrong person, damn it! I talked to Emma Stanford the night of Agatha's party. She was very curious. You know what I mean? We had some drinks. She asked questions. She..."

Victor seemed to be in real pain. He slumped over himself and lifted an arm to his chest, but Candy steeled herself to feel pity.

"She flattered me," he admitted. "It all seemed so casual at the time—her laughter and her jokes, all that money, and she was so beautiful. But later, after I heard, I knew. But what could I do? I had no proof." His head lifted, anguish blurring his eyes. "You can't prove it, either, even if you believe me."

Candy felt all the color drain out of her face. This man whom she'd loved, Amber's father, what had happened to him? What would happen to all of them? For she did believe Victor; his words had a ring to them that only the truth could have.

A look at Reuben told her that he believed Victor too. She felt as if she'd been taken from behind, and that her arms were twisted back. She was where she'd been on the beach that night, swearing to herself that she would never be a victim again as long as she lived.

Turning, she gripped Reuben's hands with a painful ferocity. Her voice sounded shrill in her ears. "How long does this go on? How long do we keep letting it?"

Reuben thought he could remember every time during his life when he'd taken the easy way out: good ole Reuben, making things right, eating it up when everyone adored him. He raked Candy's glittering, determined eyes, the hard purposefulness lining her face.

"No more," he said. "No more."

She swung around to Victor, and Reuben was surprised when she walked over and laid her hands upon his shoulders. "I'm tired of hating you, Victor. It takes too much out of me."

Tears welled in Victor's eyes. He pressed his trembling lips and looked around at the faces watching his humiliation. "You won't be seeing me anymore, Candy. I'm going back to Georgia. The only thing I ask of you is that you raise our daughter to know who I am. I don't want her to hate me.''

It often occurred to Candy during the next days that she was supremely blessed. Their lives took on the frenzy of picking up the pieces and every hour seemed chock-full of calls between Candy's publisher and herself, or plans to replace the destroyed artwork, or insurance adjustments to rebuild Agatha's outbuilding, or—and here Candy laughingly took all the credit for having discovered the missing stock—even Reuben's aggressive takeover of his father's estate.

Then there were the wedding plans. Reuben adamantly refused to take Candy to New York to live. ''You'd die in that city, my love. No, I'll do what my father always wished I'd do. I'll stay here and take care of the business, and you continue your research.''

''But what about your business in New York?''

He chucked her chin. ''Do you hear me complaining because it's going to make us money without my being there? Of course, we may just have to fly up once a month and check in on things, take in a few shows and spend a little money.'' He looked over his shoulder. ''You don't mind if we stay here, do you, Agatha?''

They were all in the kitchen, where Candy was unpacking a new rubber wetsuit and aqualung and diving paraphernalia to replace those that had been destroyed.

Agatha glanced up from where she was loading the dishwasher. ''Mind you staying in Texas?'' she asked. ''Goodness, no. I don't know how I'd make it if you left.''

Reuben chuckled. ''No, dear. I meant that you wouldn't mind if we stayed here. *Here*, here. This old barn could do with a man around, don't you think? A little repair here, a little remodeling there. Amber's room needs redoing, and—''

When Agatha suddenly burst into tears and buried her face into her hands, Candy and Reuben both dropped their jaws and looked at each other. Candy had never seen Agatha outright cry before, and Amber whimpered in alarm and padded over to the old woman and tugged on her skirt.

"Ah, Agatha," Reuben said as he went to take her into his arms, "it won't be so bad having a son, you know. I've got enough love stored up in me that there'll be plenty for everyone. Just let me share a little of it. Okay?"

Astonished, Candy experienced the same sensation as when she'd been half-conscious in the helicopter and was running her hands over Reuben's face. She'd thought then that Reuben was a strong man, one who could make up his own rules as he went along. She hadn't been wrong, had she?

She hugged Amber and squeezed her eyes tightly shut. As Reuben comforted Agatha, she whispered into the baby's sweet hair. "We're going to be a family, my precious. A real family."

The feeling of disconnection with the past remained with Candy, even into the next day. When she put on the wetsuit and gathered up her mask and her aqualung, she smiled up at Reuben and lifted her face for a goodbye kiss. Then she happily put all the stuff back down again and held him for a moment.

She gazed up at him where the midmorning sunshine gleamed across his face from the kitchen window. She ran her hands over his face and traced the arch of his brows. "You know, I don't think I even hate him anymore."

Reuben's eyes darkened with his great love for her. "Victor? You don't need to hate him, darling."

"No," she said and smiled. "My father."

Reuben stood thoughtfully at the window and finished his cup of coffee as he watched her walk across the lawn toward the escarpment. He was happy, truly happy, for the first time in his life, and he thought he could almost discard the one last piece of unfinished business that had insinuated itself in and out the past days. If she could lay Victor behind her and Ronald Burrows, couldn't he stop thinking about the fire?

Without really considering what he was doing, he placed his cup in the sink and slipped into his jacket and walked out the back door to where the ashes still smelled in the soft morning air. The day would be unseasonably warm for late November. The gulls were clawing at the updrafts out over the gulf, and the waves were hurrying in to the shore.

He studied the rubble for a moment, his hands plunged into his pockets, and absently jingled coins against his car keys. Stepping out into the silt, his shoes kicking up poofs at every step, he walked where he'd made love to Candy that hot summer afternoon. In all of the broken glass and ashes, he could see where her desk had been, the metal frame of her chair, the melted lump of her typewriter.

It came to him gradually—like a photograph in a developing solution—as he bent over and tried to pinpoint what was bothering him. He picked up a piece of iron and stirred through the debris. Straightening, he flicked a look at the house, at the gulf, then back to the ashes. He thought of going after Candy. She would probably be diving now. She'd been eager to start the tedious process of replacing her photographs.

Pinching the bridge of his nose, he made a quick decision. He trod swiftly through the ashes and stamped his feet on the grass. His steps were rapid and determined as he strode to the pickup and swung up into the seat.

It was nearly eleven o'clock when Reuben reached the huge Stanford estate in Ingleside. It was a protected property with a Tudor mansion set back among the trees and shrubs and velvet lawns. He almost ran up the twisting brick path, and when he touched the buzzer, he heard the bark of a dog.

When the heavy lock was undone and the door thrust open, Reuben pushed past the butler. "Where's Emma?" he barked. "And don't tell me she's not here. Her car's in the garage."

Emma appeared at the top of the stairs a few minutes later, and Reuben had to exert his control to keep from taking the stairs two at a time. But he waited for her to descend in all of her regal loveliness: her heavy blond hair pulled back off her face, her velvet gown sensuously rich with color. The only jewelry she wore was the ring he had given her.

Her lips trembled slightly when she reached the landing, as if she knew why he was here.

"I want them," he said, his voice the texture of steel.

Emma didn't pretend that she didn't know what he was talking about. For that, Reuben was grateful. She walked past him and into the large breakfast room that faced the east. Sun was streaming through the huge windows, and when she turned, she was probably the most beautiful thing he'd ever seen.

"Can't we negotiate, darling?" she asked softly.

Reuben took a step that placed him only inches away from her, his right arm raised. It was the first time he'd ever seen fear in her eyes. "You give them to me now, or I'm going to break that expensive nose. Then I'm going to break your jaw. If that doesn't work, I'm going to ruin your face, Emma. Permanently."

She didn't back away. She weaved slightly, and Reuben realized that she believed he would do exactly that. In a whisper she said, "How did you know?"

He leaned toward her, his lips drawn back over his teeth. "Because she kept them in a metal clipboard. One that closed down over the top. It wasn't in the meltdown, and it should've been there. I'll give you two minutes to bring it to me."

She brought it in less than a minute, and when Reuben assured himself that Candy's artwork was all accounted for, he darted a scathing look of disgust around the huge Stanford mansion. Then a final, bitter stare at Emma as she stood pale and silent in the doorway.

He turned once before he left. "If you ever try to hurt her again, Emma, you'd better be prepared to leave this country, because I'll find you."

The temperature was fifty-two degrees. Candy could feel the cold, and her air was almost gone, but she'd had to make this initial dive; she'd had to lay out in her head a strategy before bringing down the Rolleiflex and the flash extensions and getting on with it.

Tom and Miller would have to help her with the actual photography, for the flash extensions were attached to the camera by thirty-foot cables. She hadn't told them yet that her work had been destroyed.

Even with the cold, even with the troubles that had happened above the surface, a certain excitement enervated her. Because she was in love? Or because she was loved? Or because she was saying farewell to things that had dogged her past? What had she done or not done to deserve happiness after such a terrible, wasted beginning?

A school of silvery fish, round and flat as saucers, veered and careered beyond her where a small canyon opened up, full of green weeds and white algae. The sand, sloping out into a clear blue infinity, seemed to make everything so simple, and she knew, then, that it wasn't anything she'd done or figured out or worked out. It wasn't luck and it wasn't skill. She had simply chosen to give to another human being of herself without any demands of anything in return.

An unexpected loneliness came over her, and she veered around and began swimming to the shore. She wanted to

see Reuben. To tell him. . .she didn't know—to tell him that
she was healing, that everything was going to be all right.

Some yards from the beach she surfaced and let her feet
reach down to the bottom. To her surprise, and her pleasure, she saw Reuben sitting a distance down the beach. His
knees were drawn up to his chest, and his arms were
wrapped around them. He didn't move, for he hadn't seen
her.

Smiling, she didn't call out but pulled off her mask and
detached her mouthpiece and tank and removed her fins.
As she carried them and walked barefoot in the cold, swirling surf, she watched the sun, high in its zenith, glance off
him. The sun god, she thought fondly. She'd fallen in love
with a sun god.

Midway he spotted her, and he pushed back his hair and
shaded his eyes. Lunging to his feet, he came toward her at
a brisk trot. He was carrying something, and she waved at
him.

He didn't wave back. He simply kept coming, and
Candy, frowning, cocked her head as the sun twinkled off
the object he held. What. . .

Candy paused to place her tank into the sand. She
dropped her fins and her mask and mouthpiece and began
unbuckling her belt and harness as she walked. Strewing
them along the beach, she peeled rubber gear off her head
and dropped it.

Faster and faster she ran to meet him until she was heaving to breathe. She didn't believe what she was seeing just
as she hadn't believed a lot of things about this miraculous
man.

When he was still some distance away, he stopped. The
wind was wild in his hair, and he seemed ten feet tall—this
good and fine man who cared about leaving love in the
world when he died. When she saw what was in his hands,
something more profound than she'd ever known knotted
in her throat until she couldn't breathe anymore.

She felt her face twisting with tears and she didn't care how ugly she looked. She raced to him with her heart bursting because nothing, nothing on this earth could keep them apart.

He caught her in his arms, and Candy felt the hard metal clipboard digging into her waist. She guessed that his tears were because of her own tears; she wasn't sure, but it didn't matter, for salty kisses were the best kisses in the world.

She didn't know how long they stood there without saying a single word, their communication that of breaths and sounds and caresses that no one would understand but them. Finally, releasing her, he stepped back.

Candy swiped at her tears, but he caught her hand and shook his head, and they both swallowed and laughed sort of crazily because their voices didn't sound right. Then it started again, but this time it was a language of eyes.

At last Candy managed to master speech. With something resembling a laugh, she said, "Chalk one up for us?"

His smile bordered on shyness when he reached out his big hands and clasped her face and worshipped her with his eyes. "There's no more score to keep, my love. We've won. We—"

He broke off, and Candy buried her head in his shoulder. He smoothed her wet, wind-spiked hair.

"Let's go home," he said, for the future stretched out before them like the sands of her beloved sea. "Let's go home."

READERS' COMMENTS ON SILHOUETTE SPECIAL EDITIONS:

"I just finished reading the first six Silhouette Special Edition Books and I had to take the opportunity to write you and tell you how much I enjoyed them. I enjoyed all the authors in this series. Best wishes on your Silhouette Special Editions line and many thanks."

—B.H.*, Jackson, OH

"The Special Editions are really special and I enjoyed them very much! I am looking forward to next month's books."

—R.M.W.*, Melbourne, FL

"I've just finished reading four of your first six Special Editions and I enjoyed them very much. I like the more sensual detail and longer stories. I will look forward each month to your new Special Editions."

—L.S.*, Visalia, CA

"Silhouette Special Editions are — 1.) Superb! 2.) Great! 3.) Delicious! 4.) Fantastic! . . . Did I leave anything out? These are books that an adult woman can read . . . I love them!"

—H.C.*, Monterey Park, CA

*names available on request

AMERICAN TRIBUTE

Where a man's dreams count
for more than his parentage...

*Look for these upcoming titles
under the Special Edition
American Tribute banner.*

LOVE'S HAUNTING REFRAIN
Ada Steward #289—February 1986
For thirty years a deep dark secret kept them
apart—King Stockton made his millions while
his wife, Amelia, held everything together.
Now could they tell their secret, could they
admit their love?

THIS LONG WINTER PAST
Jeanne Stephens #295—March 1986
Detective Cody Wakefield checked out
Assistant District Attorney Liann McDowell,
but only in his leisure time. For it was the
danger of Cody's job that caused Liann to
shy away.

AMERICAN TRIBUTE

RIGHT BEHIND THE RAIN
Elaine Camp #301–April 1986
The difficulty of coping with her brother's death brought reporter Raleigh Torrence to the office of Evan Younger, a police psychologist. He helped her to deal with her feelings and emotions, including love.

CHEROKEE FIRE
Gena Dalton #307–May 1986
It was Sabrina Dante's silver spoon that Cherokee cowboy Jarod Redfeather couldn't trust. The two lovers came from opposite worlds, but Jarod's Indian heritage taught them to overcome their differences.

NOBODY'S FOOL
Renee Roszel #313–June 1986
Everyone bet that Martin Dante and Cara Torrence would get together. But Martin wasn't putting any money down, and Cara was out to prove that she was nobody's fool.

MISTY MORNINGS, MAGIC NIGHTS
Ada Steward #319–July 1986
The last thing Carole Stockton wanted was to fall in love with another politician, especially Donnelly Wakefield. But under a blanket of secrecy, far from the campaign spotlights, their love became a powerful force.

AM-TRIB-1

Silhouette Special Edition

COMING NEXT MONTH

STATE SECRETS—Linda Lael Miller
When David joined Holly Llewellyn's cooking class, they found themselves instantly attracted to each other, but neither of them could chance falling in love since both had something to hide.

DATELINE: WASHINGTON—Patti Beckman
Investigative reporters Janelle Evans and Bart Tagert had different methods for finding facts, so when they were assigned to the same story the clashes were inevitable...but the passion was unexpected.

ASHES OF THE PAST—Monica Barrie
Although four years had passed since Blair had been widowed, she was reluctant to become involved, until she met author Sean Mathias and a mysterious passion drew her to him.

STRING OF PEARLS—Natalie Bishop
Devon had once believed the worst of Brittany, now the past was repeating itself. Brought together again by the pursuit of a smuggler, could they find the love they had lost?

LOVE'S PERFECT ISLAND—Rebecca Swan
Alex Gilbert and Ian McLeod were on opposing sides of a wildlife issue, until the beauty of the Aleutian Islands lured them away from their debate and into each other's arms.

DEVIL'S GAMBIT—Lisa Jackson
When Zane appeared at Rhodes Breeding Farm insisting that Tiffany's champion stallion was alive, she had to discover if this alluring man was trying to help her, or was seeking revenge.

AVAILABLE NOW:

SUMMER DESSERTS
Nora Roberts

HIGH RISK
Caitlin Cross

THIS BUSINESS OF LOVE
Alida Walsh

A CLASS ACT
Kathleen Eagle

A TIME AND A SEASON
Curtiss Ann Matlock

KISSES DON'T COUNT
Linda Shaw